Lord
Edward
&
Citizen
Small

NEIL JORDAN is an Irish film director, screenwriter and author. His first book, *Night in Tunisia*, won a Somerset Maugham Award and the *Guardian* Fiction Prize (1979). He was awarded the Rooney Prize for Irish Literature (1981), the Irish PEN Award (2004), and the Kerry Group Irish Fiction Award for *Shade* (2005) and *Mistaken* (2011), which also received the 2011 Irish Book Awards Novel of the Year. His films include *Angel* (1982), the Academy Award-winning *The Crying Game* (1992), *Michael Collins* (1996) and *The Butcher Boy* (1997).

for BJR
who made me do it

The Ballad of Lord Edward & Citizen Small

NEIL JORDAN

HEAD
of ZEUS

An Apollo Book

First published in 2021 by The Lilliput Press, with the financial support of
the Arts Council / An Chomhairle Ealaíon.

This edition published in the UK in 2022 by Head of Zeus
This paperback edition published in 2023 by Head of Zeus,
part of Bloomsbury Publishing Plc

9 7 5 3 1 2 4 6 8

A catalogue record for this book is available from the British Library.

ISBN (PB): 9781803289328
ISBN (E): 9781803289298

Set in Baskerville by iota (www.iota-books.ie)

Printed and bound by CPI Group (UK) Ltd, Croydon, CR0 4YY

Head of Zeus Ltd
5–8 Hardwick Street
London EC1R 4RG

WWW.HEADOFZEUS.COM

Contents

The Croppy Boy   1

FIRST VERSE

Eutaw Forest   7
Lieutenant   15
The King's Paper   26
Charleston   32

SECOND VERSE

Elsewhere   39
Barbados   42
St Lucia   48
Morne Fortune   51
The Passage   58
This Sceptred Isle   62
Marylebone   67
Drury Lane   74
Lascia Ch'io Pianga   80
Lost   84

THIRD VERSE

Dublin   93
Frescati   102
Cockles   109
The Kilmainham Minnit   112
Pantaloons   119
Friday   124
Izod   128
Carton   133
Silken Thomas   138
Foxhunt   141
Buachaill Bán   144
Manhunt   148

The Hanging 151
Love 158
Crusoe 168
The Rivals 172
Stoke 179

FOURTH VERSE

Nova Scotia 185
Bedlam 197
Harlequin Friday 200
Maid of Bath 209
Mehitabel Canning 216

FIFTH VERSE

Gardens 223
Thomas Paine 228
Citizen 233
Pamela 237
United 245
La Mer 250
Irishman 253
Conspiracy 266
Hamburg 272
The Silence 279
The Beggar's Opera 282
The Shan Van Vocht 292
Crow Street 305
The Performance 313

CHORUS

Newgate 319

LAST VERSE

The Holyhead Packet 327
The Greatest of These 332
Orezembo 336
Consummation 340
The Curtain Call 342

Acknowledgments 345

The Croppy Boy

So I go back there, and it's a year or so after. I have myself snuck aboard the packet by one of the United Men. Amongst the horses, since that was always my job. When the light begins creeping through the grating above, I take a chance and join those clattering heels on deck.

So I see the city again, in the bottle-green glow that always seems to surround it on this rolling approach. The cathedral of masts around the quays, the pale shape of the mountains above them, like a mother, asleep.

The way my own mother slept; I remember. But memory can lie, like any informer.

Why am I here? I'm owed money, it's true. I want to walk those streets again, also true. But most of all I want to find out who played the Judas to my dead Lieutenant.

The ballast wall is almost finished, beyond the Pigeon House. I take a walk along it, towards Irishtown, Ringsend and the sleeping city.

And when I reach the old familiar places, I realize they have finally decided what he was. A hero, not a fool. A lord, of course. A mystery, a phantom, a figure from a story book that's not been written yet. Ballads sung in dram shops about him, and printed in garlands and chapbooks to be sold in the tanneries, the horse and bully markets. Telling stories of the pitch caps and the rivers of blood and of Vinegar Hill – some mountain in Wexford.

I'm not sure I like them. I always preferred the gaol bird ones myself: 'The Kilmainham Minnit', 'Luke Caffrey's Ghost'. 'The Night Afore Larry Was Stretched'.

But my Lieutenant died before he was stretched. Of a pistol ball in the stomach, in a cell in Newgate.

I wonder if, like poor Larry, they waked him in clover when they sent him to take a ground sweat.

I'm owed money, but with little hope of it. I get in touch with Lawlor, who did the family payments. Lawlor tells me they have scattered like the Wild Geese, they have gone to warmer climes, and that I could chase them for what was owed. If I could find them.

Then I think the grave is worth a visit.

He puts me in touch with McNally, who had the honour to be one of the coffin bearers. Though how he bore it with that leg of his, I find hard to imagine. He has the same stick and there's something comforting about the tapping it makes on the old cobblestones. We walk to Werburgh Street together and push open the door of the empty church and he shows me the vault beneath the chancel where the coffin was laid.

His breath makes strange wraithlike shapes in the cold church air. He's anxious to go since word was out for anyone associated. Anxiety, everywhere. It's hard to know what would be worse, the croppy's revenge or the King's.

I tell him he can leave.

It's musty in here and lonesome but not as lonesome as in the streets around Soho or the fields in Carolina when I first went on the run.

Then I stand there for what seems eternity and my only company is that ghostly breath that dies when I inhale again.

I remember many things. When my Lieutenant Lord became a citizen and gave away his title, in that room in Paris. When I cut his hair, in the croppy way.

And I suppose I wonder what gives me the right to tell his story. To sing his song. Nothing but what we've seen together. The albatross plunging into the Atlantic, the lace handkerchiefs dipped in the blood of a dead king, hangings in Charleston and Dublin and whippings in Carolina and Kildare. We've seen Harlequin Friday on the stage at Drury Lane, Dasher Daly as Macheath in Crow Street.

And then I ask myself, who gave Richard Brinsley Sheridan the right to tell the tale of Orezembo?

And the ballad, I realize, will need a title page.

So I take a broken piece of nail from the floor and scrape on the slate covering of what they had told me was the coffin.

LEF

And that's when I know his ballad will be mine too.

FIRST VERSE

Eutaw Forest

I met a fool in the forest. I'd later hear him say those words from the regimental stage in Gibraltar and hope that he didn't mean me. That forest was made of potted rubber and banana plants. But maybe one fool met another in that other forest. The one made of bald cypresses, Spanish moss and burning cedars.

And I could have left him there, but some better angel spoke to me and wouldn't allow it. And I suppose I came to love him, though love was furthest from my mind when I was pulling his boots off in the dead field with the smoking farm-house beyond. This was in another country, another War of Independence. I had run from Old Montgomery's as far as I could from his tobacco fields. My mother had died and I could hardly see the others for the tears. We had all of us heard about the King's promise to any runaways who joined his regiment, but it was one thing to run, another to find that recruiting sergeant if he even existed. So I was edging my way through that forest in Eutaw round yet another battlefield. The shooting was over and the light was dying and the carts were departing with those who were still alive, the groaning ones, and I was scouring for whatever I could find in that dark thing, all that was left of the daylight. It was called 'the gloaming' that hour, I would later learn in the fields of Kildare where he made his last home. And in the gloaming then the red jackets gleamed a little brighter than the blue ones.

He must have been deserving of someone's love, his mother's for sure though there was an annoying kind of goneness to him in those first few days, he was hardly there. He would have been gone alright if I hadn't turned the body over to get a better handle on his boots. They were of fine calfskin, covered in mud and scuffed around the outside bit where the sword rubbed off them.

Something cracked and he gave a low moan with what must have been the only breath he had left. I didn't know how but I realized later that I had cracked his shin back into place. I knew he was alive then and being alive, for some ungodly reason, he now became my responsibility. Though it could have all been different. I could have put my own bare foot to his throat and squeezed the last breath out of him.

There was a wallet on him I was sure, a watch and chain and a cigar cutter and whatever other fancy ornaments an officer carries – and I knew he was an officer now with the turning because it showed the braids on the front of his red coat.

There were stains there that weren't caused by the mud of the swamp which I knew must be blood. So I could have used my foot or just left him to die with the light. But I didn't and maybe that's what began it all. He became my charge and later I became his and we were tied together forever after for reasons I could never fully understand. Out of such accidents are we made. Out of such an accident was my mother dragged from old Tangier, chained to a plank in a hold in a ship over an ocean she never knew was there before.

Of course, it was my luck too, I was given another life after I had nursed him back to health and the life I had wandering those swamps in the Carolinas had little to recommend it. I could have made it to Charleston maybe and believed all the King's promises or I could have joined the Continentals and tried to believe theirs or I could have run away among the Santee Indians looking for my father. But I did none of those things.

I got the boots off his feet, the right foot bleeding and fitted them on my own. His eyes opened a little and I could see they were greeny-grey, not the colour of the mud on his cheeks, but close. There was nothing but mud that gloamy evening, mud that the dead bodies sank into, mud that the horses had churned. There was one horse lying in a lake of it, trying to turn over and get a hoof in the wet sludge and I thought of grabbing the reins and pulling the beast upright and doubling my luck, so to speak, but I saw the two back legs were broken and the horse would be no use for anything but feed. Then I heard him whose boots I had already fitted on my feet give another moan and say, don't leave me here.

Well, there was nothing I could do but leave him there. I wasn't going to stand upright in that dead field. I was going to keep low like one of the fallen myself. He stretched out his hand towards me and it had something golden in it, but I wasn't taking any chances. I could see the stragglers making their way towards the Charleston road and one glance back of theirs would have cooked my goose.

I could have called, I suppose. I could have shouted out, there's one of yours back here still living, but I knew it was safer to leave it till night and if he didn't live till then there would be nothing left worth saving. The watch would still be on him and whatever the gold thing was in his hand.

So I scuttled off, still bent low, to the line of trees. I had made a small shelter in the crook of a fallen tree, a covering of twigs and wattles and leaves. I didn't dare make a fire, but it was a place to sit and think until the darkness came. And it took its time, the absolute darkness. There was the sound of drums and the clinking of harnesses as the last horses pulled away, then nothing but the moaning of the wind in that dead field. A moon came out behind the cloud and I could see the shapes of the dead humped round the burnt trees, no one moving now or moaning and I tied together two branches to make a sled of kinds and I dragged it out into the moonlight to where he had fallen. Why I did this I still don't know, but maybe providence had a hand in it. But everything looked different in the dark. I blundered round the muddied trenches and it was the same moan that found him for me. A sad cry like a broken child and I found him where I had left him and it struck me then that that's what he was, hardly more than a boy.

Does your mother love you? I whispered, somebody does, as I turned him over again and settled his bloodcrusted body on the branches that I'd tied together. Then I dragged the whole contraption, and the mud made my work easy for once, the two branches slid easily through it and I had him among the trees in a jiffy and I thought with the quiet out all around that I might chance a fire.

I had a flint and I managed to light some kindling and warm some water and I said, come on, let's get those breeches off you. So I pulled them and he moaned but I knew if I didn't keep pulling he'd never make it. I pulled hard and where the breeches were the bloodiest I saw the broken bone.

I'm going to clean it now, I said, and the hurting won't stop, so howl if you want to, there's no one to hear you but me.

He said then what seemed like his first word, but it wasn't, he'd pleaded with me in the dead field, hadn't he? But it seemed like his first word when he said it.

A bit.

What do you mean, a bit? I asked, and he said it again.

A bit, something to bite on.

So I unhooked his belt from his coat that was red once and put the leather between his teeth and I went to work.

He bit right into the leather as I cleaned and foam gathered round the corners of his lips, but if he moaned again he didn't howl, I'll give him that.

I set the bone together and cleaned the muddied flesh with the water I had and tied two bits of stick around to keep it stiff.

You may not walk for a while, I told him, but you might live.

Then I went to work on the coat. I cut off all of the buttons and peeled it free of his chest like a second skin and saw then that we were having more luck there. There was a flesh wound below his armpit and a lot of blood but nothing fatal. I cleaned that too and wiped the brown hair around his chest free of the darker stuff. He had pale flesh, like a well-kept animal, which was, I was later to discover, not too far from the truth. A very well-kept specimen. And the fire was blazing now and I didn't mind for once because I imagined we were safe. All the fury of the battle was long gone. I pulled him closer to it so he could warm his outer parts.

I'm off to get us some food, don't move.

And he gave me his first smile then and it was like sunlight breaking through a cloud. His teeth were a shocking white and he grimaced and grinned and managed his next few words.

I couldn't move, he said, even if I wanted to.

What's your name? I asked him, and all that came out was *nd*.

So for a moment I thought his name was *and*.

Then he said it again, and I heard *Ned*.

What's yours? He asked, and I told him the name they had given me. Tony. Tony Small.

He held his hand out then and I thought it was a plea for me to stay. But it was just a handshake.

So I took it. And inside his very white hand I felt something hard. That gold thing. A locket, in the shape of a heart.

Is this for me? I asked him.

No, he said.

And I opened the locket and saw one of those small pictures, made of porcelain. A woman, white against dark. Her face was in profile and her hair cascaded backwards.

Your sweetheart? I asked him.

No, he said. My mother.

So it was the first time I saw that outline. The upturned nose and the lips like a delicate bow, the proud forehead. His mother had it, Georgiana had it, Elizabeth Linley, Pamela de Genlis, or the Duchesse d'Égalité, whichever you choose to believe.

Is she dead?

I thought of my own mother, and strangely my heart didn't break.

He shook his head.

Very much alive, he said.

Where? England? I knew of England from Old Montgomery. His 'sceptred isle'. His laments that he had ever
left it.

And the soldier smiled. But it seemed that even the smile
gave him pain.

No, he said. Ireland.

Is Mayo in Ireland?

Nowhere else. Why do you ask?

No reason.

But he seemed to recognize the name. Or know the place.

And maybe that's what saved him. Saved both of us. I could
have stripped him clean, taken the locket and the watch and
the cigar cutter and boots and left him to his groaning. But I
didn't. And if I had, maybe I would have ended up hanging
under the Spanish moss of a live oak with my pickings from
him being picked over by the Continentals.

Instead I left him with the image of his mother and wandered back through the woods until I saw the smoke of a
burning farmstead in a clearing. There was a smouldering
chicken coop with the smell of burnt feathers. The reds had
burnt it or the blues, but it didn't matter to me. Because
there were a few black carcasses there and I thought whoever
burnt it mustn't have been hungry, or not as hungry as me.
The chickens were black but I didn't care, it would save me
having to broil them. So I gathered up the best of them and
stripped my shirt off and wrapped them in it.

There were a few sad burnt corn rows near an attempt of
a garden. I stripped the ears of corn from the rows and
made my way back through the trees and found him sleeping there in a curl of woodsmoke. I dumped the corn in the
pot and scraped the burnt flesh and feathers off the chickens
and prodded him awake.

Time to eat, I told him. Sleeping won't keep you alive but eating might.

And we ate with our fingers then, a meal not quite fit for kings

Lieutenant

I was a fool, to ignore the pickings on his uniform in that forest and not keep running. A fool, maybe, to nurse him back to health though the world later thought me a hero for it. And he was a fool to give away his privileges, like a swan divesting itself of feathers, though all the ballads would call him a hero for it.

Old Sheil, the blacksmith in Kildare, hammering the hot metal into a fleur-de-lis and dropping it beside the other hundred pikes on the blackened floor, would have stuck one of them in me had I called the Lieutenant that. Fool, that is, not hero.

So this is a ballad of fools and heroes, and maybe you can work out which is which.

Father I only heard of, never met, and if he was anything like me, he was never small. Or 'beag', which was their term for small, in Kildare, when I began to learn their tongue. My own mother was from the Temne people near Sierra

Leone and I was led to believe she was his prize for a while and she cleaned the deerskins he sold at Silver Bluff on the Savannah River.

He called her April because that was her birth month and Small because that's what she was then. And when she got too big with me and could clean no more, he sold her for rum, linen and a gun to Old Montgomery who needed a servant and knew he would get two for one. So she had me in a barn and my two brothers with a different father and my sister called Patty all born in slavery.

At least they knew who their father was. I could only dream of mine. Or listen to her stories of him. That he was from a place called Mayo long before he ran with the Bayou Indians and skinned pelts with them and sold them to the riverboat traders. And because of that, or because of the wounds he inflicted with his skinning knife, he went by the name Skinner Mayo.

So the only house I knew was a charnel house. And the only one to love in it was April Small.

I grew up between colours, between races, but it did me no favours, I had my back opened like the rest of them, picking suckers in Old Montgomery's tobacco fields. So my song will be like me, a runaway one, somewhere between a lament and a ballad.

Not a lot of spit and devilry about it, with those double rhymes that make you smile.

> *I'm sorry dear Larry says I*
> *To see you in this situation*
> *And blister my limbs if I lie*
> *I'd as lief it had been my own station*

You see I learned my balladspeak from the servants in Leinster House and on those Dublin streets contagious to it. The mansions were very new and the streets were very old. And from the same Leinster House on Kildare Street to the River Liffey was just a walk and though I stood out like a peacock it was a walk I took most days. I learned to read from Mr Daniel Defoe and could have learned to write from Mr Ogilvie but those lessons never took. I preferred the rhyming stuff.

Those rhymes seemed to come from the air over the bridges of the river always smelling of ordure or herring or the cries of the seagulls tho' someone must have written them. All to do with thievery, swag, graverobbing and dancing 'The Kilmainham Minnit'.

Which was the little minuet the feet did after the hangman's drop and the Darby O'Gallagher's last hurrah. And if Major Sirr's two bullets did anything, they saved Lord Edward that.

So what right have I to attempt this ballad? None, I would answer, except I saw the bits that few others could see. The bits none of the ballads I've heard would ever touch on.

Because he wasn't Lord Edward then and I didn't care too much then about where Mayo was either. All I knew was that he wasn't dead though he would have been if I'd left him on the dead field. He had finished his burnt chicken and there was corn juice round his mouth and I was wearing his boots. He didn't say anything more and neither did I and I felt a strange comfort in the silence and the presence of another's body whose breathing was the only sign of life I could hear. I had been so long alone, maybe that was it, afraid of the crackling twig and the rattle of an approaching harness. I was a runaway and knew that my back would pay dearly for wherever my feet had taken me. My feet too – for Old Montgomery had whipped on the bare feet so many times that my soles were like scuffed leather.

I wondered did he always enjoy these kinds of silences, and then smelt burning hair and saw the curls around his forehead singeing from being too near the fire and I realized he was asleep, from pain or exhaustion or both. So I pulled his head back and tramped out the flames with his boots and laid him down beside the embers and covered him with the canvas I used to sleep on. And I prayed that it wouldn't rain.

But I was woken early, by steady drops. And although I was soaked, I was glad of it, for the whey-coloured light was just coming through the trees and I could hear the clop and rattle of approaching wagons. They would be coming for the bodies and I thought it best if we found a place deeper in the forest, where the swamp gave way to harder ground. I broke a few more sticks and tied them to the sled I had made the day before, so they made something like a fixed plank. Then I hauled him in his canvas hammock and settled him on it. He groaned again, still only half-awake, and I stuck the knife and the trowel and the pieces of flint and whatever other things I had in the bag and was pulling him through the trees when I felt something was missing.

What could I have left behind I had no idea. I had few enough possessions, but I trundled back and sure enough there it was, gleaming in the charcoal of last night's fire. The golden locket with the porcelain mother inside.

I picked it up with one hand and stuffed it in my pocket and I could hear the cart horses whinnying and the stretchers dropping beyond the trees and I looked through the hanging moss and I could see the coats by the carts were blue. I could have delivered him to them then and there and hoped for the best but I knew they would have killed him outright and might have whipped me bloody anyway and delivered me back to Old Montgomery, wherever he was, who would have opened my back to the fresh air again. Not to talk about the soles of my feet. And there was another thing – I was like a child with a prize I had found, a child that wasn't used to prizes and no one was taking it from me.

So I pulled him through the swamp till my arms were aching. And when the mud gave way to solid ground and the slope of the ground got harder, I tied a rope around the handles of the sled and strung it over my forehead and pulled again, with hands and forehead now. And that way we travelled for an hour or so, away from the clean-up of the dead field into the silence of the great forest. And I made camp again by a ridge over a river below and I laid him in a patch of sunlight and watched the steam rise off him as the canvas he was wrapped in dried.

He was in a fever, half-asleep and half-awake and he spoke every now and then, but if I told you I remembered the words I would be telling a lie. They were almost words, he was in that animal state where the speech doesn't know what it is.

I saw a black bear down by the white water pulling fish out with his paw and thought I might try the same but I hadn't the claws he was blest with so I tied the knife to a piece of wood and when the bear loped off I clambered down the ridge to where the salmon were leaping through the haze of spray, the sun making a rainbow of the drops around them. I tried to skewer them with the spear I had made but I could never be as fast as that bear.

Then I saw the pool below the rainbow where they were gathering for the jump and I stabbed at the biggest of them and caught him in the gut and the water turned red as I raised him out of the spray and I threw him in the grass beside me and speared some more. I had three of them by my feet, still flapping and alive, by which time the pool was all bloody and I could see them no more. So I bashed their heads off the rocks and stuck them in my shirtfront and began the climb back. And once back there I lit a fire and I knew what my plan was.

I must have known it all along, because every action I had taken since I found him was heading in this direction. Sometimes we do things without knowing it and arrive at the result. And we know then that we knew it all along. When Lily and Sam and Jesse and Boston Joe said they were running to Charleston to join the King's Ethiopian Regiment I lagged behind and hid in the woods and it was only two days later when I found them strung up in that clearing that I knew why. And most of the King's Ethiopian died anyway, not of battle wounds either, of fever. They were dumped on the roadsides as the armies retreated.

So the plan was this. I would let the fever die down. I would get him back to a walking state. I would mend the wound in his side and I would make some kind of crutch for him and we would make our way back to Charleston. And if the bluecoats found us, he was an English officer and he was my master. And if the redcoats found us, he was what he was, and I had kept him whole and I would get one of the King's freedom papers for my reward. And I took the locket out of my pocket and rubbed the gold until it shone and I opened it and I looked at his porcelain mother again. She was of an elegant race. I could tell it by the way she held her head.

Her nose tilted upwards and her mouth perfect and closed and her hair cascading backwards. Was my mother that beautiful? I wondered. When Mayo first beheld her? Before he sold her to Old Montgomery? She was, but it wasn't that porcelain beauty. Her kind of beauty could never have been held inside a locket. It was everywhere. It whispered in the trees above me, it murmured as the wind shivered the Spanish moss.

It told me I had my own prize now and there would be no more whipping. A prize that looked like a rare bird some fancy huntsman had shot from the sky. An egret or a crane or a stork. His throat, with the smears of dried blood that I reminded myself to clean. There was a wispy beard around his chin that spread down towards his Adam's apple. And his hand moved from the canvas wrapping he was in and began tugging at the bloodied coat that covered the wound in his side. I pulled his hand away since I didn't want him to worry it. But the hand pulled back again to scratch so I tied one hand to the other and when he moaned, I said, don't worry, you're not my prisoner. And I went searching in the scrub for some plantain. I found a bunch of it and mashed the leaves and the stalks into a paste between my hands and I spread the paste over the wound. There was no yellow stuff yet, just the caked blood and I dragged his body into the sunlight again so the paste could dry.

I have to leave your hands tied, and I'm sorry.

He didn't answer. Just those grey-green eyes looking at me under the damp hair.

I'll get you well, I told him, well enough to walk at least, and I'll take you back to Charleston.

He still didn't answer. Maybe it was the fever, coming and going. But his eyes told me he was listening.

21

And if the bluecoats stop us on the way, I am your servant and always have been and my name isn't Tony Small. My name is Mayo.

Some breaths came out, but there was no need for him to speak.

And if we make it back to Charleston, return the favour. Get me one of those papers the King promised.

The eyes did something then, they did something strange. They seemed to glow with a light or a promise. And it was as I had never seen eyes before. The pupils had flecks of gold in them. They were misting up with water, he must have been in pain but the wetness only seemed to make them larger. And the fire was well lit now so I gutted the salmon and skewered them on sticks and as they were browning, I found a branch with a crook in it like a dowsing rod and I began whittling away the knobbly bits.

It will be a crutch, I told him, you'll need one to walk.

And he opened his mouth and said his first real word that day. And of course, I should have known.

The word was water.

So I turned the salmon on their sticks and I clambered down the ravine again and filled my canister with river water. And by the time I got back the fish were blistering so I laid them in the grass. I fed him water, drop by drop onto those cracked lips. Then I took pieces of the browned salmon and ate myself while I fed broken bits of flesh to him.

I didn't want him to talk. Things were fine and dandy there in the forest with the smoke curling up through the trees and the sun spreading its fingers through them and the wood-pecker chattering. I wasn't lonesome anymore and could have lived like that for a long long time. And the eating seemed to take some effort from him because his eyes closed and his head fell back on the canvas and I scattered the embers with his boots that I was still wearing and wrapped the canvas around him once more. I went walking then, to get a handle on the world outside of our little dandy paradise.

It was the opposite of paradise. I climbed the biggest tree I could find and sat myself among the high branches where I could see the river and the battle site and the blue colours of the Continentals burying their dead. There was the big plantation beyond with the horses moving to and fro in rows and the blue jackets marching, and I knew it was just a matter of time before somebody found us.

And I heard movement underneath me and saw the horses of the Cherokees, and the Cherokees themselves wearing stolen military jackets, dragging someone still living on a rope behind them. He wouldn't be living for long, I thought, and when the quiet returned I slid down slowly and made my way back to where he slept. He was sleeping soundly now, and the fire was out and it would stay out.

We were three days in the forest before they found us. Three good days. Because there is a thing that happens when you wake and see the morning sun come through the huge umbrella of branches above, the jays and the woodpeckers beginning their chatter through the vines. You realize that whatever your mother lost when the Arabs dragged her through another forest entirely, is yours now. You never knew it when you dug the corn rows and pulled the suckers off the tobacco plants and thought of a lifetime doing the same. You never had it to lose, but you have found it now, with the morning sun coming through the canopy of leaves, when you realized nobody was your master, for these days at least. Except for maybe the one

23

that was managing to stand on the crutch you had carved out for him, with the thoroughly ripped red coat. But then you were the master of him, it was odd, he needed you the way a child needs its father. You take him by the elbow and lead him through the morning trees and he says, thank you Tony and you say, hush now, hush, because there are children below, Cherokee children and they are pulling salmon from the river as they have done for an eternity. You say hush now, because the thing that you have found is freedom, he has found you and you have found him and or maybe the freedom found the two of you, but all you know is it's here now. And he hushes and watches them string their salmon and vanish back into the forest because the forest is theirs. And you want to stretch this moment out because you know that now that he can walk again you have to find your way back to what he calls civilization where this freedom thing might turn out to be not such a gorgeous pantomime.

Gorgeous pantomime. It was a ghost of a phrase that would come later. Much later.

For now, you talk about how you might make it back. Take the road to Charleston or try a flat-bottomed boat along the river. But in your heart of hearts you don't want to make it back. You know whatever the outcome it will not be as good and peaceful as this. But you don't tell him that. You tell him what you know of how the forest winds and turns into swamp and of the plantations empty of everything now except Patriot militia. He scratches maps in the earth with his stick of the various rivers leading to the Charleston estuary but your knowledge of them is flimsy, and you've never been to Charleston.

And in the end it just happened. As they say in the Bible, it was. You woke up in the morning to find boots around you. Boots like the ones you wore, they knew you had scavenged them and they were tying you to the tree before you noticed that their coats were red. And he stepped out from underneath his shelter of leaves and he said, gentlemen, please. They could tell from his ripped red coat with the braids still on it, or from his posture or from the way he spoke. I will never quite fathom these things. But as soon as he spoke, they knew. They knew he was above them, they knew he had that thing they must bow down to. This man is Tony Small, my nurse and my saviour. And he untied me as they took off their hats. And he introduced himself.

Lieutenant Lord Edward Fitzgerald of the 19th Regiment of Foot.

The King's Paper

Later, much later, there would be another uniform I would stash under the orchestra pit in the theatre in Crow Street, Dublin. And had the wearer of one met the wearer of the other, one of them wouldn't have come out alive. So maybe his story is like everyone's story. A body at war with itself.

But the first uniform was the redcoat one. The white breeches all stained with blood.

And the saviour finally knew what to call the saved.

Lieutenant.

Because it was Lieutenant this and Lieutenant that as they manhandled him back through the forest on the sled that I had made.

They took bare notice of the saviour. Me. I could have scarpered, taken my chances. But his green eyes looked up from between their bobbing red shoulders and caught my own. I took it as a signal to follow.

Their regiments owned the road when we reached it and they put him in a cart with others of the wounded. They were good enough to let me walk behind it with a motley crowd of runaways dressed in bits of fancy clothes they had taken from their owners. There were soldiers riding fast in twos and threes who splashed back and forth in the adjacent swamp and there was a huge cloud of dust ahead and I could only imagine how long the carnival went and how far away the front of it was. Behind us there was the lowing of cattle and the grunting of hogs and there were geese that rattled their wings and the shouts of the barefoot boys that drove them along. But we were the lucky ones I came to realize when I got the smell that nearly sickened me and saw them lying by the dusty grass along the roadside. Nobodies like me dressed in bits and pieces of military clothing. Black or white, their faces were strangely pale and it wasn't with the dust from the processions of horse. There were blisters round their lips, necks and naked torsos and there was the smell that was stronger than the reek of the cattle and horse dung. I asked the one beside me what it was and he told me it was the smallpox and I saw the same sores on his own face and I hung back behind him because he was clinging to the cart with his poxy hands and that was my first mistake.

Because the closer we got to Charleston the more they hemmed us in and the crush ahead of me in their runaway clothes kept me back and I lost sight of the cart and the one with the yellow sores hanging on to the back of it. I thought I'd find the cart again in Charleston but having never been there that was wishful thinking. Because the road got smaller, it had to wind between the great defensive mounds they had built and I saw the runaways of the King's Ethiopian Regiment with guns in their hands and proper uniforms on their backs looking out from the sharpened tree trunks they had stuck in the mounds of earth and I wondered would I join them and wear a uniform and fight the Continentals and maybe get to stick a bayonet in the guts of the Montgomery boys. But I didn't know then the war was lost already.

There was the big square and the soldiers milling round and a line of bayonets that sent the mounted soldiers and the carts one way and sent us the other. I shouted his name but how was he to hear me in that inferno of hooves on the cobblestones, moaning cattle and the cries and the shrieks of the crowd in front of me and behind. And the afternoon sun was beating down now with that fierce Carolina heat I knew too well. I was carried with the mass of human flesh to the quays where the ships of the line waited, pointing their cannon towards the shore.

I slept on the waterfront that night and listened to the waves slapping against the hulls and the talk around me of who would get on them and who wouldn't. And when the sun came up, I heard the tapping of wood off the cobblestoned quays and saw a figure in the mist walking towards me with two fresh boots and one old crutch.

My Lieutenant, with a rolled paper in his free hand.

My saviour, he said, deserves more than a pair of old boots.

And he sat beside me on the quayside, unrolled the paper and showed me where he had signed my name. It was a certificate of service to the British Crown, he told me, as of course I couldn't read it, and it licensed me to go to the Island of Jamaica, or elsewhere, at my own option.

And I asked him where he was going.

As an officer of the Crown, he said, it is my duty to stay here.

Did the officer need a manservant?

Every officer does.

Then I might stay here with you, instead of going to the island of Jamaica. Or elsewhere.

And the saviour must have been funny that day, because the officer of the Crown smiled.

Maybe elsewhere would suit you better?

Only if you go too.

And the officer smiled again.

I could of course use a manservant. And you, Tony Small? What could you use?

A way out of here.

Come with me then, he said and walked off, tapping the stones with his crutch.

Even if we were all walking to hell, we would find ways to get in front. Maybe walking to heaven there would be no distinctions but none of us was walking to heaven. He was my way to get in front, he was the only thing that distinguished me from the others that crowded the waterfront, that slept in the half-burnt houses, thousands of runaways like me and more pressing in every day. Most of them got their papers and they thought that that was their distinction. But I had my Lieutenant. He was mine.

He led me into a stable, below the officers' quarters.

How shall I address you, Tony Small?

Whatever way you want, Lieutenant.

Edward, he said. Ned, to those who claim to know me.

Do I know you, Lieutenant?

As well as anyone here. You saved my bacon.

Bacon?

My leg. My life. You were my angel of redemption. You deserve more than that paper from King George. You deserve rooms upstairs, in the officer's quarters. But …

He looked around the byres of hay above each stall.

I can bed down here, Lieutenant.

Ned, he said again.

Ned, I repeated. I preferred Lieutenant.

You're acquainted with horses?

I glanced around the stalls, the horses' rumps steaming in the midday heat. Those everlasters that would plod for hours and never run. But maybe there was no running needed now.

I am.

Choose one of them for me. Have it washed and cleaned and ready each morning.

He turned to leave.

Ned, I called.

The word felt like a pebble in my mouth. But I needed it, to enquire as he had.

How should I address you?

Ned, in the stables. Up above, my Lord.

So, 'Lieutenant' was gone, I thought to myself. Left in the forest, with the dead.

I made a bed for myself in the byre, above the only one of those everlasters that looked like he had any running left in him. But he could only ever plod in those Charleston streets, growing more crowded by the hour. There was only one way out of there, and it was on those ships that crowded the bay and those ships could only take so many.

I slept a dreamless sleep, and an angel called my name to wake me out of it.

Tony.

I turned in the straw and saw his face, above a steaming cup.

Coffee.

He handed it to me. I had no option but to drink.

How do I like it?

How do you like what, Lieutenant?

Ned.

Ned.

I would never get used to it.

He dipped a finger in the steaming cup.

The French way. With warm milk. A spoon of honey. You'll make it in the pantry, up above.

I will?

You will. And what do you call me up above?

My Lord?

There is a charade to be played, dear Tony. Everywhere but the forest where we found each other. You might come to miss it yet.

A charade?

A game. Servant and master. Of forelocks and titles. You are my manservant, Tony. You speak when spoken to. And you address me − how?

My Lord.

You bring me coffee, the French way, at sunrise. And you ready my horse. So get to it.

And I got to it.

Charleston

We said little in the quarters up above, when I brought up the coffee and the officers went about their morning business. We played that charade, of servant and master, and some days I wished that he was back helpless in that forest paradise. That I was dripping water on his parched lips, feeding him bits of burnt salmon, not coffee laced with honey.

My Lieutenant taught me to shave with a razor and strop, though with his downy skin it was hardly necessary, and to shine those new boots, the same as my own, and each new lesson became part of the charade, the end of which would be the manservant, patiently holding the reins in the stables below till my Lieutenant came down to begin the real business of the day.

Which involved arranging a dignified exit. The war was reaching its conclusion. Though dignity was hardly possible, in those harbourfront streets, crowded with runaways, all of them hoping for what the King had promised.

Most of them similar to the manservant that guided his Lieutenant's horse. Who held those reins as if they were his sole distinction. Who kept the King's letter wrapped in oilskin round his belt.

I found the crutch that I had cut for him lying in the gutter and took it back to my straw bed. My Lieutenant hardly noticed it, he was walking better now and had no need of it, but it was a memento, a reminder of something.

And some nights I needed reminding. I wondered what would happen in Jamaica or whatever elsewhere we ended up in but didn't care to ask. There was no talk of the future and if the future was to be this, me walking behind or in front, then so be it.

There were prisoners to be taken from the berms outside the town to the waterfront where my Lieutenant would help them down to the rowboats that would lead them to the prison ships. He talked to them as he would to equals and I held the reins by the quays until the rowboat took him back. I would link my hands under my Lieutenant's good leg and hoist him back onto the everlaster. He would say, thank you Tony, I bid you good night, and the next morning the game would begin again.

Then one day after Christmas I was told to get my papers ready. There was no need to get my *one* paper ready – I slept with it, still wrapped in its oilskin cover, under my pillow of straw. And I dragged the Lieutenant's trunks behind him, who held the reins of the old everlaster himself. His leg was fully cured and he dismounted on his own in the chaos of the waterfront.

An officer beside him seemed amused by the spectacle beneath.

33

What will we do with him? My Lieutenant asked, and for one cold moment I thought it all had been more than a charade. It had been a deception, a lie. I would be sent back through the berms to the Continentals.

But no. He meant the horse.

Let your mulatto take him back, the officer answered.

You mean my Tony? My Lieutenant replied, and the smile was playing round his lips and we both acknowledged that the game had not yet ended.

Would you be so kind, dear Tony, to take the everlaster back to the stables, the trunks being loaded?

I would be happy to, my Lord.

He didn't bow, so much as incline his head.

Then I unloaded the trunks and bumped them down the steps to the rowboat. An able seaman stashed them inside. I went back up the steps to take the reins once more and guide the everlaster through the gathering chaos.

There would be no dignity to this final exit.

I took the crutch that I had made for my Lieutenant and found a new use for it − as a stick to beat my way back through those runaway streets. But the crowds were all moving like a wave, towards the harbour. I gave up the attempt then, and sent the horse running free. I had lost all distinction now, all I had was a paper, like ten thousand others. But the same rowboat was coming back and I battered my way with the crutch to the steps by the water. And the able seaman must have recognized my face because he held out a hand to take me on board.

We rowed off then, barely in time to avoid the lines of bodies tumbling from the quays above, threshing through the brine, trying to clutch the dripping oars.

I saw what shouldn't be seen. A child thrown down, missed by the outstretched arms below, skewered on the spike of a barnacled buoy. So many jumping from the quays and threshing through the water, clinging to the oars until they snapped, that the sailors had to hit their clinging hands off with the broken oars, lash them back with the knotted ropes, stab them with the marlin spikes. The ones that couldn't swim went under and the ones that could made a dark brown wave with a foaming crest of arms in front of it, heading out to the anchor ropes of the big wooden hulks whose sails were dropping one by one. And the rowboat reached a ladder that was swinging from the huge belly of the hull with the flapping sails above like giant petticoats, and I climbed, one boot after the other on the wet wooden struts. I could see them clambering up the anchor rope like circus acrobats or squirrels up a vine and the ones that didn't lose their grip were tossed back in by the sailors up above. But two pairs of hands gripped each one of my own when I reached the top of the rope ladder and dropped me on the deck.

I looked around for my Lieutenant, but the deck was all tumbling ropes and flapping sails and anchors being drawn and barefoot seamen running this way and that. There was the awful feeling then, that I'd boarded the wrong ship. And that feeling became a certainty when I was marched to the hold, told to clamber down and didn't so much clamber as fall into the knee-high water below. It was water that smelt like a latrine, the leavings of so many humans and as my eyes got used to the darkness, I could see them all around, the whites of the eyes of others, too many others, and not one of them said a word. Were they the King's Ethiopians, I wondered, or other runaways like myself? I touched the oilskin under my belt with the King's letter, and resolved to keep it close, always dry. I found a space to sit on a plank below a solid, curving piece of oak which continued on its journey through the wooden roof above us. It must have been a tree once, and we must have been all human once.

There were barnacles against my back and the planks were rotted with slime and then the whole ship pitched and rolled, and the rancid water sluiced around my boots and there were three great booms above which must have been the guns making their farewell salute.

We were on our way then, to Jamaica. Or elsewhere.

SECOND VERSE

Elsewhere

A voice came out of the darkness.

Your boots, it said. They're kicking me.

A woman's.

I looked down into the gloom below. I saw her perched on the lip of the hold's planking, up to her knees in the water that swilled backwards and forwards, like coffee in a giant cup.

You could move up here, I said.

Is there room? she asked.

I reached down, my hand felt hers, small and strong with broad scars around the wrists.

Sally was her name. She squeezed in beside me, drew her knees up so her lips could almost kiss them and told me it was strange, to be amongst so many and to not be chained.

Chains are a thing of the past, I told her, and explained the import of the paper I had wrapped in the oilskin and tucked in my belt.

For you, maybe. Not for me.

She examined it, squinting in whatever light came from the guttering candle.

Have you read this letter? she asked.

No, I said.

You can't read?

Can you?

I kept the books for my master, she said and brought the paper closer to her face.

I must learn, I said. Maybe the letter can teach me.

It's a certificate of service to the British Crown. Signed by some lieutenant. Promising freedom in return for the same service.

Freedom to whom?

To you. The bearer.

She squinted.

Tony Small.

Who makes the promise?

King George the Third.

But has he signed it?

My Lieutenant signed it for him.

She glanced around the crowded, gloomy hold.

So, are you free?

I laid my fingers on the scars around her wrist.

As free as you.

Wait until Jamaica, she said, to find how free you are. Jamaica might make you long for Carolina. If tobacco and cotton were bad, I am told sugar cane is pitiless. Like working amongst sharpened knives.

My Lieutenant has no interest in sugar cane.

And where is he now?

I shrugged.

Maybe he's up on deck, she said. With my merchant.

Your merchant?

A slaver, who has plans for us in Kingston.

And once again the fear took hold. I was on the wrong ship.

You're a free woman, I told her, and nobody's property now.

I have no paper, she told me. I am the property of who-ever takes me off this boat. And the one who got me on will be the one who takes me off.

Has he a name? I asked her.

Mr Tallentire, she said. Who said we could pay for this passage in money or work, and as I have no coin I will have to work. But I suspect his best advantage would be to sell those of us he brought aboard.

She looked at me and smiled wanly.

Unless you have the wherewithal, Tony Small. To wipe my debt clean.

We tried to sleep, pretend the ship's motion was a giant cradle, rocked by a giant hand. Her head fell against my shoulder and slipped off again. She awoke twice, once to retch into the bile below and the second time to poke me awake, point at the light flooding down from the opened hatch.

Barbados

We were brought up from the hold and taken for a walk on the pitching deck. There was roiling water everywhere and a thin brown coastline to our right that must have been the continent we were leaving. The surf washed over our feet as the ship dipped its head and the coastline came into view again.

Strange that something so soft could have caused so much trouble.

Tony Small, I heard and turned, and there my Lieutenant was, with two others in uniform, leaning on a cannon barrel, eating a red apple. I felt a wave of relief and a pang of hunger.

I made to move towards him, but a midshipman grabbed my collar to pull me back. The calico shirt jerked my Adam's apple, like a noose.

Leave him be, my Lieutenant said, he's my manservant.

The words meant nothing to the brute, but he unclenched his fingers. And I could see the smile playing round my Lieutenant's face.

I knew our charade was once more beginning.

There, he said pointing with the apple core, is the America we have lost. Will you miss it?

And I tried to think of the right answer, but in the end came up with the safest one.

It depends, I said.

On what? an officer beside him asked, without so much as looking round.

On where we're headed.

To Jamaica, the officer said. Where you'll pick sugar cane instead of cotton.

So we'll be sold. I said it as a statement of fact, and not a question.

That depends, the same one said. And why am I talking to a runaway negro, pray?

Because, said my Lieutenant, he is a free man under the English Crown. He has a letter to prove it. And he wants nothing more than to return home.

Home to Africa?

No. To Mayo.

Even worse.

Still and all. He longs for his lost kingdom. Am I right, my dear and faithful Tony?

And he placed an arm around my shoulder, still wet from the hold. Sally stared, from behind, her mouth open. The officer turned back towards his receding continent. And my Lieutenant led me towards what he called our quarters.

They were in a small cabin with a sloping roof. There was a hammock swinging from the roof and a writing table, a mess pot and a cabinet for grog and water. A paradise, after the swilling hold below.

Tell me about Mayo, my Lieutenant said.

Mayo?

Mayo. You said the word in Eutaw. I heard it, in my fever. Or was it a dream?

Maybe a dream, I said. I have many dreams.

There's a reason you're here, Tony Small.

There is. I found you in a forest.

Besides that.

So I told him. How the father I had never met sold my mother with me inside her to Old Montgomery. And the less he knew about the rest, the better.

This father's name?

Skinner Mayo.

There was a stringed instrument in the hammock, shaped like a pear, and he plucked it idly while we talked.

Do you know this tune? he asked.

I told him I didn't, my knowledge of tunes was few and far between.

Maybe your father did.

He plucked the strings with his broken nails and the dancing tune echoed round him.

'Lilliburlero', he said. About a battle between kings. In a country neither of them cared for. He took a breath. Ireland. Have you heard of it?

I shook my head.

Adjacent to England.

I told him I had heard of England. The sceptred isle. From Old Montgomery.

Sceptred isle, he said. Of course.

And who won the battle? I asked him. King George?

No, he said. King George had no part of it. William, who maybe sent your father scurrying west. He smiled.

And what do you know about King George?

What you told me.

Remind me. What did I tell you?

I am a free man under King George, I said.

And he smiled, again.

Yes, he said, so you are.

I was freed from the hold, as well. I made a bed between the rainwater barrels, of which there was precious little until our next destination. Which was not Jamaica, but Barbados and after that St Lucia and the only king that ruled in both of them was King Sugar. I was told this by a trader, the same Mr Tallentire that Sally had spoken of.

It happened like this:

I was woken by raindrops. But there was not a cloud in the starry sky. There was a gentleman, spooning water from the barrel at my head, looking down at me, amongst my sackcloth beddings. The drops from his ladle glistened silver in the moonlight.

Excellent quarters.

His English was round, and full of earthy vowels. Its music reminded me of Old Montgomery.

I must sleep near my Lieutenant.

Ah. That explains it.

He perched above me, while the whole ship, apart from the two of us, and the merchant seamen in the crow's-nest, slept.

Explains what, sir?

Why you're not in the hold. With the rest of my charges.

I was awake now and rose, asked for a sup of his ladle.

Indeed, he said, and offered it to me.

Your charges?

In a manner of speaking. I arranged their passage. Paid good money to the quartermaster.

He drew a cigar from his top pocket.

Will you walk with me, kind sir?

I said I would. I remembered Sally and wanted to know more.

They are free men –

And women, he interjected. Yes, in a manner of speaking, they are. Free now. Runaways. But how do you think they got aboard?

Perhaps a letter?

A certificate of service? To the British Crown? I have heard of such a document.

I have one myself, sir.

Indeed.

He puffed. That word again. It led to pauses.

Which explains your presence. Up here, in this balmy night. Under these stars.

They stretched, like a great foliage of pinpricks, above us.

No, sir. Their only contract is with me. I paid the quartermaster for their passage.

To Jamaica?

Good God no. Jamaica would be too kind to them. To Barbados.

And once there?

I sell them on. To King Sugar.

But you said they were free?

Free enough, on board this ship. Free enough, in the hold below us. But there's a principal to be repaid. He turned to me. He didn't smile.

And it will be. As in any business. In the market. In Jamestown, Barbados.

And I wish it was just the thought of Sally that provoked me. The thought of chains, around her thin, scarred wrists again.

But it wasn't.

It was the smell of burning tobacco, from his cigar. I had topped and suckered those weeds. And bled on them.

Tallentire placed one foot on a cannon-mount and leaned over the side. He took one last puff and dropped the cigar, into the receding ocean. I gripped his free boot, from behind. I hoisted it towards the moon above us and tipped him over. He had barely time to gasp.

He hit the water with hardly a splash and the ship of the line sailed on.

Sally was done with him.

St Lucia

Mr Tallentire had kept his designs and his company to himself. So Barbados was upon us by the time they noticed his absence. Five planters gathered on the waterfront, all with promissory notes from 'one Mr Tallentire', to relieve him of his charges. His charges gathered on deck and refused to disembark, knowing what their future on Barbados plantations would be.

So they travelled on with us.

We reached St Lucia with Mr Tallentire's whereabouts still a mystery. His charges were deposited on the harbourfront, like so many migrant birds.

What does a free woman do? Sally asked me, clutching her few bundles to her thin chest.
   You find work, I suppose, I told her. Or a husband.
   Will you marry me, then, Tony?
   I smiled. I shook my head.

Come with me, she said. Up into those hills.

They loomed across the bay like an inverted W.

We'll live like Adam and Eve. On berries and nuts.

I seem to be wedded to my Lieutenant, I answered. Where he goes, I go.

Which was to the Morne Fortune Fort, above the bay.

I kissed her cheek goodbye and dragged his cases onto the waiting cart.

The heat.

For once I was glad of the calico shirt I wore.

His red coat was damp within minutes, as the horses dragged our bones up that hill.

A volcano smouldered in the distance and I could see figures in the fields around us, bent low, moving methodically through the rows of sugar cane.

Mr Tallentire jumped ship, my Lieutenant said, which must have proved a blessing to his charges.

How? I asked.

Don't pretend ignorance, he said. They would have been sold, so King Sugar could have his way with them.

Indeed, I said.

I was finding my own use for that odd word.

In fact, my Lieutenant opined, I would hazard a guess that he didn't jump at all. But was helped on his way.

Who would commit such a crime? I asked.

One of his charges. Who knew what fate awaited him. In Barbados.

But they were locked in the hold, I said.

And the words were out before I had thought of their consequence.

Only at night, he said. Who knows what could happen, at odd corners of the ship, in the daytime?

Who knows, indeed?

That word. I must use it more sparingly.

Or even at night? What if they had a saviour? As I once had? If one of my fellow officers took up their cause? An able seaman? Or even my faithful manservant, who slept amongst the rain barrels?

We had come within sight of the gaunt fortifications, on the hilltop. Morne Fortune.

Tell me it isn't so, Tony.

I cannot, my Lord.

He sighed. Long and hard.

I see.

And he edged the horses forward, towards that mournful fort.

Then let's not talk of it again.

And we didn't. Talk, that is. For days.

Morne Fortune

St Lucia was small, as I discovered when I had time to survey it from that dismal fort. Two conical hills at one end and a lightly belching volcano at the other. I had time on my hands there, plenty of time, since my Lieutenant had abandoned conversation after the mystery of the disappearance of Mr Tallentire. I understood my duties so well that they occupied just the beginning and the end of each day. The other officers understood where my loyalties lay and burdened me with nothing else. They rode out in team most days, on business which I understood was to do with the recent departure of the French. My Lieutenant was proficient in their language and therefore much in demand. So I was left alone in the heat, with the remaining horses – my only other companions in that humid hilltop magazine being the mosquitos, the horseflies and other buzzing winged creatures which I had no name for but which I came to recognize by the weals they left on my skin.

There was a French word for this particular brand of silence, one which I learned of much later.

Froideur.

And it gave rise to the strangest feeling. I was ashamed of this feeling, at first. It was so unwelcome, it felt like shame itself. But that peculiar silence which my Lieutenant had perfected made me long for the charnel house. For the company of others, the sound of other voices, if only for the howls of outrage or the moans of complaint. For my mother's dying breath in her canvas hammock.

I would get used to it. The glance avoided, the speech withheld. As one more thing to be endured, like the horseflies, the mosquitos and the heat. And I would come to wonder, did I imagine those days in the Eutaw forest?

Meantime, the isle was full of noises.

Like Prospero's island, which I would see one year later, perched high above the stage in Drury Lane. That isle was full of sounds and sweet airs. Ariel's pipe and flute.

This isle was full of other noises. Drums at night, from the twin hills.

Rumblings from the volcano.

The clatter, for clatter it was, of insect against insect.

The buzzing of wings.

All it was missing was an actual tempest. And then it came.

A hurricane. It bent the trees into the shapes of paper theatrical streamers. Its Prospero sent peals of thunder from the cascading skies above.

Its sheets of lightning revealed my Lieutenant trying to tie down the baggage carts.

He failed. They flew into the air like matchboxes and followed the regimental tents, tumbling over the magazine walls.

I saved the horses from following them, by turning their heads to the walls, clutching seventeen pairs of reins, as the barn doors tore themselves free and flapped off like giant bats.

And when the tempest had spent itself, we inspected the damaged plantations, the fields of flattened sugar cane.

I thought of Sally. I imagined her riding that storm like a battered angel. I wondered where she had ended up.

And I soon found out, in the town of Soufriere. Or what the hurricane had left of it.

Most of the streets had been levelled. The church had survived. And the whorehouse.

After the clean-up I rode behind my Lieutenant on a mule, to the parade ground. It was next to another armoury. The horses sweated under the fierce sun and the sea glimmered like a sheet of melting lead. I stood to attention as the officers rode past the lines of men and cannon, and as a band played the tune my Lieutenant had plucked on his pear-shaped instrument. 'Lilliburlero'.

I had to walk him to the whorehouse that night. Holding the reins of the horse, while three officers behind him made jokes about what they called his maroon, walking in front.

My Tony, he said to them, would walk me to the pearly gates.

And while not addressed to me, the words felt as if they were. They were like the first drops of rain, after a long drought.

And there were gates in front of the whorehouse, gates made of painted metal that had long ago been peeled of their white in the torrid heat. There were vines tumbling over them that made them useless as gates, since the roots had embedded in the caked soil long ago, and they could never now be shut. There was music coming from the sagging building, there were frames where there once had been windows but with not a pane of glass now to be seen. I would come to know many whorehouses over the years and would learn to read the movements of my Lieutenant's heart by how many times he visited them. When his heart was broken, he would visit them nightly. When his heart was whole, he had no need. But his heart can't have been broken that night, and if it had been it was too early in our journey together for me to know of it.

I led the horses round the back as the officers entered through the front. I was tying the horses to the posts behind when someone called my name.

Tony.

And it was like the second drops of rain, that followed the first.

But this voice wasn't his.

I turned and saw her.

Sally.

She was wearing a soiled apron and was balancing a jug on her head.

Are you a whore now, Sally?

No, she said. They wouldn't take me. They want the Creole girls, born of white planters and African women.

A little like me, I said.

Was your father a planter? she asked.

And I realized how much I had not told her. About Skinner Mayo and Old Montgomery. But it seemed too complicated now.

So what do you do, Sally?

I fetch water from the river. I clean the linens. I scrub the floors. For bed and board.

So you're free?

If you call that freedom.

And they leave you alone?

If they touch me, she said, I'll run to the hills. Like Rupez Roche.

Rupez Roche?

You've heard the drums at night?

And she told me then of the villages of free slaves, or runaways, like me, who lived in the hills and had African manners. Who emerged from the jungle to sell their wares in Castries or Soufriere, on market day.

And nobody could touch them.

We could run there, Tony, together …

I did think about it. I thought about it when she lifted the pitcher from her head and gave it to my mouth to sip.

I thought about it when she said goodbye and slipped between the whorehouse doors.

And as I thought about it, I laid my hands against the glassless window of the kitchens and watched the women come and go. They would squat over soapy basins and lift their skirts and wash themselves between the legs. They would clean their faces and add rouge to their cheeks and red paint to their lips, and take the trays of food and rum and wine that the servants had laid out, balance them on one hand and make their way to the inner rooms, where the music played and the laughter never seemed to stop.

Do you want one?

I turned and saw a barefoot boy, a jug of liquor under each arm.

I could do you a favour for a shilling.

And however tempting his offer was, I told him no.

And I laid my head down on the caked earth beside the water trough and was still thinking about it and I must have slept then because a pair of boots like the ones I tried to rob prodded me awake. I opened my eyes to the red dawn in the Caribbean sky.

Your master needs some help, I heard, and all of the ss's were slurred.

I leapt up and saw an officer swaying, trying to fix his belt.

Let me help you sir, I said, but I was struck away with one end of the belt.

I would call that presumption, he said. You'd feel the whip if you were mine.

I stepped backwards and said nothing.

Well, go, he said, upstairs, maroon, your fop has need of you.

So I walked through the kitchen, and up the stairs which were draped with sleeping girls, and searched room after debauched room until I found my Lieutenant, propped between two half-dressed girls, who held his tousled head over a basin.

Too much rum, said one of them. Get him out –

The red unshaven cheeks glistening with spittle. He looked like what he was, finally. A lost boy.

And he retched then and filled the basin with his swill and they edged him upright and turned him, then let him go so he fell into his saviour's arms.

My Tony, he said. Where have you been?

I have been sleeping.

I propped him upright and turned him towards the broken stairs.

And I have been whoring, he said.

More drinking than whoring, one replied, who was pretty and had her hair dyed white.

Did it not please you? he asked.

Oh mightily, she said. Come again soon.

But her eyes told a different story. She mouthed to me silently – get him out – so I edged him back down the stairs and half carried, half dragged him through the kitchens to the horse trough outside.

I have missed you, Tony, he said.

He was helpless again. He needed his saviour. And maybe his saviour missed him too.

I had to hold the reins with one hand and keep him steady with the other on the walk back.

And he talked, at last. He talked about the Eutaw forest and the King's promise and the Cherokee boys skewering salmon with their sticks. He talked about the passage back, the ocean that we would have to cross, about Lilliburlero and the place called Ireland that awaited us both.

Sally ran, I heard, many years later. To the hills and those drums and whoever that Rupez Roche was. She had her revolution much later, the same as my Lieutenant did. And I only hope hers went better than his.

And the next week we sailed to Martinique, and then across the ocean to the great Elsewhere.

The Passage

He was the sole officer on the Martinique ship. I was given my own hammock in the hold and the ordinary seamen hated me for it. But he was blind to their hatred and deaf to their insults. He was blind to most things round him, except the pear-shaped instrument he played and the birds that would wheel around the rigging.

And after Martinique there was the passage.

My mother spoke little of it. She had made the same passage in the hold of a slaving vessel, after the Arabs had taken her to a market in Tangier. So I could only imagine hers. Not knowing that there was such a thing as an ocean, until she was chained in a wooden hull beneath it. Going to the swamps of Louisiana and to the embraces of Skinner Mayo. Which could well have been heaven compared to what came after. The Carolinas and the tobacco fields of Old Montgomery.

Maybe that's what forgetting is. What we can't bear to remember. So she never talked about that particular hell beneath these pitching waves, that charnel house where you were chained in rows and instead of fire and brimstone of the preachers there was the leavings of your guts and the saltwater that poured down from above, to clean you or to parch you with thirst, again you could never be sure. She would learn about the preacher's hell later that lasted forever. This hell just seemed to last that long. The only exit being the fever, so she must have envied the ones that didn't wake up beside her. They were dead, and their passage had ended.

So my passage was a different one. There was a ship, which heaved on the water, there were four huge sails, there were whippings alright but mainly for the ordinary seamen who came to hate me for the privilege I had fallen into. I wore a ruffed collar, I broke fast with my Lieutenant in his cabin and then walked the decks with him as the whipped ones scoured the boards on their hands and knees. He pointed out an albatross, a gannet, a porpoise, we were all God's creatures he told me and seemed to regard me with as much wonder as he regarded those wild sea creatures. But if he only knew, I was a creature of the land, the soil, always would be, the sea I regarded with abhorrence, it was the great betrayer, its large white mane had pulled my mother from her home, opened her back to the wind too many times and the thought of crossing it would terrify me for ever more. But I smiled and said yes and nodded my shaven head to my Lieutenant's godly apparitions.

And at night I had to mind myself. The cabin boys, the deck swabbers, the able seamen. If they hated the whip and the officers who wielded it, they hated me even more. The whip was in the natural order of things and I was not. I was an interloper, half animal, half crab, all sea lice. But I had my own saviour, on the deck above.

To judge by your back, they would say when I pulled off my manservant's threads each night, you've been whipped more than the whole crew of us.

I have, I told them, but never by the cat.

Dear Tony, they would tell me, we would pull out your teeth one by one, cut off that thing between your legs, feed it to the rats, we would clean this cabin of the stench of you if your master would turn a blind eye.

But he wouldn't. He would have flayed them from the yard-arm, if he had overheard.

Or if I had shared their opinion of me with him.

Snitched, would have been their word. Informed, was a word I would learn more of, later.

And here, I came to realize the enduring peculiarity of our relations.

I had crossed a great divide. I was part of his world, in a way they could never be. The world of that cut-glass decanter in his cabin, the mother-of-pearl mandolin, the gold locket with his mother's polished face that I had plucked from the Eutaw mud.

He seemed unaware of the privileges he had. Or he accepted them without thought, as the horse elegantly curls its head, careless of the fact that it is not a donkey. And that is the way with distinctions, I began to realize. The further down one gets in the pecking order the more important they become. So the cabin boy lorded it over my black self with all of the arrogance of a desert sheikh. He treated the ship-board cat with less contempt.

He won't be your master forever, they would tell me, just you wait for the Liverpool dock.

And they were right. He wouldn't be. Much, much later, he would renounce whatever privilege he had, in that evening in Paris in White's Hotel. He would make common cause with the runaway slave, the Irish croppy. Even with them, the press-ganged seaman.

But we would always have paradise in common.

This Sceptred Isle

There were two coastlines then, one to my left, one to my right, two grey and ever tilting washes, merging with two different horizons. The sun, when it could be seen, rose over one, and set over the other. Then the rains came down, and out of them came a black city that seemed to throw rain back at us.

Liverpool, the cabin boy told me.

The harbour was covered with cloud when the ship docked far out in the channel, the wharves like enormous black fingers coming out of the gloom.

There is a market there, the same cabin boy told me, where I could sell you back to Carolina, and I could buy a good alehouse with the proceeds.

I am sorry, I said, to deny you your alehouse.

Which almost made him laugh.

Damn you, Tony, he muttered. I can't go back to swabbing decks.

But he had to. After helping me load my Lieutenant's belongings onto the longboats. And as the seamen rowed us towards those wharves, I remembered the words on my freedom docket, about Jamaica or Elsewhere.

Was this Elsewhere? I wondered. It was like nowhere I had ever been before. The wind whipped the ocean into froth and the rain sheeted down and there were more warehouses on the shore than I could ever have imagined. I remembered the chaos of war and the exit from Charleston. Here was the same chaos but no war I was aware of. And yet armies of men marched over the wharves above us as the oars rose and fell and the seamen cursed the wind and we entered a world of wooden staves with cranes and pulleys above and giant nets that swung with wooden cases and bales of cotton and rolls of linen and horses dangling above them in harness. There were wooden bridges over which cattle walked, there were whole hillsides of coal, and the men that shovelled it downwards towards the barges below were black with it.

This is England? I asked my Lieutenant.

Yes, he said.

Your home?

This is Liverpool, he said, the main port of England, sometimes my home.

Where else is your home?

Ireland, he said, and there was that word again.

What is Ireland like?

And this question gave rise to a smile. As if it gave rise to a jest that would never be explained.

A good question, he said to the midshipman beside him, that you as an Irishman should be able to answer.

What is Ireland like? the midshipman repeated, in an accent like the ones they had in Barbados. It's a rathole, a

slave ship, it's a tower of Babel where no inhabitant under-
stands the other, it's an island drowned in rain and porter
and whiskey, it's a traitor's heaven and a blight upon the
kingdom and my mother, God bless her soul, still lives there.

Where in Ireland? I asked him.

Mayo, he said.

I don't know Mayo, my Lieutenant said, and looked at
me and smiled.

Do you?

The thought seemed to amuse him and he repeated the word
as he made his way down the jetty over which I dragged the
bags and roped them to the roof of a carriage. And we travelled together in silence to an inn, where a bigger carriage
awaited. I untied them, lugged them from the smaller one to
the bigger, and was clambering down when my Lieutenant
stopped my boot.

There are six other passengers, and none will tolerate a
Mayo man.

By which, his smile said, he meant me.

So what? I asked. Should I run behind?

My apologies. The carriage. The roof.

The roof. At least there was a canvas cover, roped over
the many-shaped cases. I made a pencil of space beneath it,
as the driver whipped the horses and made his way into the
English night.

There were two types of rain on that carriage. Rain from
in front and rain from above. Horizontal and vertical. I preferred the vertical but had to suffer them both.

On the ship we had shared the same deck, if not the same
sleeping quarters. But England brought a difference. As if
the ground would keep shifting with the swaying carriage

and all I could do was cling on. No warmth in that English night, no buzzing of insects, just that driving rain, that whipping canvas, with those shifting cases hemming me in like a coffin. I felt the same terror, lumbering through the English night, that I had felt in the hold with Sally. I knew what it was, the terror of the strange. That I was on the wrong ship. In the wrong country.

The carriage stopped by a waystation and as they fed the horses my Lieutenant went inside with the others and I pulled what I could of the tarpaulin over me and tried to sleep in my coffin of gilded cases. And I was ashamed to feel the same longing for my old charnel house in Carolina.

But the next morning they were hitching the two shafts of the coach onto a fresh four. I must have slept, because I awoke to see the rains had stopped. There was a chill in the air and the sun was peeking through a morning mist and I saw those rolling fields, each blade of grass touched with its piece of frost, the low hanging mist and the throaty purr of the turtle dove and a pheasant took to the air from a silvery thicket way off and I knew what Old Montgomery missed in Carolina, or wanted Carolina to be. It was this, this softness, this landscape that had a rightness to it, an order. There was a mansion tucked into the receding hills and the spire of a church peeking through the trees and I could almost see his old plantation house sitting to one side of it. Though what a vain hope, to recreate this beauty in old Carolina.

And the horses were hitched by now and I wanted to fix this image in my mind so I could remember it forever but they were striding from the inn having supped or broken fast and soon the horses were thundering through these magical hills once more. And the hills rolled by and led to another church spire and a village and a copse of silvery trees and another village but by midday the sun had banished the frost and the whole of England was bright and wet.

How strange that such a paradise could come out of a rancid downpour. Was that the way with paradises? I wondered. They always came when least expected.

Marylebone

We were three or four nights on that coach and it was midday when it ascended a hill and I saw a city below us. A river bending like quicksilver in the sun around villages that thickened into one another and became a town, which became the great enormity that the coachman told me was called London. He drove the horses towards the river which wound round one of the King's castles set among open fields and then the fields sprouted houses and the houses sprouted villages and the villages sprouted towns until the road itself became all city.

And the coach took us on, through tall and narrow streets the roofs of which seemed anxious to touch each other, the windows cracking under the weight of brick. Until we came to a house in what they called Mary le Bone where the carriage stopped and I did what needed doing without thinking, lowered the cases from the roof. There was a footman who seemed proficient in doors, the carriage door first and then the porticoed door to the house, which my Lieutenant entered with hardly a glance behind and let him know his Tony would deal with the luggage.

I was 'his Tony' now, the saviour had been left in Carolina, and maybe the scavenger too. It was, in that strange turn-about I was to find in England, as if it was he who had saved me.

The footman watched me pass, bent double with the cases.

There was a carpet on which to set them and the silence of a great hallway. I wondered should I take off the boots I had stolen, so long ago. I could see my Lieutenant's own boots ascending the stairs and stopping, then, in the sunlight that came through the window above as if waiting to be invited upwards, I heard the name I would become so well acquainted with. Lord Edward.

I saw a figure by the window and it had the same outline I had seen in the Eutaw forest. On the locket, that I knew he still wore beneath his undershirt. The hair swept back, as if shaped by the wind. On the locket, she had been light against the dark. By the window she was the opposite, dark against the light. And he said, hello, Mother darling, and she moved down one step so I could see the whole of her.

She was older than she had seemed in the forest, less an image of a sweetheart, more of a mother, and she kissed him on both cheeks and held him to her as if he was some-thing she had lost, or might lose, forever.

They moved upstairs and vanished from sight and I did what I thought I should do, I followed. And I saw them then, through a door that opened into a grand room, a man in a greatcoat holding a cup to his lips, and two by the marble fireplace, a woman and my Lieutenant. Mother and son. And that must be the father, I thought, unlike me he has a father that he knows. And the one I thought was the father turned and caught my eye. I tried to find a shadow to hide into.

He sipped from his cup and said, Edward my dear, your noble savage is blocking the light.

It was the first I heard of that phrase, 'noble savage'. Hardly the last.

This is Tony, my Lieutenant said, who's neither noble nor savage. But my saviour.

Indeed, said the mother.

And there was that word again. It implied much more than it said. A multitude.

You told us. In your letters.

Now your manservant, the other said. Or your groom?

But could this be the father? Thinner and taller, with a beakish nose and oiled locks of hair covering a half-bald pate.

The tutor, I would find out later, of the young Lord Edward. And his mother's companion.

A little of both, my Lieutenant said. And I felt, in that hushed room, with so much unexplained, that it would be a grave mistake to ever call him Ned.

Their mouths smiled, but their eyes had questions.

I moved back downstairs, where the footman smiled as well. His eyes had more contempt than questions.

His bags, the footman said, to his rooms.

Where are his rooms?

Up above, he said, follow me.

I began to pull the cases upwards.

Don't drag them. Carry.

So I carried the first of them past the grand room and this time did my best not to block the light.

Through here, said the footman and he pushed open a door that led to a room, with a four-poster bed.

I'll manage the rest, I said, although there was no hint or intimation that he would assist me.

Yes, he said. Mind the carpet. Lay out his things along the coverlet. And the groom sleeps with the horses.

He does?

He does indeed.

It was odd, I thought, as he led me to the stables. I would far prefer the bile of the seamen in the hold, the amused threats of the cabin boy to the austere distaste of this liveried servant.

But there it was.

A new world. A new lieutenant. Without doubt now, a lord.

It is difficult to get a sense of someone's life from the perspective of the stables. The brown eyes of the horses knew as much of me as I did of those living in the house. There was a cellar adjacent to them with a wooden cot and rough covers, so I didn't sleep on the straw, as I had in Charleston and in St Lucia. I slept close to the horses but not with them any longer. And my Lieutenant had vanished once more, into the great civilized world above.

A mother. A duchess. A locket come alive.

His mother's house. But not his father's.

Was it grand?

Yes it was grand to me, but plain to him, and had nothing of the grandeur of the other houses I would serve him in.

This house was in England, not the place he liked to call his Ireland.

In London, to be precise. This London, the biggest city in the world, in a village outside of it called Marylebone and a street in Marylebone called Harley Street.

His mother's house. But not his father's.

70

We were both of us fatherless, I was to find out later.

My father was lost in the forests south of Carolina, but living still. His father, the Duke of Leinster, was dead and buried in the vault at St Werburgh's, where I would later scrawl my Lieutenant's name.

Near to the Major Sirr he had done in with the dagger, who did *him* in with the pistol.

His mother came down dressed for riding the next morning and said one word to me, pointing with her crop. Amber. So I saddled Amber, the mottled mare. I placed both hands together and offered them to her boot when she said, no, we have a mount for that. She nodded down to what I was to learn was the riding block, and I pulled it forwards, stilled the mare with one hand as she placed her boot on the block and swung onto the saddle. I watched her canter through the low fields and jump the sticks and ropes that were marking them out for new houses.

I watched her until she vanished round the wall of the churchyard. In case she fell and I had to run across the same fields to help her. But she did not fall. She was good on a horse, as they all were. The other mare, Barley, whimpered behind me as if she missed her mate. Hush, I told her, hush. She'll be back soon.

But the mare's whimpering head was directed elsewhere. Towards my Lieutenant, dressed for riding, coming through the sunlit stable doors.

He pointed, as his mother had done, with the crop.

Saddle me Barley, Tony, if you please.

I got to it. I offered no clasped hands, as I had back in Carolina, but pushed the riding block to the mare's left side. And as my Lieutenant mounted, I heard him mutter.

They disapprove of you.

I had no reply to that.

They regard you as they would an oriental fever. Is that what you are, my friend, a fever I'll be cured of?

I grimaced as the horse whinnied, eager to be off.

And if so, what is the cure?

I felt myself sweating. And I wondered how a fever could be cured of itself.

And my Lieutenant whipped the mare away through the Marylebone fields.

Did it know its way home? I wondered. Because I didn't, anymore. I was an ocean away from anything I had known.

I would have liked to ride out, across the fields and the new parts of the city into the old to get my bearings. But I had only ever rode those everlasters that Old Montgomery used in old Carolina. And bareback, never with a saddle. I would learn of course, in time, when he began to open up to me again, the way he did in the lonely forest. He was like a spoiled child, that way. He would be gone to me for days even though he was still there, in all sorts of company and then without warning he would come back.

My dear Tony.

They would dress me like an Indian god and have me painted on a canvas, inside a gilded frame. And they would have been happiest had I stayed inside it. They wanted an ornament but had to make do with me. The ornament could have lived in the house. The person, in the stables.

And maybe that was their way of dealing with the most uncomfortable fact. That I had saved him. I had brought him back to life. The fact that he could gallop that horse, could even walk with such an elegant swagger was down to me. And for the moment, it was as if none of that story had ever been.

I would get used to it, like changes in the weather. The way that paradise emerged out of the downpour. That English turtle dove and the low hills, all bright with frost. The mist clears and the woodpeckers are hammering, and the Cherokee kids are pulling salmon from the river. Paradise was always close, and mostly hiding. And England, I was to find, hid it very well.

Drury Lane

There was what they call a hullabaloo some evenings later. Two footmen ran in with a uniform for me. Boots, satin pants and a button-up jacket. It hardly fit, I had to hold in my breath in case the buttons popped. The theatre, they told me, they're going to the theatre, Drury Lane. And the coach was backed in then by three grooms and we fixed the horses to it and my job was to sit behind as we drove into the city.

There was no moon. I saw the fields give way to houses that passed us like tall ships in the night, some with lights inside the windows, families at prayer, or at mealtime, or sometimes no families at all. Then the houses grew more numerous into what looked like flotillas of them, streets, with lamps at every corner, carriages, horses and passers-by moving underneath. I saw everything from behind, escaping from me like an old memory or a dream. There was dust and smoke and the whinnying of horses and the lamps from the carriages following and so much light then from the streetlamps and the braziers that the night became a kind of shadowy day. And we stopped in the widest street of all and I leapt to the carriage steps and rocked them too much with my footfall because when I opened the door the tutor, Ogilvie, froze me with his glare.

Noble savage, indeed.

But I helped her down. The Duchess, Lady Emily. She took my hand in her gloved one that was decorated with tiny pearls. She said, thank you Tony, and she could have been framed in a painting, with the gown that trailed behind her with the hood that perched above her swept-back hair. I then helped Ogilvie and last of all my Lieutenant Lord.

Was I still an oriental fever?

There was a brief glance and a wintry smile, as if to acknowledge some remembered acquaintance and I watched the trio walk between the colonnades and pillars of what the coach-boy told me was Drury Lane Theatre.

It was like a forest of lamps. A cathedral of light.

And a procession of gentlemen and ladies greeted each other by the large doors of glass, and the fans of ladies fluttered like overgrown moths.

We can have a look, the coach-boy said to me, when the horses were settled.

Have a look at what? I asked.

The play, he said. From the gods. There's a blackfella like you in it.

What blackfella?

Caliban, he said.

> *Ban Ban Ca-caliban*
> *Has a new master: — get a new man.*

So you've seen it already?

Three times now, he said. Follow me.

So I followed him. Cecil was his name, little Cecil. Through the backstage door, where he knew every stagehand. Past hanging ropes and huge velvet curtains. Up four or five sets of rickety stairs. Past the ornamental arches that he called the boxes, and up into the small half circle of bare boards he called the gods.

There was a crush of footmen and servants, young girls in bonnets too big for them, every one of them pressing forwards towards the small arched wall they called the balustrade to get a glimpse of what was going on below.

And what was going on was a procession of nobility, women in gowns that would have stopped the heart, men in waistcoats and hats in hand taking their seats in the great hall below us and the boxes that rose above them like sections of a wedding cake. There were tiers of candelabra attached to sconces on the gold-leafed walls, chandeliers hanging from the painted ceiling.

Then an invisible orchestra played and a hush descended and the curtain was raised to reveal a painted ship on a painted ocean. The waves moved against each other as the wind howled and I could see the stagehands behind the flats with sheets of metal that they bent and rolled to make the sound of thunder.

They did good work with the tempest, called up by the magician, Prospero. Less so with the island, which had no conical hills and no volcano, just a shipwreck, jutting from the blue horizon. But it was even more full of noises than St Lucia. Noises orchestrated by the spirit, Ariel, with pan pipes and drum, to beguile the shipwrecked ones.

The stage was so far below us I could hardly hear. But Cecil filled me in. This Ariel had been wrapped inside a tree by the witch Sycorax, who left the island to her son, Caliban. The magician, Prospero, ruled it in exile and used his Ariel to reclaim his lost dukedom.

But all I had eyes was for that Caliban. He was a slave who lacked the King's pardon and had to do his master's bidding. Fetch wood and water or be racked by boils and stomach pains, which seemed far worse than whipping.

The only light on this Caliban came from the mirrored candles on the floor. He twisted himself into a misshapen bundle, arms flailing against an invisible whip. He shambled from left to right, one hand to his face, making common cause with the audience below.

> *The red plague rid you*
> *For learning me your language!*

But learn it he did and he drew howls of laughter with it. He met two drunken sailors who thought he was a mooncalf while he thought they had dropped from heaven or the moon itself. He promised them the lordship of the island if they would kill his lord and master, Prospero, but his plan had the great weakness that it was overheard. By the musical sprite, Ariel, who sang invisibly and had them turning this way and that until Caliban reassured them that the isle was full of noises, sounds and sweet airs that give delight and hurt not.

So was my Lieutenant to be my Prospero and I his Caliban? I would far rather be his Ariel and help him reclaim his lost dukedom. I searched the audience below and finally caught sight of him in the boxes, behind the fan of his mother, the Duchess Emily.

There was a magical banquet, there were plots and counter plots, dancing and more songs than I could remember.

> *Full fathom five thy father lies;*
> *Of his bones are coral made;*

If I was to be his Caliban I would suffer greatly. I would follow music through toothed briars, sharp furzes, pricking gorse and thorns into a foul lake that oer'stunk my feet. I would have my joints ground with dry convulsions, have my sinews shortened with aged cramps. I would be pinched almost to death, before being dismissed.

> *He is as disproportioned in his manners.*
> *As in his shape. Go, sirrah, to my cell;*

And Caliban went. Followed by hoots and catcalls and cabbages and fruit, most of it thrown from the gods around me.

Time to go, my Sirrah, young Cecil said to me and drew me downstairs again to ready the carriage and the horses. I could hear Prospero begging for release from his bare island back to Naples and all I could wonder was, did Caliban go with them?

Help me here, Cecil, I asked, did Caliban go with them?

He thought not. There would be no place for him in the Naples dukedom.

But there was a flaw to that island drama. And I couldn't stop thinking, as the carriages lined up at the theatre entrance, as I helped them up the carriage steps, as I watched the city retreat behind me into darkness, was Caliban left to lord it over his lonely isle? Or did he find a place in Naples city? Then, when the carriage was unhitched and the horses stabled, I went, sirrah, to my cell of straw. I wondered about Sally, in her exile on her island of St Lucia.

And I awoke the next morning to find that my Prospero had gone.

Lascia Ch'io Pianga

I was grooming the horses and the sun was well up when I heard footsteps behind and turned and saw a figure silhouetted against the light, tall, with a riding crop tapping off a calfskin boot. It was the one I had mistaken for his father, with the oiled hair falling over the left eye. His tutor, Ogilvie.

You, he said.

Me, sir? I replied.

You, sir, are all my fault.

I didn't know where to look but at those military boots of mine. And he reached out his crop and tilted my face to the light.

If he had swung it back, I would have struck him hard and run. Or mounted one of those horses and galloped across the green. To another Elsewhere.

I taught him to read, you see.

So, he didn't want to strike. He wanted to tutor.

To read beyond the classics. The French: Voltaire, Rousseau. Rousseau's *Émile*. Thus, I introduced him to you long before he met you.

I do not understand, sir, I said.

His voice made the horse shiver, with those thick vowels that I later learned were Scottish.

The glorified man in his natural state.

My state was anything but natural, sir, I replied, when I first met him.

Ah. So Rousseau got it wrong.

I must learn more of this Rousseau, I said.

Can you read? he asked me.

Badly, I said.

But you *can* read. More's the pity.

There was the ghost of a smile playing round his lips that I would become well acquainted with. As if there was a jest that I was not party to.

So I asked, quietly, would my master be down soon?

You mean your Lord?

I do, sir.

He's gone, he said. On the packet to Dublin.

Dublin, I repeated. I had no knowledge of it.

And he walked forwards, with that half smile playing on his lips and raised his calfskin boot and I held my hands out to lift him to the saddle. He seemed not to need the riding block. And I hoped the lesson was over.

But I was wrong.

Take the reins, he said, and walk me to the Strand.

So I took the reins and walked him, down the half-built street towards Marylebone Green and let him guide me towards the city.

You were a runaway, I believe.

I was, I said, when I first met him.

Tell me everything, he said. We were moving past the crowd on the green gathered round a cock fight.

I found him on the dead field, I told him.

After the battle.

At Eutaw Springs.

His saviour.

In a manner of speaking.

And you nursed him back to health?

But there was something too precious in those early days in the forest, too precious to tell.

I bandaged his wound, I said and lit a fire and fed him until he could walk again.

And from what were you running, pray?

From life, I thought. And I would run from you if I could. To that Dublin, wherever it turned out to be.

From servitude.

You were born into chains?

Yes, sir.

Your father then. Perhaps he was the noble savage.

So, nobility was not to be mine, I thought to myself. I was learning. Certain thoughts were best kept in.

He was no savage, I told him, though I never met him.

So you were Lord Edward's saviour.

I saw that he lived.

And he repaid you in kind.

He got me my freedom papers, when we made it to Charleston.

And then?

And then, I told him, we took the boat to Jamaica and after to St Lucia and afterwards to here.

But there was so much I didn't want to tell. Of Sally and Mr Tallentire and Rupez Roche.

There are many forms of servitude.

I beg your pardon, sir?

Do not disappoint him, Tony Small.

I will do my utmost not to, sir.

You are the living symbol of everything I tried to lead him towards.

And that is?

And as the horse whinnied, I realized that I was getting good at this thing called conversation.

We have civilized ourselves, almost to death.

I had a dim idea of what he meant. But the talk had to stop here, as we had reached civilization in the form of the crowded streets and I held tight to the reins, guided the horse through the carriages, the passers-by, the filth and fury of the place until we reached the Strand and stopped outside a concert hall. I knew it was a concert hall from the sound of an orchestra tuning up inside.

I tied the horse to a post by the large column where there was a poster with a face that I would come to know later very well as the Maid of Bath, Elizabeth Sheridan. It resembled the face on my Lieutenant's locket, but her gaze was to the left, not the right. All of his loved ones would, I would come to realize, resemble that face on his locket. And I saw his tutor enter the splendid doors and be greeted by a pear-shaped man who I would later come to know as the husband of the Maid of Bath. Sheridan.

I leant against the horse's flank, and studied this maid's profile, on the playbill. She was seated by a pianoforte, with the outlines of floating infants behind her. I would later learn they were called cherubs. Then I heard the music of paradise from inside and the voice of an angel.

It begged to be allowed to weep. To shed tears. I could tell by the sound. And the words I would come to know, although, like most things then, I didn't understand them.

Caliban could have sung them, had he ever left his island.

Lost

I was three weeks in that Marylebone House and happy
enough keeping company with the horses. They seemed to
know secrets that I didn't. They sensed arrivals and departures that were hidden from me. They whinnied before
his mother came in for riding, as if they had sensed her
approach. She would address the horse in nonsense talk
and give me a brisk, thank you Tony, when I pulled up the
mounting block. Off then, in a flurry of dust and divots into
the fields around Marylebone Green. I would catch the
reins on her return and every now and then her profile fell
into the aspect I had first seen on the locket in the Eutaw
forest. The hair spilling out under her hat when she took
it off, framed in the doorway with the sunlight coming in
fingers from behind. It was as if a veil had been pulled to
reveal another, quite different, shadow. And her manner
would change, along with her speech.

You must get lonely, this vision said, descending from the
saddle, in that way that seemed to expect no reply.

I have the horses to keep me busy.

Has my Edward forgotten you?

Is that what he's done? I wondered.

Still, you have a home.

Home, I thought. I wondered what it would feel like.

For the moment. But we can't keep you here, forever.

I felt a dull beating under the buttons of my livery. I could lose this too, along with my Lieutenant.

I could make myself useful, madame.

You may have to. Otherwise – where was home?

Carolina, madame, I said.

Yes. We have lost Carolina.

I have a letter from the King, madame, I began. I felt an invisible bit between my teeth. My words came out strange.

The King, she said, yes. How odd. The King loses America. And sends us you, in return.

She placed the reins in my hand.

Would you consider that a fair exchange? A continent for a stable boy?

She turned then and walked back into the sunlight. I took the saddle from the horse and scrubbed her down, all of the time wondering, was I worth a whole continent? And I was backing the horse into her stall when dear Cecil came down, with more news of Caliban.

He had seen another performance two nights ago, he said. Afforded entry by Annabel the seamstress.

The seamstress?

Cecil's playgoing, he gravely informed me, was enabled by two things: his ability to sneak out at night, unhindered, and his theatrical contacts. Amongst the seamstresses, stage-hands and set-builders of Drury Lane.

And so, I asked him, did Caliban go with his master to Naples in the end?

Nobody knows, he replied. He had heard the last speech in full and the matter was still not resolved. Most unsatisfactory.

I had to agree. It was most unsatisfactory. But I was already tiring of this Caliban business.

But Cecil longed for the issue to be resolved. Maybe there was something they had missed?

We could see it again?

Three knocks on the backstage door. And we're in.

Maybe so great a flaw in that island drama did need resolution. So when the stables were put to rest, we crept out of the yard and walked, and sometimes ran, across Marylebone Green towards the city. Three knocks on the stage door, and sure enough, we were admitted. And as we climbed up to the gods, the walls around were buffeted by waves of laughter that stopped me in my tracks.

Was Prospero that funny?

Caliban, perhaps?

Cecil gestured me on. We emerged, into a crow's-nest seat in the highest gods, to see that the ocean had transformed itself. It was now a promenade, between elegant townhouses. Two servants in livery, much like ourselves, leaning on the railings.

Fag and Thomas.

Was the island growing overcrowded, I had to wonder? Or was it an island at all?

Cecil shook his head. He apologized, profusely. The play had changed. Their tempest had moved on.

The spectacle below us was in a watering place called Bath. Prospero, Ariel, Miranda and Caliban had been replaced by Fag and Thomas, Lydia Languish, Sir Anthony Absolute and the confounding Mrs Malaprop.

It was a poor substitute for *The Tempest*, we both agreed. So we made an exit and descended the stairs, as Mrs Malaprop was revealing her partiality for Sir Lucius O'Trigger.

And outside, we saw the playbill, fixed to the glass doors, which seemed to shake, with the waves of laughter from the great theatre inside.

Cecil spelt it out, and begged forgiveness for the fact he hadn't read it sooner.

The Rivals, by Richard Brinsley Sheridan.

We walked home to Marylebone and tried not to be despondent. At least our absence might not be noticed. And Caliban's fate could yet be revealed.

But I dreamed of Prospero in my stables that night. Of a tempestuous island, with the wind whipping the munitions carts and the regimental tents. My Prospero vainly trying to tie them down.

And I woke to find a sprite above me. Cecil, handing me a bowl of steaming milk. Quoting:

> *As you from crimes would pardon'd be,*
> *Let your indulgence set me free.*

Set free? I asked. From what?

From these stables. From Marylebone. You're going to Dublin.

Dublin?

Dublin, he repeated. That's punishment enough.

I asked him how far away it was.

Across the water, he said. In Ireland. Lord Edward has horses there, in need of grooming.

And when did you hear this?

A letter came. This morning.

He took it from his pocket and unrolled it. But it made as much sense to me as my letter of freedom.

Will you teach me to read, Cecil?

I will, Tony. If we ever meet again.

Why would we not?

Because everything changes, Tony dear. Prospero's island turns into the promenade of Bath.

But my Lieutenant will return here, surely?

He will. And I suppose the question is, will he return with you?

Don't alarm me, Cecil.

Alright. So I'll tell you nothing of Ireland, then.

Why not?

Because I've heard it equals Prospero's island for its wilderness and savagery.

There are savages there?

I've been told there are.

Noble ones?

He didn't laugh. He folded my Lieutenant's letter.

They call themselves Romans.

Cecil was to pack some cases for his Lordship and I was to gather my things and ready myself for travel. He brought me a tray sometime later, with cheese, a jug of cloudy beer and some loaves of bread. He told me to eat some and wrap the rest, since I would need it for the journey.

When I asked him how long the journey would be, he said he had no idea. I was to take the coach to Holyhead in a place called Wales and the packet to Dublin, the capital, he told me, of that island of Calibans.

But perhaps, Cecil reassured me, as he drove the cart to Lad Lane, it will be no worse than Carolina. At least the King still ruled there.

So his letter will mean something?

Perhaps, he said. If they can read it.

We hauled my Lieutenant's cases onto the coach roof, outside the 'Swan and Two Necks', and as Cecil tied them down, he made a bed for me between them.

Goodbye, he said, Tony dear.

I could see tears in his eyes. And that brought tears to mine. Or maybe it was that one word, dear.

Goodbye, I said. Dear Cecil.

Where is your letter?

I tapped my belt.

If you ever make it back, we'll see more of Drury Lane.

I settled myself in my bed of cases and watched him vanish in the clouds of dust the coach left behind.

THIRD VERSE

Dublin

You know the feeling when you're huddled beneath the canvas covers of the cases on the coach roof and the rain is sheeting down, heading to an island of Calibans? No, you don't. And you shouldn't. Nobody should ever be acquainted with that feeling. It makes you long for things that never should be missed. For that charnel house you'd left in Patriot America. I could only hope that what Cecil said was true. That it could be no worse than Carolina.

England was passing by me, but I couldn't see it for the rain. So I had to imagine that sceptred isle, with its church spires and villages and its pheasants beating into the silvery air. Two days later we reached a small dripping hamlet called Holyhead and I dragged my Lieutenant's cases onto the ship they called the packet.

There would be someone to meet me, Cecil had told me, on the other side. I had no idea what the other side was, other than that I was not yet on it. How many days the journey would take, days or weeks? I settled myself on the deck amongst his cases, arranged them in a small shelter around me in the event it would become my bed for who knows how many nights to come.

Dublin, Ireland. Mayo was in Ireland, he had told me, and I couldn't help thinking of the name, Skinner Mayo. Was my father from this mysterious Mayo, on this island of Calibans, or had the name attached itself to him, uninvited, like a louse to an ankle or a barnacle to a boat? And all the while the thin line of mist shifted with the pitching waves.

But the passage was mercifully short, less than a day and a night and as the sun came up I could see the outlines of a city from the sea. The water was calm, and I had to wonder how this island had earned its reputation, since at first sight there was nothing savage about it.

There was a pale turquoise light as if I was viewing the coastline through the glass of a greenish bottle. There were low mountains rising from the curve of the bay and hills like two sleeping women on either side, as if their job was to nurture the city between them. The morning sun came out then, dancing off the water and the city did seem to sleep like an ancient child, with a river curling into its breast. It was more beautiful than Liverpool or London, like the best of them in miniature. When we came to Bath, some years later, I knew then that they were cousins. There were white villas on either side of the bay and the largest of them I would discover was Frescati House, where my Lieutenant had spent his younger days, with the Scotsman as his tutor. There was a lighthouse and a half-finished sea wall and a small harbour where we didn't dock but clambered down to rowing boats which took us through the forest of ships, sunken and floating, towards the city. There was a newness to the shapes that rose above the ancient streets, great monuments with arches and colonnades and green copper roofs. And there was a wharf there, before the first bridge with a crowd waiting for the mail and among that crowd was my Lieutenant waiting for me.

His lip was between his teeth and I wondered why. Then the lips trembled and grew into a smile as I dragged his cases down the gangplank.

Dear Tony, he said. I surprised myself by missing you.

How could he have missed me? I wondered, I had barely seen him, sleeping as I did in the byre next to the horses. He had left me there without saying goodbye. But my own mouth couldn't help itself. I tried to purse my lips to prevent it, then bite them from the inside but the more I pursed and the more I bit, the more I smiled. He saw this and his smile became a grin, and then exploded into a laugh. And when he laughed, of course I laughed too. The crowd around us stared as he embraced me, me, two heads taller than him, browner than the horses that were being led now down the gangplank. There was a coach standing by and three servants dressed in the family livery.

We'll walk, he said. Let them deal with the cases.

So we walked. Along that brown river, and up the wide curving street to the left. And it was odd, I could feel the old closeness return as the crowds parted around us.

The Liffey, he said, meaning the brown river. It was a forest of small flapping sails and rowboats moving like so many water beetles. He took my arm then and led me away from it, towards a wide granite curve of colonnades.

And that's the parliament, he said, and his mouth turned downwards. My brother wants me to take my seat inside it. Should I abandon soldiering for politics?

I had no reply and wondered did he expect one. He stopped for a moment and the crowd made a half circle round us. Some children reached out to touch my sleeve. He didn't notice. He was like a rare bird again, amongst a flock of pigeons or crows.

My brother, he continued, the Duke of Leinster. Who has no need to make such choices.

The building curved away from us and lost itself in scaffolding. Like many things in that city, it was yet to be finished. He took my elbow and drew me across the street. Every horse and carriage stopped, as if by some unspoken command.

In my tribe, the eldest son inherits, and all of the rest go wanting. How is it in your tribe, Tony Small?

I have no tribe, my Lord.

And stop calling me 'Lord'.

Yes, my Lord.

Ned.

Yes, Ned.

You told me once about the Temne people.

My mother's tribe, near the river of Sierra Leone. And all I know of my father is his name.

Mayo.

Skinner Mayo.

My father was the Duke of Leinster, and I knew not much more of him.

Why was he telling me this? Here, after the days in Charleston, St Lucia, the crossing, the trip to London. He was almost a different person, in this different country. And not a Caliban in sight. The wave of unwashed faces that stared as they came towards us and we parted them like a comb through unruly hair.

Could we be more conspicuous, he asked, Ned Fitzgerald and Tony Small?

And we couldn't have been, I had to admit.

There was a stench now, off the crowd and the grubby hands of children reached out to touch me, as if my person was made of precious metal.

You have to forgive their curiosity. They haven't got much colour in their lives.

But their curiosity had become a ferment. They pressed about us like a crowd around a baited bear. And we didn't so much walk up those streets as were carried.

The King, he said, has lost America. And he is afraid he might lose this island too.

How would he lose it?

The way he lost America. But we are Geraldines and have one purpose in life. To keep it safe for him.

He grimaced. He didn't seem to relish that thought. He took off his hat then and swatted away the poking hands of the children.

This walk was a bad idea.

And he took me by the elbow then, to hurry me on. The streets stopped, as if they were a bad idea and gave way to a stretch of tangled field. There was a large mansion beyond them, huge metal gates that were already being pulled behind the carriage that had taken our cases.

And this, he said, was my father's house.

We stopped by the gates and the crowds stopped too. Three footmen pushed them open with a grind of metal. Three more pushed the crowds back, and we stepped inside. Then the gates were closed behind us and the crowds surged forwards again, the hands of children pushing through the metal bars like so many blades of grass. And we walked towards what he called his father's house.

It was not so much a house as a small city. Bigger than the parliament building, two arms of granite curving round on either side of a pebbled drive. An immense façade of cut stone with three levels of windows, each smaller than the one below.

I had never seen so many windows, reflecting the morning sun. He walked towards them, his boots crunching on the rough gravel, towards the liveried footman waiting on the steps.

This is Tony, he said to the footman. My dear Tony. You will show him to his rooms.

So I had rooms in this house. Wonder of wonders. I watched him vanish through the open door into the gloom inside. The footman stared at me, through slow-lidded eyes.

Is it Tony? He asked. Tony what?

Tony Small, I replied.

Strange world, he said.

And yes, I agreed with him. It was.

Folly, he said.

Folly, I wondered. What was the folly?

Folly me.

He meant follow. So I followed his boots, up the marble stairs and became aware of bodies filing in like ghosts below us. Servants all of them, filling the hallway below, staring upwards.

You'll have to get used to it, the footman said. The staring.

I will, I said.

Because you are quite the whatdyacallit?

The what?

The spectacle.

And more spectators gathered, at the top of the marble stairs. To the left and to the right, faces, peering out of open doorways, maids in kitchen clothing, servants in livery. As we walked towards them the faces ducked back in, the doors stayed open and I could see the wide staring eyes in the shadows.

We headed towards a smaller wooden staircase and I saw them crowding the threadbare carpet above us, like curious owls. We walked up those stairs and he clapped his hands briskly.

Give him some peace, he said. He's new here.

Does this house ever end? I asked, as we made it to yet another staircase. Uncarpeted this time.

Never, he said. And it's still being built.

A girl stepped back, like a dutiful shadow, to give way before us and then she followed behind.

This is Molly, he said. She'll do your room.

Do? I asked.

Yes, do, he said. What a servant does.

You mean I have a servant?

You have a servant to do your room and her name is Molly. And my name is Jeremiah.

Jeremiah.

Jerry for short.

Molly smiled at me, all teeth and red cheeks, and curtseyed. I bowed. I was unused to such deference.

And this, said Jeremiah, is all yours.

He pushed open a small door. There was a bed, beneath a skylight, in the sloping ceiling.

I walked inside. No more beds of straw, beside the horses.

Mine, I repeated.

Yours, he said. And Molly blushed and curtseyed again. She whispered something to him.

I suppose, he muttered.

What did she say? I asked.

She wants to know if she can touch you.

Touch me?

Said she's never seen the like.

So I reached out my hand, towards her face. She bent backwards, like a startled kitten.

Go on Molly. I don't imagine he bites.

She rubbed her fingers off my palm.

He's real, she said.

Real, he said, just the colour of that wardrobe. And you will take him through his duties, now, Molly. I'll leave you both to it.

Molly curled her hand through mine and led me back through the corridors and took me through my duties. Into my Lieutenant's bedroom first, where a large four poster was surrounded by his cases. She laid out his clothes and showed me his shaving bowl, his razor and his strop. She led me through the backstairs down to the kitchens and showed me where the water could be heated. Down to the stables then where his horses were chewing at the straw that once would have made my bed.

You know horses? She asked.

I know horses, I answered.

Look after the horses, she said, and the rest will look after itself.

Could it be that simple? I wondered. Had I arrived in some paradise?

You are an odd thing, she said. Can I touch that hair of yours?

You can I said, and bent my head towards hers.

Soft, she said, who would have thought it would be soft?

And it was another of those questions that demanded no answer.

I was made the same as you, I told her.
Who made you? She asked.
The same god that made you.
Well now, she said.

Frescati

But it was that simple, I found. In the first weeks, at least. There was a small bell by my bedroom doorway that would be rung by an invisible hand and wake me before the light broke. I would pull on my boots and my livery in the whey-coloured dawn and make my way through that maze of corridors, of half-awake scurrying servants and find Molly in the kitchens with the water and milk warmed and the freshly made bread and a small saucer of honey because my Lieutenant liked honey in the mornings. I would wait outside until I heard him move, and pray to God he woke before the water had gone cold and I had to make the long trek back down to the kitchens again.

I would shave him then as he broke his fast by the large window that allowed him a view of the fields and the city beyond. Every year, he told me, it continued its slow crawl towards his father's mansion and would one day spread those new streets around it, streets of brown sandstone and tall windows of barely mottled glass. The idea of glass entranced him. It was glass that enabled those streets, he told me, glass that allowed them grow so tall, allowed the light through to their ornate interiors, and if he could build a city made of glass he would.

I would dress him then and prepare his horse and sometimes gallop with him in the fields behind his father's mansion. He taught me how to hold the reins, how to stand in the stirrups in the English style. Horses were made for flight, he told me, as if he wanted to escape from everything he knew as well as the dark mansion behind him. I would ride him down to the parliament then, which, he confided, might one day be his melancholy destiny, if he couldn't escape that too.

He would vanish inside and I would stay with the horses and endure the stares of passers-by and the children's rhymes that seemed to arrive fully formed, as if they'd always been there.

Some days we would ride out to the south wall along the strand where the ships of the line sat out on the bay like painted toys on a painted horizon. We would gallop until the horses were spent and then walk them to the villa where he spent his childhood, Frescati. My mother's house, he would tell me, as if to draw an absolute distinction between the city of servants that was his father's and this childhood home. He would walk around the lawns in front of the white-stuccoed building with each window shuttered as if in search of something lost among plants that had withered with the winter. A large cypress tree that branched into two forks, among the leafless birches. They had moved there after his father died, he told me, and the Scotsman Ogilvie had supervised his education.

We would let the horses feed on the unkempt grass. He would stare at the shuttered house, as if it held some forgotten secret.

Then one summer's day we finished our gallop and the shutters were down. There was a table set in the Italianate gardens, with servants running backwards and forwards from the open doors, the windows glittering like mirrors in the sunlight. His mother and the Scotsman. He ran forwards and embraced her and I knew that whatever had been lost had been found again.

I took the reins in hand and tethered the horses to the cypress. I listened to them crop the grass and tried to imagine the conversation that I couldn't hear. Mother dear. My darling Edward. The Scotsman, Ogilvie, rose and pushed the hair back from his forehead and held his hand out, waiting for a greeting. But Edward turned as if he was hardly there and waved instead at me.

Tony! He called.

His mother turned to me then, her eyes half-closed against the sunlight.

He beckoned me again and I walked over.

So, you are still his Tony? She asked me, with just a hint of amusement in her voice.

I am his Lordship's servant.

A little more than that.

More and less, I thought. Sometimes in the haybarn, sometimes in the house.

You must have tea, she said, and gestured to the chair beside her.

I took this as a signal to sit and the servant boy poured tea into a cup, with a smile on his face. His smile grew as I drank, on the assumption I would spill it. But I denied him that pleasure and managed the tiny cup, between finger and thumb.

You should dress your Tony, his mother said.

He is hardly naked, my Lieutenant answered.

In more than Leinster livery. He deserves a costume that suits his physique. That has some of the magic of the Orient.

He's from the Occident, Mama, he said. America.

Oh, fiddlesticks. You know what I mean. Don't you, dear? And she turned to Ogilvie.

Bright Orient pearl, he said, alack too timely shaded …

Dress him with fantasy. Poetry. And America, as we all know, is too prosaic. How many of us have seen such an exotic creature?

Exotic, my Lieutenant repeated. And I knew he wanted done with the conversation.

Pantaloons, the Scotsman said.

Just the thing. With slippers of gold. To go with your Arabian steed.

Roberts can paint them both.

My cheeks grew red, but no one noticed. I would later learn the word for it. Blushing. As the conversations flew around me, about me, I would redden from my crown to the pale soles of my feet. And the soles of my feet were pale, as Molly informed me, one languorous afternoon. She gave me reason to blush then, too.

You must stay the night, Edward, she said. Both of you.

She rose, suddenly. And just as suddenly, it seemed, afternoon tea was over.

And let us show the house to your Tony.

They walked and assumed his Tony would follow. Which I did, three or four feet behind her, to avoid stepping on her train. The servant ran ahead of us, shoes scraping off the granite steps, and pushed open the large wooden door.

She gestured me ahead of her and I walked inside.

Frescati, she said.

There was a spectral hush in there and the sense of old ghosts. I heard the footsteps of the servants echoing. I had no idea where my Lieutenant had gone.

After the Italian –

Naples, I said, still thinking of the play. Caliban. The island.

No, not Naples, she replied. Frascati, nearer to Rome -

I saw another marble staircase, another ornate hallway, a huge picture by the wall, a geometric row of windows looking out on the Irish Sea. More of that glass. But it was warmer than his father's house, with carpets everywhere, soft drapes lining the windows.

He spent his childhood here, she told me. A home away from home. After the Duke died.

She glanced across the edge of the marble banister, where Ogilvie walked with her son into another room. More windows, blazing with sunlight. Books lining the wall. I remembered Prospero.

> *My library*
> *Was dukedom large enough.*

The Duke, she said. His father.

A portrait of a young man, seated, against a stormy sky.

I could see the resemblance. I caught the eye of my Lieutenant, with his substitute father, through the open doorway, in the other room.

She seemed to read my thoughts.

William was his tutor, then his stepfather. Come –

She was whispering now and held one hand to her pursed lips. A secret? I thought. I am to be the bearer of a secret?

She took my hand and my hand was shocked rigid. But she seemed not to notice. She drew me through a small door, under the shadow of the staircase. Down a corridor, through another door.

There was a boy's room. Bookcases, lining the walls. An array of toy soldiers on a wooden tray. A desk, beneath a small window. A garden outside. A portrait on the wall of a boy I immediately recognized as him. The same wide open, surprised eyes.

His room, she said. His books. His Latin primer. And his Greek. William tried to interest him in something more than toy soldiers. Do you read, Tony?

I shook my head. I felt that blush, again.

She flicked through them reading the titles.

Divine Songs.

'How doth the little busy bee.'

Émile.

Have Edward teach you. Or better still, William.

She placed the books back on the windowsill.

But perhaps the garden taught him most.

She looked out the window to the garden outside.

We have always looked east, she told me. Some look west, we look east. Warmer climates. They suit him. Laburnum, jacaranda, bougainvillea. Magnolia. One of the great virtues of empire. The flora they brought. Should go with your pantaloons.

Was it a habit with them? I wondered. They used words either like a miser or a spendthrift. I heard few syllables for days, then an explosive flow of them.

Look after him, Tony.

Yes, Ma'am, I replied. And I wondered what she meant.

I used to be his only confidant, she said. But sons grow up and mothers cease to know them. He sends me letters, but what do they tell me of his heart?

He sends me no letters, Ma'am.

But you have his ear. You brought him back to life.

Was that to be my duty? I wondered. And I realized I had known it was, ever since I had returned to him in that dead field, lifted him onto the wooden sled and asked him, does your mother love you?

And when I look at him now, I see a young man that is rootless. Restless. Without purpose.

I cannot provide him with purpose, Ma'am.

No. But you can confide in me. Every now and then? And let it be our secret?

So, I was to be the guardian of secrets. A confidence. And I wondered how long this privilege would last.

I joined them for dinner. A confusion of plates, different knives, forks. I kept my eyes on him and followed his progress through them. Oysters. Flatfish. Late spring lamb. Her eyes met mine over her tilted wineglass and she smiled, as if to seal it. Our secret.

Another servant led me to a bedroom. There was a white smock laid out, across the bedclothes. I was to wear it, apparently, rather than sleep naked.

There was a book by the bedside. All I could read of it was the title. *Pamela*. And the pictures. A maiden, by a lawn, before a house not unlike Frescati. In a drawing room, a young man kneeling before her. One hand to her forehead. She was in a battle, it seemed, between virtue and vice.

The next morning a tailor was summoned along with a sketch artist, who drew pantaloons in red, a pair of golden slippers and a satin waistcoat. Into a room they called the parlour, with a painted ceiling of pink and white clouds. I was measured and bound, my thighs and my biceps. I was found to be six foot, two inches tall.

A giant, Lady Emily said. But a slender one.

Cockles

We rode back to Leinster House together. Was I his equal now? No, but that feeling had come back. Whatever happened in the Eutaw forest. When the sun pushed through the umbrella of Spanish moss. When the Cherokee kids pulled salmon from the river. He would have died without me then. And this life, as the horses' hooves threw up fountains of spray around us, was ours and no one else's.

There were children scrabbling for cockles in the shale beyond the waterline. My Lieutenant rode through them as if he hardly saw them. But they saw him. When they heard the first thump of our hooves, they knew to dart away back towards the tiny cabins that lined the dunes, that looked like overgrown barnacles. A barefoot mother emerged, her dress twisted into a rope around her waist, a wickerwork basket on her head. She was as poor as my mother had been, in Old Montgomery's, in Carolina.

I was learning, about the odd contradiction between servant and master. How the lines between them can blur into oblivion like a strand of hair you bring too close to your eye, so you can't see it anymore. He began to need me again, and in that need there was a strange reversal of servitude. I could make myself indispensable, for the thousand daily routines that surrounded his living. And in my servitude there was the shadow of mastery.

I saw it reflected in the country around me. Those great houses depended on a mass of people that the inhabitants hardly saw, that could well have been invisible. But I saw them. I had shared their condition. And I had got what they had not, a paper from the King.

We all see different things. I saw that mother, knee-deep in the brine, pulling seaweed from the rocks. He saw his Tony, raising arcs of spray along the shore. But he had eyes, and a heart, that just needed to be opened. And he would be educated. As he was by those children's books, by the garden in Frescati. Facing east, as his mother told me. And strangest of all, he would be educated by one who had no education. As he would tell me later, in a feather merchant's shop in the Liberties.

Me.

So should I take the blame? Since all it would lead to would be the Newgate cell and him waiting in it with Major Sirr's lead ball in his gut, waiting to dance the Kilmainham Minnit?

Look after him, Tony, she said. And did I fail in that duty?

Maybe I did. I saw what he didn't see, and I saw what he would lose by seeing. I saw and said nothing. I saw him give away his privilege. I could have said, you are separated from that mass by an accident of birth, by wealth, by title and all of those things you want to throw away. How will you survive, amongst them?

He would have said, the way you did, Tony dear.

Let Thomas Paine take the blame. Let Rousseau take the blame, whoever he was.

The Kilmainham Minnit

Molly could read. She pulled ballads out of her smock like a magician pulling flowers. She sang them while I read lying on the straw in the stables. While the horses shifted below us.

> *When to see Luke's last gig we agreed*
> *We tipped all our gripes in a tangle*
> *And mounted our trotters with speed*
> *To squint at the snub as hed dangle –*

Luke Caffrey, she told me, sliced one too many gullets with what she called his toaster. Which I understood to be a blade, not meant for toasting bread. So his last gig was his Kilmainham Minnit, the small dance his legs would make while dangling from the drop. And it wasn't only his legs that would shift, she said, whatever hung between them would dance too.

In death? I asked her.

Yes, she told me, that fine gentleman is well known for its last minuet.

> *When we came to the mantrap and saw*
> *Poor Luke look so blue in the gabbard*
> *To save him I thought I could draw*
> *Me toaster from out of the scabbard —*

Her voice was soft and lilting but her eyes were teary. Her own betrothed Oscar was in Kilmainham as we spoke, awaiting judgment. Which was why 'Luke Caffrey's Kilmainham Minnit' affected her so.

> *His pushing block prissey came in*
> *After tipping the scragboy a dusting*
> *Her stuff shop was up to her chin*
> *Like a crammd foul with tenderness brusting —*

You see she loved him, Molly said.

Who? I asked.

His prissey, she said.

And I had to ask her what a prissey was.

Oh now, she said. Don't act so innocent. Pushing block prissey? Were you born yesterday? She asked. Have you never walked down Temple Bar? South William Street? Don't they have pushing houses in Carolina?

Ah. I pretended to understand.

And I learned that Luke loved his prissey the way Oscar loved his Molly. And her Oscar was arraigned, she told me, for riotous behaviour when the tailor's corporation rode the fringes.

The fringes? I asked.

The franchises, she said, that marked the boundaries between the different trades.

Her Oscar had let whiskey get the better of him and lost the run of himself. Took down two watchmen along the way.

Tell me more, I said.

About Oscar?

About Luke Caffrey. I laid out the printed ballad on the straw. It smelt of rough perfume. I wondered did her skin smell the same.

> We lent him a snig as he sed
> In the juggler tis there that the mark is
> But when that we found him quite dead
> In the dustcase we bundled his carcase
> And sent him to sleep in the clay.

Sad verse, she said.

It was sad. But it was made sadder by what she told me next. Her Oscar had spiked one of the watchmen with his toaster who was lying in the Royal Hospital with his bladder all aflame and if he ever croaked it that was her betrothed for the drop, and the only hope she'd ever have of seeing her Oscar again would be his ghost in sweet Bully's Acre.

So she should visit Kilmainham now, she said, before her dear Oscar's last gig.

I brushed a tear away from her cheek, dusty from the straw bales.

Will you come with me? she asked.

What good could I do?

You could push him vittles through the bars. I'm too small to reach, you see. And if you did that, maybe, I'd be your pushing block prissey for a while.

No need, I told her.

Men, she said, just want one thing. Don't tell me you're any different.

I can try, I told her, to be different.

She took my hand in hers then and brought it back to her cheek.

You can try, she said.

She took a pie and some sausages from the kitchens and I walked with her when the sun was going down past South William Street where what she called the pushing houses were. The ladies sat on the steps with their rouged faces and their tattered stockings and she knew most of them by name.

I can get you a cheap one, Tony. With Dolly.

Dolly?

My good friend Dolly. Maybe she'd do a man like you for free?

Why would she do that?

Curiosity, she said. She took my hand and brought it to her breast. I could feel the pie she had hidden, underneath her shawl.

I would wager she has never known skin like that.

She led me down to the river where the fishing boats were pulling in their nets and the air stank of mackerel. The light was falling and she drew in close beside me.

Can I pretend you're Oscar? She asked, now that the light is going.

Only at night, I said.

Night, she said. Kind of hides you.

The smell of mackerel was overwhelmed by the smell of burnt barley.

That smell? I asked her.

Barley. She said. For the porter.

Porter?

Have you not heard of porter? She asked. Black, like you. My Oscar made the uniforms for all the drawmen at St James's Gate.

It was rich and peaty and it smelt like burning sugar cane. But we lost the fumes of it as we passed the chimneys of the brewery. A more pungent smell took over. Whiskey, she told me, from the Liberties distilleries, then both were over-whelmed by the smell of cattle. I could hear them moaning in a dark field to my left and soon a new set of towers stood out against the sky and the waxing moon. A light or two gleamed within them and as we drew closer I could see the bars outlined by the guttering movement of the candles within. Kilmainham Gaol, she told me.

She threw stones against the barred windows. There were whistles and mutters of words I didn't understand: juggler, duds, sweater, pissey, ketch, squeezer. It was as if her ballads had come to life. Shady talk, she told me. The language of those who had no wish to be understood.

Give me a lift now, she said. So I took a muddy shoe between both hands and hoisted her upwards. A face appeared at the bars above.

Oscar, she said.

Molly, he said, my darling Molly, what've you brought me?

Pie, she said, and a bottle of cider. Push me higher, she said down to me, I can't get to his blessed hands.

So I pushed both shoes upwards and settled one on each of my shoulders. Her petticoat fell over my face and I stood there in the darkness of her underthings. I heard murmurs and kisses from above and then her knees crossed each other in some kind of passionate movement. I gripped both ankles with my hands then and pushed her higher.

He's like a circus strongman, she said to her Oscar above.

But I can't stay like this forever, I whispered.

Hold me up, she said, a few moments more.

So I held her up and the kissing went on and her knees crossed themselves again and I tried to look everywhere but up those petticoats. There were more voices from the barred windows adjacent. Muted cheers and catcalls and jokes about his ghost giving his Molly a better fol de rol than the living Oscar ever would. And either she got tired of it then or there must have been some danger up above.

Goodbye Oscar, she said, I must go back to earth now.

Take care it's not you for the drop, Oscar said and there was a flurry of movement above then, the rapid slap of wooden clogs off bare flagstones.

The Slag's coming, Molly said, and I managed to grip her by the waist and ease her downwards.

God bless you Tony, she said and kissed me on the lips on the way down. I held her there to prolong the kiss and felt her tongue dart like a small fish against my lips.

And no dallying we'd better scarper.

So I placed her like a doll on the grass below the gaol wall and she was off like a hare across the fields. I lumbered after her.

He would indeed be hung, her Oscar, like the ones in the ballad she read to me, but I didn't know that then. He would dance the Kilmainham Minnit and die with his feet to the city and she would wake him in clover and send him to take a ground sweat. She probably knew that as we walked back towards the smell of herring from the river and burnt barley from the brewery. She knew the way of things for Oscars like hers which might account for the melancholy way she held my arm to her breast as we made our ways home.

Can I be your prissey for tonight at least? She asked, as we may our way up from the river past the pushing houses in Temple Bar. I'll teach you more reading, if you'll let me.

What about your Oscar? I asked her.

Oscar wouldn't mind you being him for a while.

And the thought did intrigue me, as she led me past the painted prisseys on the steps.

And I'm clean, she said, I'm cleaner than any of those doxies.

So we kissed once, to the great enjoyment of the ladies of the steps.

Your Lord and master, she said, knows each one of them by name.

We kissed once more, in the windy fields by the gates of Leinster House. And I had the pleasure of hoisting her up again, over the perimeter wall and she dropped down the side and made it to the side gate and let me in.

Where? I asked, as she kissed me again in the shadow of the great house. I had to hope no one was looking.

The stables, she said. The horses know you and won't make a whimper.

And sure enough in the stables the horses shifted their feet on the barley-strewn floor but didn't make so much as a whinny. So we had the straw to cover us. And afterwards she took another ballad from her smock and began the promised lesson.

> *His music excels all carillon bells*
> *His stroke's more sweet than a warbling chorister*
> *No flute or guitar can ever compare*
> *To the musical hammer of Darby O'Gallagher.*

So this Darby could dance?

None better, she said. Except maybe you.

Chorister, I asked her. What is a chorister?

Choirboy, she said and chewed on a golden piece of straw. And you have to let me cry a moment for my other Darby.

Oscar, you mean.

Yes, she said.

Oscar, who'll soon be dancing his last gig.

Pantaloons

I stroked her hair, brown against the yellow straw as the sun came up and told her that I would plead her Oscar's case with the one she called my own Lord Edward. But as things turned out, I had to plead my own case first.

I was summoned to the great parlour where a costume was arrayed on a long couch, a chaise longue I learned it was called later. A costume for a carnival, I thought, but no, my Lieutenant informed me, these were the oriental duds designed by his own mother, with the hearty approval of his stepfather, the Scot.

Pantaloons of silk, a jacket of velvet, the colour of oranges and a belt of white leather. I could feel Molly's eyes through the crack in the open doorway while I tried them on, I could hear her snigger, a kind of chortle in her pretty nose and I thought then that she didn't deserve my pleas for her Oscar, so I pleaded for myself.

Please, my Lord, must I wear them?

Ned, he said, and he didn't hide his own amusement. And if you would please my mother, Tony, you must.

So I stretched my arms, as they wrapped me in coloured silks, and the tailors stitched and chalked and snipped.

We rode back out to Frescati that afternoon. The wind bellowed out the pantaloons and sleeves and made me long for the Leinster livery of old. These duds as Molly would have called them invited nothing but ridicule. The cockle-picking children ran after us in a swarm and I had to marvel at their skill at rhyming. I was a 'foreign fruit in a Nancy suit' or 'a blackfella in orange and yella' and my only relief came when I whipped his horse into a gallop and I found the escape of the cascading tide. I begged him once more to be rid of the orientals but he told me, and at least had the grace not to laugh, to plead my case with his mother.

But his mother, when we reached Frescati was fulsome in her praise of them. The tailor, she told him, had done my physique proud, had added a touch of delicacy to my savage grace, had accentuated the nobility of my bearing.

He is shy of them, my Lieutenant said, afraid of ridicule.

He must think of them as ceremonial, his mother told him. When we wear taffeta, he wears silk.

And, he is freezing.

There was a cold wind that day, and it didn't deserve the name summer.

He is used to warmer climes, the Scot said. But, by God Sir, do those garments not suit him?

We had tea again, inside this time, because of the weather. The summers in Ireland were often cold, I was to find, colder than the winters in Carolina. But I was happy, I realized, despite the cold and the laughable duds. I was happy because she was happy, because my Lieutenant was happy and they both were always happiest, I came to notice, close to that house, and around each other.

I wandered from room to room with the Scot in my wake. He seemed to have a plan for me, his 'oriental', as he had for everyone that crossed his path. And when I entered the library and was fingering the leather spines of the unreadable books, I discovered what it was.

My education.

He had little Latin and less Greek, he said.
Pardon me, I said. For I genuinely didn't understand.
You have Shakespeare in your hands, sir.
Forgive me, I said.
Do you read, sir?
I have begun learning, I told him.
Under whose instruction?
Molly's.
Molly who?
Molly the kitchen maid, I told him.
I would wager she had even less.
Of Latin and Greek? She has none, but she reads the ballads.
Which ballads?
Luke Caffrey's.
I am not familiar.
'Luke Caffrey's Kilmainham Minnit'.
Intriguing.
It tells the story, I told him, of Luke Caffrey's friends and their attempts to rescue him after he has danced the Kilmainham Minnit.
It's a dance?
I think, sir, I told him, it means minuet.

A minuet is a dance, indeed. But I have not heard of the Kilmainham variation.

I think it means the movement a corpse makes after the drop.

The drop?

The drop after the hanging.

I must confess to being puzzled.

This was Molly's world, not his. I thought it better not to mention Darby O'Gallagher.

It is the world of street ballads, sir.

I looked around the library. The bound volumes. The embroidered drapes. The light coming from the booming sea.

Far from this one.

Very far.

Yet not so far at all, I thought. The world of those who served in it.

Though I must commend you for your efforts.

Thank you, sir.

You might be better served by the Psalms. Or *The Book of Common Prayer.*

I know prayers to speak, sir, but not to read.

Have you heard of Shakespeare?

I have seen *The Tempest*, I told him. 'Ban Ban Ca-caliban, has a new master, get a new man.'

Wherever?

Drury Lane, I told him. From the gods. With the boots, Cecil. I saw you in the box below.

Kemble, he said, made a good hand of Prospero.

Though he left a great mystery behind him.

A mystery?

Did Caliban travel back with him?

With whom?

With his master.

To where?

And I wondered had we seen the same play.

To Naples, I said.

I have no idea. It is a play, he said. A fancy. A dream, as Prospero tells us.

I would swear they went to Naples in the end.

And perhaps they did, sir.

He took a volume from the shelf.

But if reading is your goal, you could do worse than begin with this.

He placed a volume in my hands.

I read, hesitantly.

The Life and Strange …

the next two words defeated me.

Surprising Adventures … he said.

of … I had no difficulty with that.

Robinson Crusoe, he said, *of York, Mariner*.

He smiled then, in that way of his, as if there was a joke I was not party to.

There is a Caliban in this tale as well, he said.

Another Caliban?

But his name is Friday.

Friday

We rode back to Leinster House that night and he allowed me change from my oriental duds as I stabled the horses. So I was spared the laughter of Molly, who came in after teatime.

I have a book for us, I told her.

A book, is it? Are the printed ballads not enough for you?

No more of Luke Caffrey and Darby O'Gallagher, I said. I have *The Life and Surprising Adventures of Robinson Crusoe.*

And who is he when he's at home?

A mariner, from York.

I took the book from my shirt and showed her the strange illustration. A man with two fowling pieces on his shoulders, barefoot, with a straw hat.

'Who lived eight and twenty years,' she read, 'all alone on an uninhabited island, on the coast on America, near the Great River Oroonoque.' Do you know it? She asked.

Do I know what?

The Great River Oroonoque?

No, I said.

But you know America?

I know Carolina, I said. The Santee river. Charleston. The Eutaw forest. I have never heard of the Great River Oroonoque.

She began to read then, as I brushed down the horses for the night. 'Of a man born in the city of York, 1632, of good family. Who was the third son of the family and not bred to any trade', and whose 'head began to fill early with rambling thoughts.'

Rambling thoughts? I asked her, what are they?

I have them often, she said. And I should have rambled off with Oscar when I had the chance.

This Robinson Crusoe, we learned, ignored his father's advice and took to sea. For London, at first, where a tempest on the way put the fear of God into him, destroyed the ship and had him wandering on foot into Yarmouth. And what he called an obstinacy that nothing could resist led him on foot to London.

That storm, Molly asked me. Have you ever known a storm like that?

I have known several, I told her. And the wonder always is how the calm afterwards makes one forget the tempest of the night before.

The light was falling as she ended the first chapter. And I resolved to attempt the second on my own, by candlelight. For she read out the title to me, 'Slavery and Escape'.

Though 'Slavery and Escape' had to bide its time.

I lit a candle in my garret and fell asleep before the second chapter. I awoke with the dawn light coming through the window and the candle burnt to the stick and the stick overflowing with frozen wax.

Reading tired me. My mind, like Crusoe's, began to fill with rambling thoughts. It wandered back to Old Mongtomery's, to the blood staining the tobacco plants, to the morning I tried to wake my mother on her wooden pallet and realized she would sweat no more. It was more exhausting, I came to realize, than physical labour. I had begun my adventures in reading with my King's letter of pardon and continued them fitfully on my journey across oceans. But I was far from mastering the art. And what kind of slavery Robinson endured, how it compared with the captivity of April Small, what kind of escape he managed, all this would have to wait because Molly knocked on the door and told me to get about my business, the master was on the move.

I took the stairs two at a time, had his milk and honey by the windowsill and was heading back down to heat the water for shaving when he told me not to bother. I was to meet him in the stables, ready for travel.

And does this mean, my Lord, that I wear –

Your oriental outfit, he said.

There was a familiar smile playing round his lips. He was not beyond teasing.

I beg you, my Lord, I would rather any other punishment than that.

The days of punishment are gone.

But not for me.

I could feel my cheeks burning already.

Do you insist, my Lord?

I insist on nothing. But would you disappoint my mother?

Ah.

She is enamoured of that outfit, sir. She has hired an artist to memorialize it. We are to meet her in Carton House.

Carton House. I had not heard of it.

His father's other residence, he told me, in Kildare, the rather gloomy seat of the Earls of Leinster.

So I climbed back to the bedroom where I had to bend my head when standing. I put on the orange shirt and the crimson vest with the white sash for a belt and the billowing pantaloons. I made my way back down through the woken house, and at the landing of every staircase met a sea of smiling faces. I remembered the cockle-picking children and could have provided rhymes to their giggling. And I was ashamed to admit to myself that I feared the days of ridicule almost as much as the days of pulling tobacco.

And Molly joined me on the humiliating trek down to the stables.

The book, she said, let me have the book.

I want to read it.

You can't she said, you haven't learned reading yet. Leave it with me, I'll help you through it.

On my return? I asked her. Do you promise?

I promise, she said. And I'll keep it here, with the memory of Darby O'Gallagher.

She lifted her blouse then and placed the volume underneath it.

Izod

We rode by the pavement along the river. The barges were being loaded on the quays and the morning sun gleamed in reflection from the windows across the way. A swarm of children followed us and I heard a version of the same rhyme chanted, about an 'apron of yella to clothe this blackfella' and as I crossed the Essex bridge to get beyond them I heard the rhyme that would follow me for many years to come.

> *You maidens so pretty in country and city*
> *Come hear my ditty about Tony Small*

The smell of burnt barley from the distilleries, from the barrels they rolled across the cobbled curve to the barges on the river.

> *That Indian fella in orange and yella*
> *Black as an umbrella or an old cannonball*

My name, I asked my Lieutenant, how do they know my name?

We are their theatre, he told me, they make drama where they find it and what they don't know they invent. And whenever they invent, they rhyme.

And we quickened our ride to leave them behind. The rhyming children, the smell of offal and burnt barley. So I would be that forever, I thought. That cannonball fellow in orange and yella.

The sun was blocked by the dark walls of yet another prison which he told me was called Black Dog. Was this city full of prisons? I wondered. Which reminded me to make good my promise to Molly about her Oscar. So I asked him had he any further thoughts.

Oscar, he said. You must remind me.

He's for the drop, I told him.

The drop, he said. You mean hanging? Remind me why?

He spiked a watchman with his toaster. During the fringes.

And I quoted what I remembered of Molly's verse.

> *When to see Luke's last gig we agreed*
> *We tipped all our gripes in a tangle*
> *And mounted our trotters with speed*
> *To squint at the snub as hed dangle.*

You are learning Gaelic? He asked me.

It's not Gaelic, I told him. It's from 'Luke Caffrey's Kilmainham Minnit'.

Minnit, he said. A bastardization of minuet. Ballad rhetoric. You would do well, Tony Small, to perfect your English first.

We left the city behind us then and galloped by the river until the horses got tired and we let them drink by the weir of a village called Chapelizod.

There was a church spire peeking over the bridge behind the weir.

The chapel of Iseult, he told me. Iseult, who was betrothed to the King of Cornwall. And the king sent his nephew, prince, Tristan, to escort her back across the water. But they fell in love, which always seems to lead to tragedy.

The tale seemed to move him more than the predicament of Molly's Oscar.

Tragedy, he told me, as he brought the water from the foaming weir to his lips, is the second cousin of love. And kings may marry where princes cannot. So she threw herself in the waters here and drowned and they built a church to remember her. Chapelizod.

Not Iseult? I asked.

No, he said. Izod. The native version. Always a bastardization.

Molly loves her Oscar, I said, the way Iseult loved her Tristan.

Can we compare them?

We can compare the drop.

Drop, he said. Iseult was drowned. Not hung.

So I had to rest my case. For the moment, at least. Molly and Oscar could hardly compete with Tristan and Iseult. They had no church, no weir. Just the walls of Kilmainham and sweet Bully's Acre.

We passed through a run of smaller villages then whose names he barely knew. I came to remember them, with time, on subsequent visits. Strawberry Beds, Lucan, Leixlip. We kept the river to our right insofar as we could, until the big one parted from us and we followed a smaller one called the Rye. And the road then led to a large set of gates surrounded by the vast wall of what he called his father's demesne.

The gates were open, as if the acres inside were no longer worth defending. There was an irregular line of beech trees tracing a path through the overgrown lawns, a herd of spotted cows grazing on either side.

I spent my childhood here. I remember thinking it was haunted.

And it had a spectral look. A hundred windows, flickering with the last of the evening light.

And was it, my Lord? Haunted?

Only by my father. The Duke of Leinster. He confined himself to the east wing. He seemed dead even then.

The fourth house. The first, Harley Street, in Marylebone, the second in Dublin. The third, Frescati by the sea and now the fourth, Carton, biggest of all. The sun was setting to the west by the time our horses reached the house itself. There were three large hounds, the biggest I had ever seen, sleeping in the last rays of sunlight on the great steps. They could have used them for hunting runaways in Carolina, I remember thinking.

Wolfhounds, my Lieutenant called them. Irish wolfhounds. The Duke breeds them.

The Duke your father?

No. The Duke, William, my brother. My father has been dead a long time.

Our horses were taken from us and we were led inside. An immense darkness reigned in there, the shadows of servants flitted, as if not wanting to be seen. And a man who could have been his father came down the great staircase.

Edward, he said, you came.

I did sir, he said, and I brought a companion.

From the Orient, I gather?

No, my Lieutenant replied. From the Americas. Carolina.

Ah. He seems Moorish. Levantine. Oriental, for sure. If he hunts, see that he changes costume.

They talked then, of hunting, of improvements to the demesne, of tenants, of some tribe they called the Whiteboys. And something descended on me, like a theatrical cloak. It was odd, given the orientals I still wore.

Invisibility.

Carton

The fourth house. It was as large as the other three put together. Inside it was like a small city, sheltered from the sun and rain, windows facing parkland that fell away from them to the pencil lines of trees that led to the distant gates. I could see the glint of water through the windows, of artificial lakes. It was as if a sleeping lion had dropped from the sky and stretched his paws around the land he imagined to be his alone. The lion's mouth was the entrance hall, with the stairs curving up above, where the brothers stood and talked, their voices growing indistinct as I wandered. Its paws were the different wings and I walked through the east one now, as the servants scurried through the shadows. I should have kept to the shadows like them but felt I had been granted the freedom of this interior city. There was a room with strange decorations from the Orient and I entered it and understood my outlandish costume at last. I would later hear it called the Chinese room and consider myself lucky to have been spared the indignity of a Chinaman's hat.

Everything was carved, fashioned, made, as if to distinguish it from the barbarous wilderness outside. Yet everything seemed neglected, dusty, even ancient, as if the wilderness has somehow infected it. I passed through a room full of wooden scaffolding, as if in the preparation for a hanging. But there was no body swinging from the transom above, instead an elegant pair of heels, and a bewigged man, working on the plaster decorations.

Eeet never ends, he said.

You mean the house, sir, I replied.

No. Renovations By the time we have finished one ceiling, another needs work. The damp, he said. This Irish climate.

And you, he said, as he turned to me.

He had a waxed moustache and a trimmed beard. He had an accent I had not yet encountered.

Like me, a foreigner.

Yes sir, I agreed.

From where?

Carolina, I said.

The Americas, he said. Like me, you are far from your home.

And you, sir?

From the kingdom of Naples.

Do you know of a Prospero there?

Prospero, I do not recall. Is he a Moor, like you?

He brushed the plaster from his hair. Come work with me. I will soon turn you white.

I know nothing of plasterwork, sir, I told him.

Ah, he said and whistled through his teeth. What is – how do they say – your function here?

Horses, I said.

Ah. They do love the hunt.

I visited the stables. They were a village unto themselves. And in the yard outside, a groom led an untamed stallion round in a circle.

Make a great hunter, he said, if anyone could break him.

He has not been ridden?

By many, but never for long.

He held out the reins to me.

The same colour as yourself though. So, you're welcome to try.

He led the stallion to the mounting block.

He has no saddle –

No. Not yet. Whoever rides him might saddle him. He smiled, briefly, showing blackened teeth. Go on blackfella. Give it a go.

It was a challenge. I could see other grooms gathering.

You're the Lord Edward's groom, aren't you?

I nodded.

Should be no bother to you.

So I took the reins and mounted.

What a sight, he said. Orange and yella.

Yes, I said. The blackfella.

The horse whinnied, once, twice, then ran and took the fence. I managed to hang on and heard a cheer behind me. I knew that a fall now would open me to ever more ridicule so I grabbed a fistful of mane and dug my heels in, hard. He took off even faster, as if his gallop had been merely a trot. Through an orchard, where I had to bury my head beneath his loping neck to avoid being whipped by the overhanging branches. Still the apples fell around me like hailstones. The thundering hooves and the cascading balls of fruit then a broken wall faced us and he leapt and my head crashed through an arch of boughs and the horse curved back down to the turf below and he met it with his stride and twisted his haunches once and then twice to unseat me. But I gripped his mane harder and made no attempt to slow him down. If I had I knew his twisting haunches would have tumbled me to earth. I clung on and dug my heels again to see if he had any more speed in him and the wonder was that he had. I remembered the old everlasters I had learnt to ride in Carolina and compared to them he was a different species. He jumped a river and passed a row of yew trees and I glimpsed row after row of mossy gravestones through them. Towards a lake up ahead, with brown water and a scimitar of white sand and a herd of deer appeared and scattered like a seed pod blown by a monster or a god and then the sand was beneath his hooves, and cascading sprays of the brown lake water. And the water finally worked its magic and slowed him down. I guided him in deeper and his stride slowed gradually to an exhausted halt. There were flecks of white foam on his mouth and his mane and we were both deep in the stillness of the lake.

I made cups of my hands and ladled lake water over his neck and his heaving flanks. He whinnied in submission and dipped his head. And I knew he was mine now.

A salmon leapt for a mayfly and startled him with its falling splash.

Hush, I said, and rubbed his wet black hair.

His ears pricked, as if he had language.

That was you, riding me, I said. Now let me ride you.

I edged his head sideways and guided him back towards the white sand. And when we reached it, I dug my heels in gently. He trotted then, with a beautiful loping stride and I nudged him into a gentle canter, towards a great perimeter wall beyond.

No horse would have ever leapt that. And he turned left there, as if he knew it. He followed the shadow of the great wall then, round the whole demesne, which was like a miniature, manicured country, barricaded from the wilderness beyond. Nature had been tamed, within this immense, rambling grey granite paddock. As this horse had been tamed. And I wondered had he a name.

The wall led us past a crumbling, ancient abbey with a round tower next to it. Abbey and tower were set in a bed of ancient oaks. They looked picturesque, too pretty to be true. I would later learn they were not true. They were what the Scot called follies, ruins built as ruins.

The oaks led to fields with spotted cattle grazing. Gardens beyond them and a maze of trimmed hedges. Beyond them again, the stables, congealing in the afternoon sun.

My horse indeed had a name, as I found out from the other grooms. Setanta.

They made a forest of arms for me and wouldn't let me descend to the mounting block, they had to lift me from his sodden flanks and deposit me on the straw-covered cobbles.

Setanta? I asked them, when the cheering subsided. Has it a meaning?

The boyhood name of Cuchulain, they told me.

And who is Cuchulain?

King of the Whiteboys, they told me, long ago.

And who are the Whiteboys?

There are no Whiteboys, they muttered. Who said Whiteboy?

You said Whiteboy.

There were Whiteboys once, they said. But they've long been levelled. And his name is Setanta. Ask the master can he be yours.

Silken Thomas

I was relieved of duties almost entirely in that house. My Lieutenant stayed up late and woke later, only asked for the occasional shave. Meals were irregular, and the Fitzgeralds broke their fast close to lunchtime. The only excitement came from rumours of the hunt.

I dreamt I saw a ghost the first night and wandered from my bed and quarters to follow it, down a series of long corridors to a pair of windows blown open by the breeze. I looked out over the fields and distant hayricks, like shadows of themselves in the moonlight and saw a figure cross the lawns, dressed in a top hat with feathers spiking from it, dragging the carcass of a deer behind him. I wondered was it my father, the ghost of the father whom I had never met and had no hope of ever meeting. Skinner Mayo, who followed the Cree trails and hunted the Indian way. He turned towards me in the moonlight and he doffed his hat.

Why here, father, in this distant unknowable land, why come to me here and not in Carolina?

I saw a blackened face beneath the top hat and beneath it the rough shape of a white shift. The ghost of my father, in a woman's dress. The vision walked on then, dragging its booty of dead deerflesh and was consumed by the shadows.

And I found myself by those actual windows and wondered was it the dream that brought me there or the ghost that I had dreamt.

But no, the figure I had seen was real, I could see the tracks in the grass the hind legs had left.

I turned and wandered back the corridors to find the door I remembered as mine. But there were so many doors, so many corridors. I heard footsteps behind me then, and hid in the shadows of the great organ above the stairs. This house, like Prospero's island, was full of noises.

It was a duke alright, but not Prospero. The Duke of Leinster, a bottle of hock in his hand. He mounted the last few stairs, unsteadily, and swayed at the top.

Thomas, he muttered, Thomas.

He was staring at the shadows beyond me.

He lost his footing and would have tumbled back if I had not stepped from the organ loft and gripped his elbow.

Silken Thomas, he muttered. You belong in the tower, not here.

I drew him gently from the precipice of the huge staircase and asked him who this Silken Thomas was.

My ancestor, he told me, who rebelled against the King and was drawn and quartered for his troubles.

He stopped then and stared at the great maze of shadows below.

Forgive me, he continued. He was hung and headed. Not drawn. The King gave him that.

The Duke had lost his boots. Or left them somewhere down below. I let his stockinged feet lead me, towards the great oaken door of his quarters. The stockings, I noticed, were silk.

And his ghost wanders here and wonders what went wrong.

What did go wrong? I dared to ask.

He forgot, he began, and his foot slipped. I had to steady his elbow.

He forgot?

Correct sir. He forgot he held his title at the King's pleasure.

Ah.

And you sir, who gave you your freedom?

The King, I told him.

I remembered my paper, wrapped in oilskin. Perhaps now I knew enough letters to read it.

Never forget.

And I vowed, never to forget.

Foxhunt

That house seemed built for ghosts.

The rooms, leading to other rooms through ever diminishing sets of doorways. The wind, moaning down every chimney. The boards creaking underneath the frayed carpets and the tinkling chandeliers above them. The paintings of Silken Thomas and his mercenaries with the silken fringes dangling from their helmets. The dukes that succeeded him, all covered in dust. The man-made ruins scattered round the demesne. The dawn mist that shrouded the avenue.

I awoke one morning to find it still clinging, long after the sun should have risen. There was a waferish circle of light trying to pierce the grey. The beech trees were like soft pencils with nothing beyond.

I heard the sound of horses but couldn't see them. A ghostly horde and I thought maybe Silken Thomas had returned. Then I saw splashes of red through the grey mist as if an invisible hand above was bleeding. Another rumble of hooves, and the mist dispersed as if the hooves brought their own wind with them and I saw red-coated riders coming through like a blood-soaked cavalry.

I heard a blast from a trumpet. I remembered Old Montgomery's readings from the Bible and wondered had the end of days come. But no, it was the hunt. The Kildare hunt followed by a pack of yapping dogs.

So, I was relieved of my pantaloons at last. I was dressed in a red greatcoat and high black boots. I mounted Setanta in the stables and joined the hunt in the cobbled yard. A great ocean of yapping dogs and shifting horses. The red-coats drank from pewter mugs and smashed them off the cobblestones, and I was one of them now. He makes a fine figure, Lord Edward's blackamoor. I heard variations of that more often than I could count. Then there was a tootle on the hunting horn and we headed down the avenue, like one large beast with a hundred or so legs. At the gates the horn blasted again with more purpose this time and the ride-out began. Across an empty field at first, and we rose in one undulating wave over a low stone wall. Across a small river, over an ancient bridge that led to a broken village, the thatched roofs of the houses almost touching the muddy ground. Women huddled in shawls and gathered children beneath them, lest they make a sudden dart underneath our hundred hooves. Then we found an open field with a circle of trees around a mound of a hill and the hounds burrowed into a culvert and a fox darted out and the chase was on.

All I could remember of the hunt was not the jumps, the yapping hounds, the whoops, the tumbles into muddy ditches, but the farmlands our hundred hooves trashed beneath them. We ran the fox to ground in a field of barley, ready for reaping but when the hunt was over and the fox was a mangled carcass there was no barley left. A farmer and his three stalwart sons gazed at us blankly, from a cabin beyond. There was a dull, burning resentment in their downcast eyes that I recognized.

What will they do for barley now? I asked the master of the hunt, as we rode past.

They'll be well paid for their trouble.

But I saw them spit, three times, in the dusty ground beneath our horses' feet.

Buachaill Bán

There was a carriage in the forecourt when the hunt returned. His mother stepped from it, and the dogs for some reason surged around her.

It's your handwarmer, my dear, said Ogilvie, descending behind her, kicking them aside with his boot.

And it must have been. Her delicate hands were buried in a whorl of dark fur.

Lord Edward jumped from his horse in his mud-spattered boots. But it was my eye she caught, through the sea of red coats. She pulled one hand from the fox-fur and waved.

Every head turned.

A favourite, muttered the groom, when he dragged up the mounting block. I hear she has a favourite.

We rode out to another demesne that night, that of the master of the Kildare hunt. And Lady Emily may have had a favourite, but I was not asked to dinner. I ate with the servants and listened to the traffic to and from the great dining room, the platters with the spitting pig, the oiled mounds of pheasant, the steaming potatoes. The liveried feet ascending from the cellars, with bottle after dusty bottle. I sat in my room then and listened to the laughter, the singing, the bibulous jokes, the tinkling on a harpsichord. And through the window I saw movement on the lawns.

Another ghost, with the top hat and the blackened face and the white woman's dress. He stood just beyond the edge of lamplight the great windows threw on the lawn. I could see his head, under that feathered hat searching from left to right across the house façade. As if to be certain he remained unseen. Then his head tilted upwards and his eyes met mine.

I could see dim shapes of other white dresses, moving in darkness behind him. Men, or ghosts, in the shifts of women.

Then he tipped his hat, mockingly, and bowed. He stepped backwards, delicately, into the shadows, as if he didn't want to leave a trace on the manicured lawns.

I asked the stable boys about it in the morning.

An buachaill bán, they said, you saw him or his ghost. Was the moon shining?

I remembered the candlelit lawns. No moonlight.

Then it wasn't Captain Moonlight.

It was the first I had heard of this Captain Moonlight. The ghost that walks, the night avenger that leaves burning hayricks and gutted cattle.

They had blackened faces, I told them.

Like your own, they said.

Would the buachaill gorm make a buachaill bán?

What's a buachaill bán?

A buachaill's a boy. Buachaill bán's a Whiteboy.

I was readying the horses for a picnic. Four of them – one each for my Lieutenant, Lady Emily, Mr Ogilvie and me. And as we rode down the avenue, there was an odour of burnt straw. We passed gutted cattle in the fields, underneath the smouldering hayricks.

His Herefordshires, my Lieutenant murmured. The Master will not be pleased.

It never ends, does it? His mother said.

I felt it was not my place to ask what it was that never ends. But I knew ghosts hadn't done this. Let the Kildare hunt deal with it, Ogilvie said, and quickened his horse into a canter.

He wanted to educate us in ruins. It was a countryside of ruins and he was a connoisseur of most of them. The Hills of Uisneach and Tara, the ruined graves of Nowth and Dowth, the valley of St Ite where the streams run uphill, the water won't boil and the trees won't burn. So we rode, through the shabby hills in the low sun to the grounds of a ruined abbey alive with red poppies. And Ogilvie sketched, as I opened the basket and spread a linen cloth over the meadow of wild strawberries. He told me of an ancient race of kings and high kings, of saints and scholars, with a savage grace entirely lacking in its degraded descendants.

Read Macpherson, he told me. And you'll find this country has an epic to rival Homer. *Fingal.*

Father of Ossian, my Lieutenant smiled.

Supposedly, his mother chirped.

So you believe O'Connor? He asked.

And Doctor Johnson, she said. They are fakes, my dear.

Scottish fakes, my Lieutenant said, follies, manufactured ruins.

Still, the Scot continued, as his pencil continued its fluid shiver of his notepad, even a folly has its own aesthetic.

146

Is this, he asked, any less lovely than the Duke of Leinster's folly?

He held out the sketch then, of the gravestones, the ruined arch of the abbey and the round tower behind them.

It seemed beautiful to me, magical. But I kept my mouth shut.

Manhunt

There was another hunt assembling around the demesne stable-yard when we returned. But this was a hunt with bloodhounds, with whips and shooting pieces and the riders wore black, not red.

Stable the horses, my Lieutenant told me. We want no part of this.

So I led his and mine into the barn inside where the oats and barley tumbled from the sacks and the stable boys smoked their pipes on the haystacks, watching the goings-on in the fading sunlight outside.

And they wanted no part of it either.

The gentry, they told me, have their own rules.

But this was a hunt more familiar to me, I could already see that. It was a hunt for people. I pictured the horses, fanning out across the trampled barley-field. The farmer dragged from his cabin. And from what I had seen of that country-side, there were no forests in which to hide.

It would be a hunt by moonlight, they told me. For Captain Moonlight.

I was invited to dine at the table that night. My Lieutenant, his mother, Mr Ogilvie. The Master was riding out, with the hunt.

We could hear the distant yapping of hounds. The conversation was of the same Macpherson, of Doctor Johnson, of Scottish myths and Irish legends. I had to marvel about what was left unspoken.

And I saw what was not spoken of around dawn, from my bedroom window. The hunt, returning, down the misty avenue. It had had some success, it seemed, for last in line behind the horses a barefoot youth staggered, his hands bound by a rope to a rider's saddle.

I recognized him from the ruined field of barley. And as I prepared the horses for departure, they were strapping him to a construction of beams that they wheeled into the stable-yard. The grooms called it the Triangle. I would have called it a whipping post.

The hunt had found a dress stained with the blood of a Hereford cow, thrown down inside a well. And as the Master and my Lieutenant were saying their goodbyes, by the front steps of the great house, I could hear the whipping begin.

I remembered the sound of those strokes. The whistle through the air, the crack and the cry of pain, always louder than the bullwhip.

How many? I asked my Lieutenant as we rode down the avenue.

How many what? He seemed pensive, absent.

How many lashes? I asked him.

With the Whiteboys, he told me, they lose all count.

And he whipped his horse into a gallop and my horse dutifully followed.

And we rode back to Carton. Once there, it was as if the thing never happened. We picnicked around more ruins, and all admired the artistry with which the Scotsman sketched them. The Abbey at Mellifont, the tombs at Brú na Bóinne, Nowth and Dowth, what they called the Lia Fáil at Tara. He told me more of Fingal and his son, the poet Ossian. Forgeries, perhaps, but like these ruins, the only remnants of the race of heroes that once walked this land. A sad contrast to the churls that walk it now.

Churl. It was a new word to me. As ugly as that triangle. And I wondered was he churl or hero, the Whiteboy tied to it.

The Hanging

Molly had her fill of Crusoe. He was captured into slavery she told me and made his escape with a boy called Xury who he himself sold into slavery before he settled in Brazil and on his way back to lead a slaving expedition he was shipwrecked near the Great River Oroonoque where he dragged provisions from the ruined ship through the waves that nearly killed him on the shore. And she liked the description of the waves crashing, they were waves bigger than any she had noticed here. The ship stayed out on the bay where it was shipwrecked and he swam back out twice, retrieving nails and implements and what vittles he could until those same waves took it under. He built a shelter then and dug deep into the ground and despaired of rescue and spoke only to God. He had the ship's dog and two cats for company and when the island was visited by cannibals, he captured one of them on a Friday and named him Friday. If he had captured him on a Saturday he would have named him Saturday, she supposed, or Sunday for that matter. Anyway, she had wearied of the tale and gave the well-thumbed book to me and told me to labour my way through it if I had the patience that she had run out of.

So I began to read. Slowly, very slowly at first, my finger tracing each of the words, inhaling the smell of Molly's skin since she had kept it tucked into the space between her blouse and apron at work. She smelt of chaff, Molly, of flour and of woman's sweat. She would ask me daily what my progress was, had he been captured yet by the Moors at Sallee, had he made his escape with Xury, had he sold Xury yet to the Portuguese captain for ten years if he promised to convert to Christianity. And my progress was slow, to tell you the truth, what with the horses and my Lieutenant's morning habits and his visits to the parliament where I would stable the horses, make my way inside to the gallery and observe the speeches on the round stage below. It was the season, of parliament, of the theatre, the Lord Lieutenant's balls in Dublin Castle. I would dress in my Leinster livery or my oriental finery and lead his horses to one or the other. And all of the time I moved through Crusoe's life, page by laborious page. I fell asleep to the imagined roaring of beasts on the African coast, the sound of the wind on the rigging, the howl of the cataclysmic storm, the crash of the waves on the island shore.

And two things happened during those long months I spent with Crusoe. Molly's Oscar was hung in Stephen's Green and my Lieutenant fell in love.

I would get used to him falling in love. It drew him away from me and back again, with the rhythm of a pendulum that caught him in the stomach, lifted him off his feet, bore him off into an unknown landscape and deposited him back again, spent, longing for me and the whorehouse. And when

I grew more adventurous in my reading, I became familiar with Cupid and his fanciful arrows. But my Lieutenant's Cupid seemed to use more than a bow.

I would get used to hangings as well, my acquaintance with the scaffold and the drop and everything that preceded it – the hunt by the militia, the triangle and the whippings – would grow over the years until it drowned in a river of blood. But a first hanging, like a first love, can never be forgotten. I had seen corpses dangling before of course, Boston Joe and his friends in the Carolinas, deserters in Charleston, but always the aftermath, never the event.

I came down one morning to the kitchens for the honey and milk and heard sobbing from the pantry. I opened the door and found Molly sitting on a sack of meal, her eyes running with tears and her face white with flour.

What is it Molly? I asked and she began about her hopes for a reprieve or at the very least a sentence of indentured servitude in the colonies, Carolina or New England.

You're from Carolina, aren't you Tony?

And the bell rang then that I knew was his, which only made her cry more.

Go on Tony, she said, run upstairs and attend to the master and leave me to cry on here.

So I ran upstairs and I poured him his milk and his honey and I shaved those delicate cheeks and I rubbed him clean with the towel and returned to the kitchen which was full now with the business of the morning. I opened the pantry door again, and no sign of Molly. So I walked out to the stables and I found her in a hayrick there, drying her eyes. She had no more crying left, she told me. She had hoped, she told me again, for a sentence of indentured servitude for her Oscar but there was no Carolina or New England left since the King had lost America. She could have joined him there and had some kind of life, though he hadn't asked, the bowsie, after three years courting, he had never asked. And now he found himself sentenced by Judge Moynihan to public hanging on September the seventh with six others in Stephen's Green. And her only hope of a life with him was if she grabbed his corpse before the breath went and stuck a dagger in his windpipe.

Or does that only happen in ballads? She wondered.

I had no way of knowing but I walked with her again that evening up the river past the brewery to Kilmainham with two stolen bottles of hock in my pockets and Molly with a pie under her skirt. I lifted her up to the barred window again, two hands under her dainty shoes but there was no Oscar there to greet her, but another unfortunate who told her that her Oscar had been transferred to the new built prison at Newgate. So we walked then, back down to the river and followed it till we saw the spire of the cathedral. Molly took a sip of the bottle and passed it to me and I passed it back to her so by the time we'd crossed the river and reached Newgate the bottle was empty.

Thanks be to Jesus we have two, said Molly.

But the gaoler took the other and demanded tuppence more, so she gave him half the pie as well, so she was finally admitted to her Oscar with very little left. I could see them through the bars. He crumbled the pie into bits with his fingers and fed himself with one hand while the other rubbed her tear-stained cheek.

There'll be seven of them, the gaoler told me, on the seventh and the whole city will gather for a look. Two murderers, three thieves, a rioter and a witch.

A witch? I asked him.

Lizzie Doyle, he said, who skewered unborn children with a hatpin. Will you be there?

I said that I might.

Keep your face well covered, he told me.

Why, would they hang me too? I asked him. I had to wonder, if that fancy took them, what protection my letter from the King would provide?

And he changed the subject then, told me about this new built prison, from which the only possible escape would be the mechanical drop.

Mechanical? I asked.

With a swinging trapdoor. For the hangings. A miracle of carpentry, soon to be finished. If her apprentice is lucky, he'll swing from it. If not, it's Stephen's Green where they've nothing but the tree. They lead them there on horseback, put the rope around their neck and whip the horse goodbye.

And Molly returned then, to put an end to the ghoulish conversation.

Come with me, she said, to Barrack Street, and we'll drink some more.

Which we did. An evening of long lament, with her friends, all pushing block prisseys. Some apprentices joined us, from Tailor's Hall and they drank to her Oscar and planned his escape. A rope dropped down from the Newgate window, or if that didn't work, a toaster through the gullet so his breath came back. I hadn't the heart to mention the mechanical drop, as they planned the journey through the night with Captain Moonlight, her Oscar passed from one Whiteboy cottage to another until he made it to Wexford and a boat bound for France.

What's wrong with Carolina? Asked Molly, and they assured her that nothing whatsoever was wrong with Carolina except that the wine merchants from Wexford headed only to France.

But as the night wore on even that plan lost its urgency and was dissipated in a river of drink. I would see more of that in the future too, plans hatched over a bottle, lost at the bottom of a bottle. But there were no informers then. At least not yet. And by the evening's end, there was no more plan.

And the Newgate carpenters must have been tardy, because he was hung the next Saturday, in Stephen's Green. I met Molly in the stables that morning and she was dressed in her finest.

If anyone asks us Tony, she told me, we're heading to the fair.

Which fair? I asked her.

Donnybrook Fair, she told me. Because if they knew I was acquainted with a felon, I'll lose more than my job.

You'll lose nothing, I told her.

I'm not favoured by the Lord, like you, she said. I'm a kitchen skivvy, from Thomas Street.

You're a Lady, I said.

In widow's weeds, she said.

There were crowds gathering around the leafless tree to the north end of the Green. There was one branch, almost as thick as the trunk and I could see that the bark had been rubbed bare around it. There were cake sellers and thimble pushers and three-card-trick men and ballad singers and I kept my arm around Molly in the press of people. We could hear the jeers beginning and see the missiles curving through the air. Stones, potatoes, rotten fruit. We could see bare heads coming towards us, raised above the crowd by the horses they sat on. The loudest jeers were for the pale young woman who sat backwards on the horse, her hands tied behind her. And when Oscar's turn came there was a surge forward as if from an invisible force within the gathering.

The 'prentices, Molly told me. But the watchmen beat them back and the rope was looped round the hanging branch and the horse pushed back from it, unwilling it seemed, to go under. It resisted, whinnied and brayed, kicked two of the guards who pulled the bit and the reins. Maybe it shared Molly's liking for Oscar. Until it finally reared, bucked and galloped through the scattering crowd and he was left swinging, his face to the river. His body twitched as he swung and his legs danced for a while till he gave up the ghost and hung, silent.

I would have happily danced it with him, she said. And now take me home, Tony Small.

So we went to Leinster House, if we could call that home.

She cut him down that night, with his apprentice friends, and they tried piercing his gullet, but the breath was long gone. So either the ballads were wrong, she told me, or they'd left it too late. They took his body to a pushing shop in South William Street and they waked him till the morning when the tailors rode his body to The Naul, where his people were from.

Love

At least hanging came to a conclusion. Love, I was to find,
rarely did. I saw her first catch his eye from the parliament gallery, during the debate about the Policing Act. I
was many rows behind her, leaning against the back wall
with others of the servant class and all of us bored by the
theatre on the parliament floor below. It was crowded with
lords, all of whom had an opinion to express on what they
called 'riot, papistry and rural and urban disturbance'. My
Lieutenant seemed as bored with the proceedings as we
were. He bore his politics lightly then. He was unconcerned
with the burdens that came with his lordship, he wore his
privileges as yet with unconscious ease, arrogance, some
would have called it, and I would have called it grace, since
it suited him. I was pondering the moment when Crusoe
saw the ship finally sink below the waves when I caught the
glance and knew it wasn't for me. It was for her, the lady
that leaned with her bare shoulders over the gallery parapet.
She had a fan and brushed her cheeks with it, as she gazed
at the theatrics below. Her hair was brown, and cascaded

backwards in a kind of contained fury, as if it carried a silent wind with it.

So whatever this Cupid was using, it was more than an arrow. I could gather its force from seven bodies behind her. I could measure it by the movement of her fan that stopped, briefly, by her rounded, rouged cheekbone and when his eyes fell back to the floor, it resumed its shiver, like a hummingbird's wing. I saw his eyes search out the form of the speaker and then be drawn back and upwards to meet hers again, so the fan slowed its movement again to a series of slow, languorous strokes and then fell still once more. It perched by her left ear this time, which was decorated with a pearl. I could only imagine the eyes that looked back at his.

They were blue, I would find out later, the kind of blue that is made all the more startling by the luxuriant darkness of her hair. And the fan rested and her face turned slightly, as if to display her charms better to the gaze below and I saw her long eyelashes flicker and I felt his gaze steady from below and a blush spread over the side of her cheek that faced me, a blush that was bloodier than the rouge she had dabbed it with. The face turned back then, so the fan was obscured, but I felt its resumption of movement by the shiver of her thumb. Her companion leant a head gently towards her and must have followed her glance below, because he looked away and languorously crossed the tiles of the parliament floor.

I knew my place. I had to move too, and did, rushing down the stairs to reach the stable before he did.

He rode the short distance up from College Green to his father's house in silence. He jumped off the mounting block with barely a word and I stabled the horses alone.

But two days later we rode out on a warm autumn day to Frescati and there she was, on the lawns, at tea with Lady Emily and Mr Ogilvie, the same fan performing its dance around her eyelashes and her cheekbone. I could see the full shape of that face that had arrested him on the parliament floor. Almost oriental in shape, wide cheekbones, a delicate, almost non-existent chin, the startling blue eyes and the frozen tempest of the brown hair above it all. Was it only me, I had to wonder, that saw the resemblance to his mother? The memory of the muddied locket in the Eutaw forest? Maybe each porcelain face looked the same to me. The hair, for sure. Everything else though was smaller, softer, too wide and too small, she was like a lapdog wrapped in a flowing dress, but the overall effect was both coquettish and enchanting.

Her name was Lady Catherine Meade, Molly told me. Molly learnt this from Prunella, Lady Emily's parlour maid and seamstress who instructed us in the rituals of courtship. My sentimental education came from Molly and Molly's came mostly from street ballads, so we both needed more civilized instruction.

The daughter of the First Earl of Clanwilliam, Lady Catherine, Prunella informed us, was the heiress to a considerable fortune, but a very late arrival to the ranks of what she called 'the gentry'. Lord Edward, as the younger son of the Duke of Leinster, with a questionable inheritance but an impeccable pedigree, would come with certain advantages and certain impediments. But then, no match is perfect, Prunella informed us sagely, and Lord Edward has ambitions for a military commission, does he not? And Lady Catherine will come with an inheritance and a large estate in far-off county Down.

All of which seemed a world away from the quivering fan she fretted her painted face with on the Frescati lawns. But such, I was to discover over a succession of glances, enchantments and whispers, were the mysteries of love. He would be gripped by them in an instant, pulled from me into a welter of brooding silences, the predictable rhythm of our days would be thrown into chaos, there would be journeying, there would be absences, there would be gossip round the stables and the kitchens, a whole series of unspoken gestures to be interpreted by dear Molly and the unbearable Prunella, and at the end of this long saga of what she called 'courtship', were departures, sudden and unexplained.

I next saw Lady Catherine in the forecourt of Dublin Castle attending one of the Lord Lieutenant's balls. It was the Castle season, Prunella told us, as if we didn't know already, the parliament in session. There was a crush of carriages in the forecourt, my Lieutenant had exited his, with Lady Emily on his arm, the horses ahead were scraping their hooves off the cobblestones, the carriage wheels sliding forwards and back when the footman behind me opened the carriage door and the steps slid downwards and a high-heeled shoe with a pink rose embroidered into the braid of the toe placed itself on the upper step and seemed to freeze there, as if waiting for further service. A rose-coloured stocking ascended from the heel towards the folds of a pink dress, which wafted back and forward in what wind there was until a delicate hand, clutching the same fan, touched the hem of the dress, as if bidding it to be still. Then a head leaned out of the carriage door and the same brown hair was topped by an arrangement of feathers, a diadem I suppose would be Prunella's word for it, something less, anyway, than a hat. Her small lapdog face sat uneasily beneath it, those pencilled eyebrows gathered themselves into a frown until the footman took her hand and helped her down the steps. As she walked across the cobblestones, I wondered how I would describe the spectacle to Molly. It was an imitation of beauty, rather than beauty itself. An older woman hurried in small scurrying steps from behind to join her. Her mother I had to presume, which presumption was later confirmed by the omnivorous Prunella, the Countess Clanwilliam.

Did you hate her then? Molly would ask me. Not then, I would reply. Only later.

Age did not suit that clan. Her mother was, and again I could only presume, the image of what Lady Catherine might become. The daughter walked straight and the mother walked crooked, both weighed down with more apparel than the human form was designed to bear. The daughter's nest of feathers pointed towards the stars, the mother's towards the bejewelled figure with the mace who guarded the castle doors. He banged his mace off the flagstones as they passed through and roared something incomprehensible to me, their names and titles, I could only assume. And as my eyes followed their passage up the staircase, the last thing to disappear were those delicate shoes, with the same flower embroidered on the back of each heel.

There was music playing from the glittering windows above, a blast of trumpets which I would later learn was called an obligato and which was used, Prunella told myself and the breathless Molly, to announce each significant new arrival to the Great Hall. The Duchess of Leinster and her favourite son would have been worthy of one, though the jury must stay out as to whether the Countess Clanwilliam would have been afforded the same honour.

Anyway, the carriages began to move then and I rode the back of mine through the Cork Street gates to the stables behind and so was denied any further soundings from the great ball inside. Which would have begun, Prunella informed us, with a cotillion or as the French termed it, a 'contre-dance', of groups of four – two couples facing each other across an imaginary square, and Lord Edward and Lady Catherine could well have faced each other, and during one of the several figures of the dance crossed the invisible square towards each other, meeting eyes and touching hands.

Prunella drew a square in the sawdust of the kitchen floor and had me dance my Lieutenant's steps while she danced Lady Catherine's, Molly and Samuel the bootblack commandeered to fill out the four. All hands would have been gloved, she told us, and she wound a tea towel around her hands to demonstrate. So she moved, her towelled hand touching mine, in a contrariwise motion.

I'd prefer an old-fashioned slip jig, Molly interjected and raised her skirts to demonstrate the footwork of the same.

That's why you'll never be a lady, Prunella cautioned her.

No more than yourself, Molly interjected and slipped my arm around her waist and drew me into a dizzying whirl.

And as for my partner here, would he ever make a lord?

Savages, said Prunella, have no place at a cotillion, or a ball for that matter.

Even noble ones? Asked Molly who had tired of dancing by now, and was slaking her thirst with a jug of buttermilk from the table.

But Prunella was right. My place was in the stables, with the other grooms that night, their glowing pipes illuminating the empty carriages and the gently shifting horses, as the ghostly music echoed round us from the ball beyond. And my Lieutenant, when the ball had finally ended, took no more notice of me than the horses did.

I rode with him north two days later. Across the river at the Essex Bridge, down Sackville Street, through the older, grander squares that were the principal city. And with the city behind us we passed through a succession of small villages: Drumcondra, Donabate, Swords and one miserable hamlet called The Naul, where I assumed Molly's Oscar was surely buried by now. My Lieutenant said little as we rode, made no mention of the destination to which I already knew we were headed, Lady Catherine's family's estate in a county called Down.

There was a carriage, he muttered, that we could have taken, but this road he was now travelling needed to be experienced, to be felt. He had lived too long in a country that he knew little of and if he was to marry into Down, he would get to know the road there.

So marriage was the goal, I knew now, and Prunella had been right. Those few moments I had witnessed were part of what she called courtship. But the way was murky and undistinguished and seemed to wrap us round with dampness as we rode on. We came to a walled town, by a bend in a river that gleamed almost pink with the last of the day's light, and he said we should lay our heads there. The river was called the Boyne he told me, the town called Drogheda and we stopped by an inn on the poor main street next to a building called the Tholsel. There were acquaintances that would have been more than happy to provide better hospitality, he told me, but that would mean explaining his presence there. So we ate barley soup and potatoes on a bare table next to the kitchen and I slept on the floor by the foot of his bed, to be woken by the grey light coming through the curved window and the ringing of the Tholsel bell. I made my way downstairs, through the kitchen to the stables and was given a bowl of buttermilk by a curious boy.

Are you Melchior, Caspar or Balthazar? he asked me. And I told him I was neither of those three wise men, but the manservant of an Irish lord. He whistled in wonder. He had thought the opposite was the case, that the beardless youth who had not yet awoken was one of the many servants of mine. I laughed at that and told it him it might one day be the case, but for the present my job was to saddle these horses and prepare them for the road. And he helped me then to secure the buckles and the bridles while he asked more about my origins.

I was from a country, I told him, that hadn't yet been dis-covered, buried deep beneath the ocean whose murky light accounted for my dark skin. And I was caught in a net by a fisherman and dragged to the shore and sold at market, which accounted for my current state. But I had high hopes for my freedom, I told him, and to someday return to my place beneath the waves. He appreciated my candour and told me he himself was from a race that had one day ruled this island, but a series of savage tricks of fate had led to their current state, which was of various forms of servitude. The cruellest of them all, he told me, had been the Battle of the Boyne, where possession of the town he lived in and the countryside surrounding passed to its current owners. But what was won could be lost again and what was lost won, he said, and the conversation ended on that mysterious note, because my Lieutenant came out of the scullery door and we resumed our journey north.

We reached it around evening. A dark house in an untidy estate, a miniature Carton that seemed to me, as we rode towards it, built for nothing but ghosts. The windows glittered with the last light and I saw her again through one of the larger ones, next to the entrance, another fan worrying her face like a dark moth. I slept in the stables there, as of old, my presence inside being unwanted and I heard the spirits moan round me as I tossed and tried to sleep in the straw. I held both horses and walked behind them along the lough at Strangford, the last in a line of chaperones, dressed once more in my oriental duds. I saw her arm rest upon his elbow, I saw her fan cooling his face, swat off a buzzing fly. Another day they rowed on a boat along the lake while the chaperones kept pace along the shore. I lay beneath the horses in a bed of thyme and clover and listened to the soft dip of his oar. Everything was hushed, much more was understood, it seemed, than spoken. And there was music that night, while I paced the lawns and saw a hare sitting upright, its ears pointing towards the moon. Music from the pianoforte drifted round us both and a female voice that trembled. Hers, I said to the hare and hare nodded. Or it seemed to nod, as she seemed to sing.

We rode back then, in twelve long hours of black silence. Love never seemed to make him happy, communicative or restful. It brought that silence round him, like a cloud, and I returned to the kitchens of Leinster House to find Molly knew more of the progress of his suit than I did. Through Prunella, of course. Lady Catherine had another suitor, her mother disapproved, as did his, they both of them could do better, him with a dowry, her with a noble lineage. And whatever the outcome was to be, it was not to be marriage, it was a return to England for him on the packet and we both watched the city depart in the strange greenish light of the evening and he confided to me that at a time like this, he wondered would he ever return.

But for once I wasn't thinking about him. I was thinking of those city streets. I was wondering why they felt like home. I was thinking of Molly. I hadn't bid her a proper goodbye.

Crusoe

I read more of Crusoe on the packet and wondered would a storm blow up to suit my Lord's mood.

He was 'my Lord' now. My Ned was a distant memory.

He paced the decks until the night came down and he retired below while I tried to sleep above, curled up between his cases. And no storm came, just a gentle wafting wind that took us to a scattered group of hamlets which gave me my first glimpse of the harbour called Holyhead.

He makes a home in a cave for himself, then a garden, then a farm, keeps company with the drowned captain's dog. Crusoe that is, not me. I travelled to London with my Lieutenant, carried him home from brothels, nursed him through the fevers he acquired there.

Crusoe meanwhile planted seeds of barley and saw them grow, read the Good Book, abandoned his cave after an earthquake and built what he called his castle. Civilization is a fine thing, I thought, but its absence might be finer.

I learned more of Crusoe's island, waiting with the horses outside a gaming house, a theatre, a club, than I did of the great city of London. Such was the magic of reading. Crusoe mapped out his island, lord of it all. I travelled to Woolwich with my own Lord and watched him learn to grind saltpetre into powder, blast empty buildings with cannon in a field.

We travelled to the Channel Islands and Gibraltar checking munitions and fortifications, in the company of Lieutenant Sirr, later to be Major, who would later come to a reckoning with my Lord which no one could have predicted from their exchanges in Gibraltar.

I was reading by the Moorish Wall one morning, built, Lieutenant Sirr informed me, to repel the Barbary pirates from the African coast.

So if that was Africa, I wondered aloud, staring through the giant blocks, where was Algiers?

There, Lieutenant Sirr pointed, to a thin blur behind the spray, behind the white-capped ocean. And nothing good ever came from it. Or from your Africa.

My Africa? And again, I must have said it aloud.

My Tony, my Lieutenant interrupted, is from the Carolinas. The King's lost continent.

Forgive me, Sir. I took him for a Moor.

I nodded my head. What I didn't say was, it was a Moor enslaved my mother.

He apologized again, profusely. And he was all politeness as he described the wall's defensive capabilities, against the Moorish hordes.

There would be none of that politeness, some years later. Lieutenant Sirr would fire two shots from his regimental pistol, one of which would lodge in my Lieutenant's gut, the other in his shoulder. And in return my Lieutenant would leave his stomach open with his stiletto dagger. All this would happen in a flurry of goose feathers, in the attic of Murphy the feather merchant's house in Thomas Street, the Liberties.

You could have never dreamed of that outcome when I next saw them both, on the stage in the regimental hall. The play was *As You like It*, by William Shakespeare. The forest – a line of potted rubber and banana plants – was called Arden. I could have made a better job of it myself, and would, much later. The heroine was a sapper wrapped in a gypsy shawl with a black mantilla covering his barely shaven beard. Lieutenant Sirr played the exiled Duke while my Lieutenant played a melancholy vagrant, Jacques. Did all Dukes have to suffer exile? I wondered. First Prospero, now this one. Anyway, this Duke's sorry exile was in a forest made of rubber, banana and monkey-puzzles in which my Lieutenant happened to come across a fool. A motley fool, a miserable fool. And I was glad then that the forest so little resembled our own in Eutaw. He couldn't be referring to me.

Could Lieutenant Sirr act? No, he could hardly play himself, let alone a duke. But my own Lieutenant played Jacques to perfection. His melancholy gave rise to roars of laughter and brought that forest to life. And I only wish their destinies could have ended there.

But that was the way with fictions, I was realizing. They were sometimes better than facts.

We journeyed through Spain then, two itinerant fools. On horse and mule.

I read more of Crusoe on the journey. Crusoe fought with cannibals, rescued one of them from a certain death and

Molly had spoiled the story for me here, since I already knew he caught him on a Friday.

Crusoe, after many and sundry adventures, made his return, bringing Friday with him and journeyed through Spain towards home. And, oddly enough, his journey mirrored our own. Up from Madrid, they travelled, as we did, towards Pamplona and through the Pyrenees in the hope of a return to England. We crossed the Pyrenees with less adventure, though. Crusoe waded through snow, fought with packs of wolves and his Friday made much sport with a bear. But we ended up like them, back in his England, where the further adventures of Friday are left unwritten. So I had two now to wonder about, Caliban in Prospero's Naples, and Friday in Crusoe's England.

Crusoe married. My Lieutenant wasn't as lucky. He fell in love again.

The Rivals

Georgiana was her name, and she took a bit of my heart too. I saw her first on the lawns of that great mansion in Sussex, home of the Duke of Richmond, a house that was splendid in its pillars and its whiteness, that seemed, unlike the houses of his family in Ireland, to belong in the rolling hills among which it rested and to be quite empty of ghosts. There was croquet on the lawns, a small forest of parasols, and hers was the one whose shadow my Lieutenant followed, two mallets in hand.

I saw her next in the Theatre Royal in Drury Lane. The stage so far below us that I pulled Cecil back from the edge of the gods, afraid that he'd tumble over. He had missed the play once already. He wanted to catch every word of *The Rivals*, by Richard Brinsley Sheridan.

Fag and Thomas, so small down there, by the painted promenade.

Fag says to Thomas. Or was it Thomas says to Fag? From so far up above, it was hard to tell.

Why then the cause of this is – Love – Love, Thomas, who …
has been a masquerader ever since the days of Jupiter.

Love was indeed a masquerader and not to be understood.
I had reason to be afraid of it. Everything I loved died or
disappeared. I had loved my mother, until she was as thin
as the slats of the wooden pallet she died on. I had loved
Sally until she disappeared. I was afraid to love Molly in case
she disappeared. I had tried to love the ghost of my father,
whose disappearance was never in doubt. When he came to
me in dreams, always with fish in his hands, for some reason,
a broad river like the Santee behind him, an old crushed
top hat with a feather sticking from it. I had even loved
Ketchum, the young Montgomery's dog and took great pleasure in the fact that the dog loved me more than Montgomery. Even Ketchum disappeared, after a beating. Molly loved
Oscar, who was now taking his ground sweat, and practised
loving Oscar on me. But my Lieutenant loved with a different organ, one that obeyed strange, precautionary rules,
one that was all anticipation and precious little pleasure and
whatever pleasure he gleaned from his loves was exercised in
what Molly would have called the pushing shop. And each
love had its bitter aftermath and ended in a journey.

And I was the audience to all of them, like Cecil, leaning
over the gods, trying to glean what I could of the drama, the
love story, from the chatter of the servants, the gossip of the
grooms in whatever house my Lieutenant visited.

She sat beside him now in a theatre box decorated with
something like marzipan. The box had its own mirrors
and candelabra, and its own drama, more refined than the
drama onstage. Which was written, Cecil whispered, by Sheridan, the corpulent figure seated to his left.

Georgiana was some kind of cousin to my Lieutenant. Both of them cousin to James Charles Fox, who sat another seat behind.

A Whig, Cecil told me. He could only disapprove. Of the politics, whatever about the play.

Cecil preferred masques to comedies. Prospero to Sir Anthony Absolute. So he found the drama in the box more captivating than the drama on the stage, where love did its business with Lydia Languish, Jack Absolute, Lucy the maid and Sir Lucius O'Trigger, and Mrs Malaprop. The gales of laughter it gave rise to passed him by.

And this Sheridan could well have played Sir Lucius O'Trigger. While Fox himself would have made a fair hand of Sir Anthony Absolute. Any of the dowagers behind them, Mrs Malaprop.

But the spectacle of my Lieutenant and this Georgiana, we both agreed, could have graced any stage. As Ferdinand and Miranda. Jack and Lydia.

Georgiana's hair was brown and piled high on her beautiful crown and her porcelain profile managed to outdo the image I had first seen on that muddy locket. She had one dangling from her own elegant neck. I knew the name for the image inside it now. A cameo.

Could we have done better ourselves, Tony? Cecil whispered, as we scurried from the gods mid last act, to get ready for the exit.

The duel's a bluster. Faulkland reveals himself to be Jack Absolute, Lydia forgives him, and as for Delia –

Mrs Malaprop? Please, dear Cecil. Don't spoil the ending for me.

Both carriages faced each other outside, and my Lieutenant's horses scratched their heads off of Georgiana's. The theatre emptied then and I saw the propriety with which he made his goodbyes, a kiss on her gloved hand, a small theatre of bows, and I saw her face turned towards him as her carriage passed on its way.

He left his mother home to Harley Street and ordered me on to James's Street, where I kept the horses ready until the sun came up. He emerged then and claret had loosened his tongue, made him almost my intimate once more.

Fox, he told me, advised him against the business. The Duke of Richmond was without heir and her brother would inherit the title, which made her a pearl of great price, one perhaps beyond his paltry means. But the heart knows what it wants, does it not, dear Tony? And I was dear Tony again and so moved by the fact that I told him that it did. I helped him from the carriage, through the dawn light on the staircase into his bedroom, as the staff was going through its morning motions.

And it was past mid-afternoon when I was called to him again, in the library, where he sat sealing a letter in an envelope.

Letters, I came to realize, were the guardians of what he called sentiment, carried by me to the penny post, or conveyed by me, by hand, to whatever residence she stayed in. I rode this one out to her uncle's house on the great river, and waited on the terrace, with its view of the city and St Paul's, while she made her reply. She carried it out herself and placed it in my gloved hands and I was afforded a full and open glimpse of those eyes that had captivated his.

He calls you his Tony, she said, with a wisp of a smile playing across her lips.

Yes Ma'am, I answered. Tony Small.

And can you keep a secret, Tony Small? She asked.

What secret, Ma'am? I asked.

This correspondence is our secret, she said. This letter is for his hands only, and any reply only for mine. Can I trust you with that? To keep it close to your heart?

Inside my breast pocket, Ma'am? I asked.

Hidden from the world, she said. So fly to him now, with this secret. And when I see you again, have another secret in hand.

I plucked some roses from the garden and wrapped it in the petals. It seemed to deserve them. I rode back then, along the river, the letter in my breast pocket near the organ that she called the heart. It seemed to beat, as I rode, with a pulse of its own.

Did she touch it to her lips? He asked me, when I delivered it back to him in Harley Street.

Yes, I lied. And the lie seemed to please him.

He brought the embossed paper to his nose.

It smells of roses.

She wore one at her breast, when she pressed the letter to her heart.

The lie seemed to please him more.

And what does your heart tell you, Tony?

It tells me love has been a masquerader, my Lord, since the days of Jupiter.

Where have I heard that before?

The Rivals. Drury Lane.

You're quoting Sheridan, Tony?

He does see the humour in affairs of the heart.

Have you ever loved, Tony?

Yes, my Lord.

So you understand.

I do.

Oh Tony, he murmured. Dear faithful Tony. Should I reply at once?

It might be better, my Lord, to appear a little less eager.

Though Darby O'Gallagher was never less than eager, I remember. But I wondered what part Darby may have to play in this romance.

Less eagerness, more nonchalance, you say?

I nodded. Though the word was foreign to me. I was beginning to enjoy the elaboration of this little drama.

A reply before bedtime, do you think?

Morning, my Lord, might be better.

I was tired from riding. One hour to Richmond, another hour back.

Morning, yes much better. If she awakes to the sight of you, with my reply in hand.

It would remind her of you, my Lord.

Indeed it would.

And even lovers' needs must sleep.

Lovers, he sighed. Are we lovers yet?

The thought seemed to fill him with melancholy, which had to be dispelled somehow. Which meant little sleep.

So I drove him in his coach and four to Drury Lane, where the theatre was ending. I waited with him, until Sheridan emerged, with his party of rollicking Foxites. I drove them from hazard room to hazard room, from White's to Brook's to Almack's. I waited and kept the horses still as the market stalls set up around me and saw him emerge just before dawn, still full of the fumes of romance.

Back in Harley Street he said, with the elaborate care of the inebriated, Tony, bring me paper and pen.

I brought him paper and pen and stood while he copied out the dictates of his heart and placed it in my breast pocket while I rode, in the light of the new dawn towards Richmond.

And there I waited, on the river terrace, until her Ladyship awoke. And when a footman came with a silver platter outstretched, I placed the letter on the gleaming plate and I waited, watching the pink dawn rise over the dome of St Paul's. Until her footsteps echoed on the floor behind me.

Tony, she said, holding the letter to her upturned nose, could this scent be his?

Yes, my Lady, I lied. I knew it was mine.

It smells of manhood, muscle and purpose.

He is a soldier, my Lady.

He means to stay in his commission to the King?

He does, my Lady. He is at the King's service.

As we all should be, Tony. Despite the King's incontinence.

Incontinence, Ma'am?

I was collecting new words by the hour.

Of the brain, Tony. Madness, in a word.

So the King was mad now. I felt a sudden panic. And I wondered where I'd left my mad King's letter.

Stoke

Stoke. Her father's house. In that perfect England I first got a glimpse of on our way from Liverpool. Nothing of the grandeur of her uncle's but it had a quality all of its own. Those soft deciduous trees half hiding the dwelling. My Lieutenant should have married her. The house would not have buried him, the way Leinster House and Carton did, eventually. The countryside green, low modelled hills that seemed wrapped in mist every time we rode there. Even I could imagine a future with her in it. But. The but, of course, was her father, Lord Lennox. Perfumed letters delivered do not a match make.

I began to understand this ardour, this thing called love, a love that Darby O'Gallagher could never have rhymed. It was to do with promise. The promise of rolling English hills, of a garden set amongst them, a house or several houses beyond the garden walls and beyond them, shimmering in the haze of the afternoon heat, the spire of a village church. The England that I saw when I came off the packet, that those plantations in sweltering Carolina mocked by their rude imitation, an England that was always promised and so rarely encountered that maybe only the King himself lived in and was the only true 'elsewhere'. So this was what love promised him, this elsewhere, promised by that oval face that tilted towards us behind the casement window as I guided the carriage round the forecourt.

The promise, and the procession. As they both walked around the artificial lake, her gloved fingers lightly resting on his arm, followed by the group of hooped skirts that were their chaperones, followed by me and her father's groom, leading the horses, should they ever need them which they never did.

He has as much hope as a snowflake in summer, the groom whispered.

Why ever?

I was getting good at this thing called conversation.

Her father. Lord George Lennox, the great-grandson of a king.

And was that king mad too?

Who knows? Charles the first or second. So, she can do better than this lieutenant, he muttered, and I wasn't sure if he wanted to elicit a reply.

His father was a Duke, I hazarded.

A Duke of what, he almost spat. Of a wilderness called Leinster? His uncle is another Duke, of Richmond, which to my mind makes them cousins. There are so many reasons, apart from your own dusky presence, to be against this match. And besides, he said (he seemed to revel in his own access to the Stoke household), there is another.

Another what? My heart went cold. I could see a future of early morning brothels, my drunken Lieutenant needing help from door to carriage.

Another suitor. You come on weekdays, he on weekends.

And they walk the same path?

Henry Bathurst, Lord Apsley, and Lord of the Admiralty for three years now.

Wouldn't it be kinder to let my own Lord know?

Kindness has nothing to do with such matters.

But she was kind enough to weep, at least.

There will be no more secrets, she told me some weeks later on the terrace in Richmond. But many tears. And this letter is sprinkled with them. Will I see you again, Tony Small? She asked, as I slipped it next to my heart.

When I bring his reply.

I don't expect one, she said. And I shall miss you both. You as much as him.

And she took my arm, to my shock and surprise, and led me down towards the river.

So this is goodbye? I said. I felt the tears welling up. For both of us.

Unless you'll accept my patronage. Enter my employment. But that, I am afraid, would be crueller to him than this letter.

And she kissed my cheek and whispered goodbye. Adieu. Farewell. If there were more words for the thing, she would have found them.

Look after him, Tony.

Which is what his mother said.

And I did my best, as the visits to Drury Lane soon resumed. To White's afterwards, with Sheridan and a bevy of his play-girls. I would sleep in the carriage outside until they both emerged in the pale dawn, the comedian supporting the unsteady Lord. To the whorehouses in Southampton then, where he rejoined his regiment, Georgiana having accepted the bountiful hand of the Admiralty Lord.

And his heart must have been truly severed because we were on-board a ship soon thereafter, heading towards the cold wastes of what piece of America the mad King still retained.

FOURTH VERSE

Nova Scotia

I knew he thought of it as a return. To paradise. Those days in the forests above the Santee River. And I did too. I needed to return, to something, somewhere. But I suspected it wouldn't be paradise.

The reality was the rocky outline that came through the Atlantic mist, flecked with something like snow, although it can't have been snow because it wasn't yet winter. It was white heather, the kind of heather, they told me when we landed, found in 'the old country'. The old country being Scotland, which must have been a more windswept, wetter version of the Ireland we had left. It seemed to please him, and he claimed Scottish roots until I reminded him ever so gently that old Ogilvie was his tutor, even if lately his mother's husband but never his father. And he said, now that you mention it Tony, I have never been north of Hadrian's Wall.

Scotland or Ireland, it was a dismal vista. Small stony hills and fields barely worth the tilling. Enclosures cropped from the Micmac Indian lands. The King had written more letters, my Lieutenant told me, called the Halifax Treaties. So there were farms, carved out of the Micmac forests, cabins built from the trees they felled, ramparts to protect them from the Micmac spears, from the guns and powder they had sold them during the Continental wars. Not to mention whiskey. The garrison in Halifax to protect the lot, surrounded by ramparts, always damp from the ocean spray.

The trek across the marshes then, to his regiment in St John's. I worried less about the Micmacs' arrows than about the leeches. And it must by then have been summer, because the flies came. Clouds of those flies, whole tempests of them, bluebottles round the ears of the horses, midges round our own. He took to wearing a cowl of burlap draped from his regimental hat and cotton gloves underneath the leather. I suffered the flies, their ravages didn't show on my skin, didn't raise those reddened welts like they did on that creamy English skin of his, but he didn't seem to care. He loved it, perhaps as much as, or more than, I hated it. He would chat with every cottager, break fast in every home-stead, talk about that damned Rousseau, man in his natural state, unencumbered by primogeniture and title, 'When Adam delved and Eve span, who was then the gentleman?' Did he want me to answer? I was never sure and wondered why he had come so far to speak to impoverished home-steaders. He could have found poorer specimens at home. I thought of the cockle-picking children around the strands of Frescati. He had to cross half the world to find out what he should have seen through his bedroom window.

We were mapping the country. Why? I asked him. Does Paradise – if that's what it truly was – need a map? Leave it to its own devices. The Iroquois who paddled us to St John's needed no map. The drums that sounded through the dripping forests tracked our own progress. Told them that General Carleton's 54th Regiment was mapping their world with a theodolite. To triangulate this paradise, plant their flag on it and find their way home.

Then the freezing rain came and after it the snow, banishing the flies, and paradise finally showed itself. No more clouds of buzzing horseflies, midges, mosquitos. The muddy lakes turned into fields of crystal. The rivers turned to threads of silver; each pine capped with its mushroom of white. I never imagined cold could be so welcome. Ice could transform a waterfall; snow could make a forest passable. We travelled on netted snowshoes through forests empty of mosquitos. We skated the lakes. We covered miles on our bladed shoes, dragging toboggans behind us. The ice gave us wings. We chased deer and moose across the St John River. We skinned them and roasted their flesh by the frozen shore. We quartered the meat, dragged it behind us through the snow until we reached the St Lawrence River.

It was frozen too, and made a glittering pathway all the way to Quebec.

Barges, immobile in the frozen river. Logs, pinned beneath the ice, tracing their way from them to the shore. Ice-caves round the shoreline which we crawled inside of, laid our bedding on the glassy floor. We lit fires by the entrances, drank our tea of melted snow and woke to see the Mohawk children pulling salmon from the holes they had cut. And if paradise could have been frozen in a moment, this was it. We swapped our slabs of mooseflesh for raw salmon and char and burnt them to brown crisp for breakfast.

He was given leave from his regiment in Quebec but declined the offer of a passage home. Maybe he knew Georgiana was being fitted for a wedding dress in Richmond. Maybe he hoped she would change her mind. Maybe he just didn't want to return. So he plotted a journey, through the Great Lakes, down the Mississippi, if we could find our way to it, to New Orleans. So we set out, when the snows melted, into a world of flowing water once more.

Niagara. A distant roaring we could hear, through the forest. Then, when the undergrowth gave way, what I thought was another burning cloud of midges, dissipating into the midday sun. But it was spray. Spray, from the curving falls that augmented the thunder, the closer we approached. And for once I had to share his sense of ecstasy. We were witnessing the endless birth of something. Something already old, if that makes sense, something from long before Adam and Eve trod the new earth. Something eternal, something still being born.

I needed another language for what I saw there with him. I watched it with eyes that could barely register. I needed the eyes of a moose, or a Kodiak bear, of a leaping salmon, to comprehend it. There was splendour, there was wonder, there was nature, unadorned and it was here. And if we got too close, it would obliterate us both.

He wanted civilization to melt, the way the ice melted.

Civilization, I suspected, is what doesn't melt. It feeds on what it finds and keeps on growing. Civilization is Fort Niagara, below the falls, is the lighthouse that sends its beam over Lake Ontario. Civilization is even the Iroquois longhouse below Fort Erie, sleeping thirty or more, with us on the hardened mud floor. Chief Joseph Brant's daughter is offered to share your bed. That is his civilization. You decline. That is yours.

They made him one of theirs. Their tribe. They called him 'Eghnidal'. They gave him a letter, from the Chief of the Six Nations. So we both now had letters. Maybe we were both at last free. And for some reason I remembered Lady Emily.

You should write to your mother, I told him, after the ceremony. Though he had no need of a mother now, having been adopted by all of the Six Nations. The whole earth was his mother.

Indeed I should, Tony. I should tell her I have been offered the hand of several princesses, of the Iroquois tribe. Each of them more than a match for Georgiana. And if you found yourself a bride, we could rule a little kingdom together.

But as we rode out, three days later, our canoes were carried by four Africans, whose scarred backs told me they were someone's property.

Is it possible, I asked my Lieutenant, that the Iroquois Chief keeps slaves?

He has learned all the lessons of empire, was my Lieutenant's reply.

And this is one of them?

Sadly, yes.

So there was slavery, I was to understand, even in paradise?

Then let us be uncivilized, my Lord.

Indeed.

Yes, I thought. Let us melt.

But I wrapped his letter of freedom with mine, safe inside its oilcloth.

I needed the oilcloth. We had to cover our bodies in bear-grease again, shoulder our canoes from Lake Superior to the St Croix River and paddle our way through the growing corn and the spring forests. And when the bronzed Mississippi began to gleam through the cathedral of trees, the buzz of the mosquitos became a roar and an odour drifted through the forest that made me, for some mad reason, think of my father.

When we reached the bigger river I saw the source of the odour, the thought and the buzzing.

Barges, piled high with pelts and waiting for more, from that vast interior. Trappers, unloading their mules of their burden of pelts, blackened by clouds of attendant flies. The stench was unbearable, but I was drawn towards the source, like one of those insects, myself. Deerflies, mosquitos and bluebottles by the piles of pelts, bear, moose, deer and even silver fox, waiting, like us, for passage downriver.

We arranged ourselves on a lumber-barge, on which the smell of resin replaced the smell of rotting hide.

I thought I knew what a river was. This was a whole universe of water, winding its way towards an estuary somewhere at the back of New Orleans. No need for a paddle, the barge needed only a tiller to guide it through the endless flow of murky brown. The corn grew ever higher in the clearings on the bank. Cultivation thinned the forest, as we journeyed down.

But as the river took us around each bend, another wharf or a floating pile of pelts would reappear, blackened by its buzzing veil, spreading its stench over the brown waters.

The accents were Spanish now, and as we drifted further south, I heard my Lieutenant speaking French. I asked him to enquire amongst the trappers and traders and auctioneers of steaming skin about a Skinner Mayo, no matter how their stench offended him. We were in Indian territory, bordering the region of the Continentals and this itinerant brotherhood crossed every border because pelt was pelt, needed to be trapped and skinned, brought to the stations on the great brown river, traded and sold.

And somewhere near the Chickasaw Bayou, we got word of that name. A Choctaw named Blue Salt had made his acquaintance. As his name implied, a trader of salts, medicinal ointments and occasional skins, he was heading back to the bayous that fed the great Mississippi and could take us with him.

So we rode with him, and when the rivers got in our way we put the horses on the rafts. We followed the old Indian paths and when they failed us, we hacked out our own. The Skinner, he told me, is a man of habit, and like most trappers, he turns up again in spring to sell the pelts he has collected through the winter. He has so many children he cannot count, but he prides himself on the fact they all remember him. And when they seek him out, he always gives them his cheek.

We came to an old bayou station close to Louisiana where more river barges waited, their mounds of trapper skins growing by the hour. We asked about Skinner Mayo and were told he was expected, any day now. My Lieutenant had despaired of this quest and returned to the Chickasaw ridge. And one day I was sitting there by the jetty, considering the same option when a flurry of dogs came thrashing through the swamp. Wild things, with matted hair and studs around their collars, hunting dogs, but they seemed to recognize the jetty, the liquor sellers there, they jumped up and down and around them like familiars. Skinner Mayo's dogs, I was told. And I awaited his arrival, then two Cherokee women came out of the thickets sitting on ponies, and behind them a kid on horseback, pulling a dead moose on an improvised sled. There were mules then, each of them laden down with skinned pelts, each with their clouds of horseflies and mosquitos and behind them came their master, wearing what had once been a top hat with a feather skewered through it. A profusion of skins, tumbling down from his shoulders. A hawklike face, like the raised surface of some ancient coin, burnished copper by the sun but sliced by deep lines that showed the white beneath. I was reminded of those peeling silver birches in the forests up north.

The dogs sniffed round his ankles. They smelt of animal grease and swamp. I stood and tried to catch their master's gaze but the eyes made no acknowledgment. Green eyes, like mine.

Good day, I said, and he stopped his horse and repeated my greeting.

Good day. If you're buying, he said, we will auction them tomorrow.

I'm buying nothing, I said, but I am seeking something.

Can it be trapped, hunted or skinned? He asked.

Neither I said, and I ventured closer.

That pungent thing. Animal grease and swamp. Could a father smell like this? The dogs, worrying his legs. A whip came down and sent them snarling.

Is this a riddle? What can't be trapped and hunted? Can be shot, maybe –

It was a threat of course, so I came out with it.

The man who was my father.

And the bayou was never silent. But it felt so, suddenly. All of the buzzing retreated.

Was or is? He asked.

Was and is, I told him.

He swatted a fly from his birch-marked face.

He barely acknowledged me, but his blackened teeth worried his lower lip and I knew that he knew something. The blazing thing that would set my wandering pulse to rest.

I followed him, around that haphazard village, behind the dogs, which followed him everywhere.

I have enough dogs, he told me, I don't need another.

I am no dog, I told him, my name is Tony Small. I am a freed slave from Eutaw and my mother was once yours.

Mine, he said and stopped, and those eyes still avoided mine and flickered towards the river.

She was yours, I told him, and when she was big with me you sold her to Old Montgomery for a rifle or two.

So then, he said, I gave her a better home.

You may as well have tied her to a whipping post, I said, and me into the bargain.

I feel an accusation, he said. And don't like to be accused.

Then consider yourself accused, I told him.

Of what? He asked.

Of selling my mother into slavery I said. Along with her unborn child.

I have too many children, he said, to acknowledge them all.

Well you can count me amongst them.

Your name?

Small. Tony Small. And your name is Mayo.

They do call me that.

And I have journeyed here from the country you left.

What country is that?

There was a tinge to his accent, like the bayou French.

Ireland.

Ireland? He asked again. What would I know of Ireland?

Your name, Mayo.

My mother was a Cherokee from the Chattahoochee River, he said, my father Spanish. I was named after the day I was born. Premier mai. Primero de Mayo.

He took a knife from his belt and picked his teeth with it.

I hunt skins for a living. So they call me Skinner Mayo.

I felt a strange breath pulled out of me.

He raised the blade to my chin and tilted it upwards.

But your eyes are mine. Mis ojos.

He returned the knife to his belt.

I could skin them out with this knife for your affrontery. But I won't

He edged his horse forwards.

So will you ride with me a while?

And I rode with him. Behind the mules, the women, the dogs, who seemed to know their way.

The same mound of black flies followed the pelt mules, like a pair of dark lungs.

You seem melancholy, he said to me and I could hear again the bayou French from the syllables. Have I disappointed you?

I carried a different story with me, I told him. An Irish story.

We all need a story, he said. And mine is the bayou. I was thrown into the world here. I will leave it here.

I could see the bronzed Mississippi, gleaming through the peeling trees.

And your mother? Her story is over?

I nodded. It was. As was, maybe, mine.

I left my bayou father to his mounds of skins and made my way back upriver to the Chickasaw Bluffs.

I feared I had lost you, my Lord said, waiting for a log boat to be fully loaded.

I lost myself, I said, and when he asked me to explain, I told him about Skinner Mayo who had as much knowledge of the Ireland we had journeyed from as I had, when we first met in our Eutaw forest. Meaning, none at all.

Premier mai, he said, in his impeccable French.

Primero de Mayo, I said.

So, my dear Tony, we both got it wrong. But at least we laboured under the same illusion.

What is that illusion, my Lord?

The illusion of belonging. And you are still a mongrel. Like me.

We boarded the wooden boat, almost sinking with its weight of logs. And I had to admire the captain, as he managed that giant paddle and let the flow of the river take us towards New Orleans. And as the brown current wound us on its way, I had to wonder what comic destiny was playing its hand. I belonged more to these passing swamps and bayous than to the Ireland to which I was returning. I had taken its balladspeak too much to heart. And as that giant paddle guided us past the river plantations, as the sunlight glittered off the sweat of the bodies heaving the hogsheads of tobacco onto the waiting barges, I wondered what other illusions could be shattered.

And I found out, in New Orleans. The last illusion to be shattered was his.

There were letters waiting, from his sisters, his mother. Georgiana was now Lady Apsley, wife of the Third Earl of Bathurst.

The thing about bad news, he told me, was that by the time you get it, you realize you have known it all along.

And I burned with shame. I had known it since she had given me that tear-stained letter, in Richmond, by the river. I knew even then that her tears were false.

There would be no brothels either, though the city was full of them. Maybe he needed companionship other than mine for those pleasures.

At least, dear Tony, we have each other.

He said this on the vessel home, another ship of the line, and the guillemots were plunging, making white plumes out of the ocean.

I had my own berth this time, with a hammock to rest in, like his.

And we are equals, at last. Two mongrels, on a pitching deck.

We rounded a coastline, on the way towards Liverpool. Two blunt-billed birds flew by the rigging. The gannets poured down to the waves, from a white cloud above.

Ireland, he said.

Your home? I asked.

And I wondered why it was even a question.

Not yours, anymore?

I shook my head.

Maybe we have to invent one.

Bedlam

We made our way across the city of London and got our share of stares and I wondered how Crusoe's Friday had survived on these streets. Maybe he hadn't? We at least had tattered suits to wear and could have passed for New World traders, come to flog our wares at the great house in Harley Street. My Lieutenant's face almost burnt to my colour by the sun. The grooms on the front steps, who were now dressed like major-domos, pointed to the tradesmen's entrance.

Then Cecil called, from behind the open doorway.

Tony, could that be you?

I told him it was not only me, but Lord Edward beside me and the major-domos turned to grooms again, walking backwards, bowing as they went. They took our walking sticks from our unwashed hands and we stepped through the entrance and up the marble staircase.

There was a flurry of excitement as we ascended. Servants, running up and down in livery we had never seen before. A pear-shaped gentleman, whom I later remembered to be his cousin Henry Fox, came to the living room doorway and talked in whispers about how indelicate it would be for us to make an entrance.

My Lieutenant seemed to understand and drew me to the landing above.

We waited.

Is it because of me, my Lord?

Call me Ned.

His eyes were blinking. Tears of loss, or shame.

Because of our dress?

The Ned didn't seem to belong here. It had been left in the bayou, or in New Orleans. Lord was more appropriate.

And my Lord shook his head.

And a kerfuffle at the door below us let me know what the matter was.

Georgiana. One hand on the arm of Apsley, Earl of Bathurst, who was dressed in a mushroom-green greatcoat, his hair combed into a kiss-curl on his balding head. He kept his eyes on the carpet.

She allowed hers drift upwards as if searching for Edward.

My Lord's eyes were closed by then, his head turned away, as if even blinking had failed him.

So her eyes met mine. A furtive, barely perceptible smile. Her free hand rose slightly, clasped and unclasped itself. And the hand seemed to say what she couldn't.

Goodbye, my Tony.

Forgive me.

I wish it were otherwise.

It somehow said all of those things. And I wish I could have told her of the freezing winter, the trek through the snows to Niagara, the barges high with pelts, my bayou father, the winding river to New Orleans. All because of that little thing they call the heart.

Cecil opened the front door and the incoming breeze flurried the hem of her dress, as she moved outside. It lifted the kiss-curl on Lord Apsley's bald head. An echoing bang, and they were gone.

And as if that was the signal, then the living room door opened. His mother, the Scot, sisters, cousins. They kissed and they cried and they excused themselves. We had interrupted a luncheon. If only he had sent word.

We had crossed a continent to be here and should have sent word.

This strange process, called manners.

Or politeness.

He said he understood, his face colder than the frozen lakes we had left behind us. And before the door closed, I glimpsed the remains of the interrupted meal.

Harlequin Friday

Lo, Tony, you look darker than you did before, if that were possible.

Cecil was laying my things on the bed in the attic room. I could think of nothing but the oddness of the situation. I had a room, and not a byre. I had a servant at last. I have out Calibanned Caliban, I told him.

You have out Fridayed Friday.

I wondered where he had heard that name.

So have you read it, Cecil?

Read what?

The Life and Adventures of Robinson Crusoe, Mariner, of York?

No, but you know I attend the playhouse. Grimaldi's playing *Harlequin Friday* in Drury Lane.

Harlequin Friday. He was a clown, apparently, played by the great comedian Grimaldi. He ran from assorted cannibals, dressed in black mask, in a play written by that other great comedian, Sheridan.

So, we went.

The playbill read:

Robinson Crusoe; or, Harlequin Friday, a grand pantomime in two acts, by Richard Brinsley Sheridan.

I thought you hated Sheridan?

But I like Grimaldi.

And after a long tattoo of knocking, we made it through the
stage door, to a perch behind some packing cases where,
through an obscurity of hanging ropes and stage flats, we
got a glimpse of Grimaldi in black mask and a harlequin
outfit perform a ballet of knocks and tumbles with a group
of charcoaled cannibals.

You could play one of them yourself, Cecil whispered.
Saved them the charcoal.

I am no actor.

Neither are they.

They were acrobats, though. They made the audience
howl, in vast caterwauls of laughter that swept through that
ocean of playgoers. And Robinson Crusoe, Mariner of York
had little to do with their antics.

I drove my Lord there some days later. With a party. Sheridan himself, his wife, Elizabeth, their child and my Lord's
cousin Charles James Fox. I sat with the carriage outside
and listened to the gales of laughter that made it through
the doors. When the applause had died and the crowds
spilled from the foyer onto the street, Sheridan emerged,
and I realized who the real comedian was. It was him, the
playwright. He walked unsteadily through the doors, tripped
coming down the steps and turned his subsequent tumble
into a bow. Grimaldi couldn't have elicited more applause.

London was Sheridan's that night. He made his way through the throng of admirers, had me drive the gentlemen to White's, and drive his wife and child home.

Elizabeth was her name. She seemed pensive, with her boy sleeping beside her. I drew the horses to a halt, outside their residence in Savile Row and helped her from the carriage. I remembered her face from a playbill in the Strand. Her voice, echoing round the dusty street. And somehow I knew I would know more of both as I carried the child from the carriage to the steps.

Don't wake him, she whispered, as I handed the sleeping bundle to her footman. She thanked me, and I caught a glimpse of her profile against the candlelight, inside. And I saw what I had remembered. It could have been his mother, on that locket in Eutaw.

Once more, I thought, as I drove the horses back to White's. The gentlemen emerged, the worse for wear, some hours later. I drove them from gaming club to bawdy house, until my Lord surprised me by asking me to take him home.

I had come to know the movements of his heart by the brothels and the bawdy houses. When we visited them, it was broken. When he tired of them, it meant only one thing.

Love, and more letters.

I discussed the matter with Cecil, who expressed his preference for the broken heart, over the unbroken.
Why, so, Cecil?
This was in the stables, where I was readying the horses for a trip to Bath.
Would you not prefer the bawdy house to the stables, Tony?

I have known bawdy houses *with* stables.

The whores then, to the horses?

Courtesans, Cecil, I corrected him. And when he spends his time with the courtesans, I spend my time with the horses. Never with the whores.

And there is a difference, Tony, between courtesan and whore?

The courtesan lives upstairs and dresses better. The whore would generally be contiguous with the stables.

Are there brothels and bawdy houses in Bath, Tony?

I suppose we'll see. Cecil.

I liked Bath. It was like a miniature Dublin, and like Dublin, seemed always under construction. Fawn-coloured brick and geometric windows. And while I'm sure Bath had its fill of brothels, we visited none of them. We visited the house of Elizabeth Sheridan, née Linley, the wife of the comedian.

And so it began, the comedy.

And as with all of his comedies there was a lord, a lady and a Hibernian clown.

But there was a portrait, first.

He was waiting, for Sheridan, in the living room of his house in Bath and I was waiting on him. Above the pianoforte was a painting of Elizabeth at a painted pianoforte, with two painted angels singing behind her.

Cecilia, he murmured.

Who? I asked.

Patron saint of music.

Or were they angels? Her face in profile. Their faces raised, to adore her.

Reynolds, he said, captures what the heart should see.

Her face in the painting was drenched in light. Where it came from, I had no idea. From the fingers of sun, pushing through the cloud, behind them?

And then she entered. And I could see where the light had come from. She carried it with her.

My husband's in Brighton, she said. Detained by the Prince of Wales. If we're fortunate, we might have his company for dinner.

She looked at both of us and smiled.

Or unfortunate, as the case may be.

Unfortunate, as it turned out. Sheridan never turned up. They had dinner alone together, served by Jeremiah, the butler, and Mildred, his wife.

We ate what was left, in the kitchens.

He has business with the Prince, Mildred informed me.

And we all know what business that is, her husband muttered, his large rear-end coming first through the door.

With the Prince's ladies.

If you could call them that, her husband almost spat.

She does need some consolation, Mildred opined, as she carved the duck into slices.

An actress she could tolerate. But a countess?

Married to a Viscount. What does that make her?

A trollop, if you ask me.

So there was to be a lord, a lady, a Hibernian clown and a countess. All this comedy needed was a Harlequin Friday.

Sheridan missed dinner that night, breakfast, lunch and dinner the next, and I thought we would miss the comedian entirely, until on the third night I walked his elegant garden, listening to the echo of her singing over the small, moonlit pond, when a figure behind the willow tree spoke.

Let me weep, it said.

I recognized the voice.

Lascia ch'io pianga

A pear-shaped shadow behind the cascade of branches. Unwilling, it seemed, to enter the house.

Has there been music? Sheridan asked. Every night?

No, I told him. This was the first.

Ah, he said. I should have stayed away. Until her voice had worked its magic. And it has magic, you would agree?

I could only say yes.

And I suppose I must face it now.

Face what, sir?

The music.

He emerged, from behind the willow tree. And as always, he seemed the worse for wear.

You again, he said. His 'Harlequin Friday'.

He appraised me with those eyes that must have been startling blue once, and smiled.

You could play him, one day.

Play who, sir?

Harlequin Friday. Grimaldi's getting on. Finds the acrobatics arduous.

He placed one hand on my elbow.

Announce me, sir.

Announce you?

Member of Parliament for the borough of Stafford. Owner of the Theatre Royal, Drury Lane. Comedian of note. Husband to that voice. There are rules in situations such as these.

There are?

And a sudden surprise is not one of them.

So I led him towards the drawing room doors, as he hummed, to his wife's singing.

Il duolo infranga
Questo ritorte

Something about a duel, he muttered, translating. Within these twisted places.

But there would be no duel. No glove thrown down, impossible anyway, since his small hands were gloveless. I knocked and made my entrance, announced him to them both, saw her rise from the pianoforte and embrace him, and saw my Lord embrace them both.

And if the comedy had already begun, it was one Sheridan had not yet written. Where the husband welcomes his own betrayal. Where the wife betrays him, because he has already betrayed her. Where the lover seems to love them both.

A rum comedy, Cecil complained, being well acquainted with Sheridan's own.

And nothing made sense, I did agree. But there was some hope, at least. That love, which never made sense, would at least keep my Lord from the bawdy houses.

And there was love, I could tell, because I could see it on her face, each time I delivered her yet another of his letters. The blush that perfected cheeks already perfect.

Will you wait for me, Tony, while I compose my reply?

I would wait, happily, underneath the weeping willow, throwing bread to the ducks. Sometimes her husband would join me. Sometimes he would laugh.

Sometimes she would sing, still writing.

Lascia ch'io pianga

Comedies of this kind, Cecil informed me, had their rules. And if these rules were broken, there could be nothing funny about them. Sheridan, of all people, should know that.

That there was a child expected, nobody could doubt. Her dresses began to swell around the same time as the light began to leave her face. She sat by the pianoforte, which did its best to hide that inconvenient fact, and sang, 'Let Me Weep' and both lover and husband did weep, as if they knew their time with comedy was ending. The portrait reminded me and them, and indeed anyone who watched what she had resembled once. The cough that interrupted her 'Let Me Weep' only made all three of them weep more.

The child broke all of the rules, Cecil agreed. Nothing funny about that. This comedy was in danger, unbeknownst to itself, of slipping into tragedy. Duel, divorce, indignity would follow, as night follows day.

The comedy, if that's what it was, had moved by then, from Bath to London. Then it bounced between them, like Mrs Malaprop in Sheridan's own *The School for Scandal*. The comedy took place in drawing rooms, theatre foyers, gaming clubs and aristocratic bedrooms. It involved hidey-holes and secret gardens, curtains, cupboards and sculleries, and the interior of many a hansom carriage, ferrying the principals from one to the other. Kisses, blushes, petticoats raised and lowered, promises of undying love and enmity, assurances of friendship that would outlast both. It involved me ferrying letters between all of the principals and in the end me ferrying a newborn infant in swaddling clothes down a snow-swept avenue, by which time nobody was laughing.

Although there was one comedic detail left. A 'touch', Cecil called it, that reminded him of the great comedian's glory days.

The husband claimed the child to be his, while the whole world knew otherwise.

Maid of Bath

I was the Maid of Bath, she told me.

I was wheeling her down by the wharves in Southampton, and the ship's rigging tinkled like a thousand metronomes. She was rounded with child now and every time she coughed, she needed her handkerchief.

The sea air, my Lord had told me, would do her some good. So we both awaited his arrival from his regiment in Portsmouth.

Born in Bath, a maid of Bath, *The Maid of Bath*. It was a play, Tony, written by Samuel Foote, before my husband's glory days. Lacking his wit, almost entirely, but not without merit. So I was the Maid of Bath, in fiction and in fact, if you can appreciate the difference.

I assured her that I was beginning to. The fiction was that the child she was bearing was her husband's, Richard Brinsley Sheridan, dramatist, member of Parliament, lexicographer and drunk. The fact was that the child was my

Lord's, honorary chief of the Six Nations, Lieutenant of the 54th Regiment.

My parents, you see, had arranged a marriage to a man who could have been my grandfather. A time-worn old plot, of course, but I outwitted them in a manner that any dramatist would have envied. I ran off with Richard Brinsley Sheridan for France knowing full well the whole of London would be talking. You see, I did love my small, pear-shaped Irish playwright for as long as he loved me. Which would not be, as my dear mother had warned me, for very long at all. I married him in France and came back to marry him, more respectably, in London. Everything with Sheridan, you see, had to happen twice. And we returned to find my play already written by a rival playwright, Mr Foote, who had the gall to call me 'Kitty Linnet'. And it was popular, Tony, that Maid of Bath but the crowds came not for the wit or the repartee or any literary merit. They came to see scandal.

And my new husband, who had more talent in his left ear than Foote in his whole unmanageable body, persuaded me to grace the boards in this barely disguised version of myself.

Which became a great success, Tony, and a scandal and led to a duel, two duels, in fact, one which my comedian won easily, even comically, and another which left him for dead in a field near Bath. He lived to tell the tale of a small sword through the body and a bullet in the thorax, Act five, Scene two of *The School for Scandal*, if you've ever seen it. Not my scandal, his entirely invented one. He was always better at invention than reality. But the double duels made Mr Foote's rather limp theatrical version of the same events more popular than ever. Which led to me singing for the King at his pavilion in Brighton before the madness took him over. As the true Maid of Bath, not Kitty Linnet anymore, but Elizabeth Linley. Then Gainsborough came to paint me, as myself, and Reynolds came to paint me as St Cecilia. Do you know of St Cecilia, Tony?

The patron saint of music, I ventured.

The same. And you've seen the portrait?

I had, I admitted. Many times. And she had seen me see it.

Well you know then that there is a certain comfort in being preserved against the ravages of time. I was beautiful once, Tony.

You still are, Ma'am.

No. I am consumed by something from within. The child, you think, Tony?

I hope not, my Lady.

But it was visible, even in the chair. The wheels of which creaked, bumping over the cobbles. The main weight the cushions bore seemed to be inside her. She was a paper-thin, elegant wrapping for something yet to be born.

I cannot let myself regret it Tony.

Regret what, Ma'am?

Another scandal, I suppose. Well, let them gossip. Let my husband claim it as evidence of his continued vigour. But we both know the truth, Tony.

Indeed.

That was the word that kept giving.

My husband's affections wandered as a matter of course, after too many losses and too much port at the Foxes' but I wouldn't have minded that so much. It wasn't the port or the claret or the ladies who gathered there late at night, hardly worthy of the name. Actresses, like me, but with less care for their reputations. No, it was the princesses, the duchesses, the maids-in-waiting for the eye of good King George, the ones for whom sentiment meant more than a quick fumble over the billiard table, they took more than his eye and the discharge from his Irish prick, they took what he thought of as his heart but what I came to recognize as his ambition. He needed a title to satisfy that, and knowing he could no longer marry one, he could at least captivate one. And as he wandered, so eventually did I. Don't you find that Tony, that the soul knows what is missing even before the mind does?

The soul. And being grateful that she credited me with one, I said, I did.

Perhaps the soul is tutor to the mind, Tony?

I am certain Ma'am, that it is.

So my soul desired its mate, before my mind knew the lack of it? Is there a word for that, dear Tony?

Soulmate, I repeated.

I knew the word by now. She had tutored me well.

And my eye had already begun its roving but didn't know until it fell upon Edward.

And I could see him now, waiting, where the pier met the horizon. The garlands of white the wind drew from the ocean made his greatcoat stand out, like a figure in a Reynolds seascape.

And I knew this was my cue, to ask, when did you first meet him?

The theatre, where everybody meets. My husband had a farce – a whatdoyoucallit –

A pantomime –

A harlequinade. With a name you should recognize. Friday. And across from him, in the box, I saw those startling green eyes, the sad eyes of a younger son, without fortune and without apparent purpose and I thought perfect, he'll demand nothing of me, take nothing from me. But he did take, dear Tony, he took what was left of my heart.

I didn't remind her that I'd driven her home that night.

She coughed then and the sound made me think of everything I didn't want to. The spume travelling from her lungs to her lips. Like the white flecks on the horizon. I leaned down and placed the handkerchief into her tiny hand. But when she handed it back, it was flecked with red.

What a contretemps, she murmured. I can only thank the Lord my parents didn't live to see it. But, she said, coughing again, and I had to tilt the chair back, for fear she'd cough herself out of it.

I want you to promise me, Tony.

Promise you, my Lady?

Promise me that he will see this child of ours when I am gone.

Gone? You will be gone, my Lady?

Oh don't lie to me, you savage. If I live to see this child born, it will be a miracle. But I would rather die of his child than of this damn consumption. Whichever takes me first.

Heads bowed as they passed us. She had not lost her beauty. As her weight declined, it was as if the ghost inside her was coming to the fore. And that ghost had its own unearthly beauty.

I want him to know her, Tony. And don't ask me how I know it is a she. Women know these things, Even half-dead ones. Left to my husband she would die as I am dying. Of neglect. Promise me you will take her to him.

So I promised. And I pushed the chair towards the figure by the pier side. He was done with his regimental duties and the evening would be theirs alone. He took the handles from me, kissed her paper-thin cheek and said, until tomorrow, Tony.

He guided her towards the harbour-side inn. And I kicked my heels for the afternoon. I counted the ships of the line, in the bay. I watched Mr Punch beat his wife on a breezy circus cart. I improvised a rod and caught three mackerel and cooked them on the stony beach. I untied the horses, and while one of them grazed, I ran the other on the sandy stretch of foreshore. I made a bed of the carriage seat, and was woken by the dawn, over the English Channel. The sky over France was pink, as if the clouds were washed by the bloody doings beyond.

I bridled the horses, and wheeled the carriage round to the inn, to find them both by the harbour's edge, his arm around her swollen waist, as they looked at the same red sky over France.

She walked with me, Tony, almost the length of the pier. There is hope, yet.

There is, my Lord, I said. Though I could tell from her eyes, as I lifted her into the carriage seat, that she knew there was none.

He helped me with the business of the wheeled chair. She took the glove from her hand so he could hold it with his own as I eased the horses forward, soft as we go, clip clop, extending the exquisite melancholy of the moment. So I drove her back to Bath, as he resumed his duties with the 54th.

His regiment was preparing for war.

He would resign his commission within the month.

The child would be born.

The Maid of Bath would die.

In that order.

And what amazed me was how all of the characters and props needed for a comedy remained intact when it made its shift to tragedy. The Hibernian clown still played his part. There was still a lord, and a lady, there was a bemused audience in Bath, and in London beyond, as always, hungry for scandal.

There were hurried arrivals and departures, whispered gatherings behind closed curtains, there was silverware dropped, gasps of horror, there was even a Mrs Malaprop, whose confusions only gave rise to tears instead of laughter.

Mehitabel Canning

As the Maid of Bath declined, Mehitabel Canning wiped her fevered brow, changed her blood-soaked linens, imposed a spectral hush on that house in Bath.

Her consummation, I'm afraid, is too well advanced.

I think she meant consumption. Although I wasn't sure.

All we can do is elevate her discomfort.

Alleviate, Elizabeth had to whisper.

And alleviate she did. Or elevate. With prayers. Whole rounds of them, as if there was a competition to find out who could last the longest.

Elizabeth always lost. Her eyes would close, exhausted. Mrs Canning would continue.

Blessed be the fruit of thy wound.

She meant womb. And perhaps I heard it. But wound was more appropriate.

The child when it was born was a tiny thing, paler than a snowdrop and as she had predicted, a little girl. I carried her in my arms as my Lord wheeled her mother round the garden in Bath. I rocked her to sleep as her husband wailed and wept over his wife's declining form. I held her in the carriage to London as the two men wept over their impossible affection. Love, I came to realize, was even frailer than this creature in my arms. I rocked her in her cradle upstairs in Savile Row as her mother sang her last song in the drawing room below. I held her at the funeral, where they both bore their loss with the stoicism of gentlemen. I handed her to our own Mrs Malaprop, Mehitabel Canning, at the graveside. I asked my Lord, as we departed, would we ever see her again.

He promised we would. And although he was good at promises, this one he didn't keep.

The death of love, once more, did its unlovely thing. He nursed his broken heart in company.

But it was different company, this time.

I will be away, Tony, I don't know for how many nights.

You do not need my help, my Lord?

No, Tony. In certain circumstances, a manservant can be a hindrance.

I asked him what circumstances those were and received the silence as reply.

He rode out the next morning and the silence grew, in the house, empty of everyone but servants. His mother was in Ireland with Mr Ogilvie. All of the liveried ones avoided me, except Cecil, who filled me in with tales of bloodletting from across the channel.

I asked him which channel that was.

The French one, he told me, not the Irish one. Yet. The King had already lost America. He was fearful now of losing Ireland, and maybe England too.

I drew a sketch, as he talked. Of Amber, the Duchess's fine horse. It was on the Duchess's embossed notepaper.

I asked Cecil for an envelope, and had him inscribe it, as his writing hand was better than mine.

To Miss Mary Sheridan, Cherry Cottage, Wanstead. In fine copperplate.

I rode out to Wanstead with the letter in my breast pocket. I thought it would be safer than the penny post, and besides, I had another end in view.

There were indeed cherries, on the path to Cherry Cottage, Wanstead. They were blooming that spring and fell around me like flakes of pink, rosy snow. I knocked on the cottage door, and as an answer to the guarded surprise of Mrs Mehitabel Canning, proffered my letter, which I had carried from my Lord's residence, Harley Street.

He can't visit himself? she asked.

No, I told her, his affairs have taken him elsewhere.

So, he sends his manservant, Tony Small?

Yes, I told her.

And he never will, will he, visit?

His heart is broken. Mine is not.

Not yet, she replied.

And I echoed her. Not yet.

And she smiled at this. Stood back from the door. Had I said something funny?

Tony Small, she said. And Mehitabel Canning. In loco parenthesis.

Was this another Mrs Malaprop turn? I had to ask her what it meant.

In place of family. You, Tony Small, and I.

And she took my hand then and led me through room after tiny room.

Sheridan never visits. But we still had hopes for your Lord. And here —

In a sun-dappled kitchen, sketching her first letters with chalk, on a board —

Is little Mary.

She turned and smiled.

Is every angel's hair that peachy blonde?

Does every angel sit by a deal table, with the sunlight making snowdrops of her cheeks?

Tony, whom your father sent. You remember?

She nodded. She seemed to.

You should stand, my dear, and curtsey.

She did that. Then she ran into my arms.

She's walking, I whispered.

Yes. And running too.

I took out the letter and had to show her how to pull it open.

From whom? Mrs Canning asked.

Lord Edward, I lied.

Your father, Mrs Canning said.

Horse, little Mary said.

He has taken up drawing? Mrs Canning asked.

I nodded. And the child, at least, believed me.

There was an apple tree in the garden, with a swing beneath. I held her in my arms and sat on the seat and pushed. And every push brought the apple blossoms falling. She kept wanting higher, so the more I pushed, the more the blossoms fell. Until I could hardly see the forest beyond for the falling blossoms.

Which was called Epping, Mrs Mehitabel Canning said.

FIFTH VERSE

Gardens

He never visited, though I did. Twice more.

She came to call me dada, which made Mrs Mehitabel smile.
   Too many fathers, this child has.

One of them, Sheridan, was in France. He had fallen in
love with a young Pamela de Genlis, whose face reminded
him of his first glimpse of the dead Elizabeth. Another St
Cecilia, Mrs Mehitabel told me. She would have the same
effect on the actual father, my Lieutenant, when they eventually met, in Paris. So Elizabeth would live on. Like a porcelain profile, in a locket.

Has your Lord vanished? Cecil asked.
   Maybe no longer mine, I thought. But I answered: maybe
he's gone home.
   So, this was never home?
   No, I said. Home for him is always somewhere else.

Elsewhere. I remembered the Eutaw forest. The trek to
Niagara. The Iroquois longhouse. Eghnidal, the new-made

Chief of the Six Nations. And it dawned on me. My Ned, my Lieutenant, my Lord, was inventing a home. An Elsewhere.

Meanwhile his mother asked me to her house in Dublin – Blackrock and Frescati. I tended the gardens under Ogilvie's instruction, packing the black earth round the plants that bent under the wind that tried to whip them into the Irish Sea. The Scotsman had theories as elaborate about gardens as he had about noble savages. I was not to subdue the landscape, or beat it into submission with hoe, spade and barrow, but to cultivate it, from the Latin *cultivare*, to improve by reason of its grooming by one human being, me. He had a vision of a house leading to a garden which enhanced what he called the symmetries found in nature, guided the eye towards them, so wilderness and cultivation lived in some essential harmony that expressed his ideal vision of the harmonies of the ideal world.

Like the villa 'Parisi-Borghese' in the original Frascati, on the outskirts of Rome, he told me. The gardens of the late Renaissance might never be surpassed, and Italianate landscapes, with their descending tiers of cultivation, their verticals of cypress and umbrella pine are far from the Irish variant, but this Celtic wilderness, Tony, still has its charms.

And so I laboured, moved earth from one hillock to another, tilled the long fields down to the sea into passable versions of a lawn, planted sapling cypresses and yews, and wondered was I myself to be one of those charms. I was spared the indignity of my oriental costume and allowed wear dusty gardening duds with a cocked hat of my absent Lieutenant's, when the sun shone.

And the sun did shine, betimes. When it did, Lady Emily would make a perch beside me, in an elegant hat of her own, reading his letters aloud. His heartsore laments over his abandoned daughter.

They called her 'it', which was strange. To me that small bundle of bliss would always be Mary.

It was surely better, Tony, she confided, that Sheridan acknowledge the child as his. A regular upbringing was the least it deserved, being of quality.

She deserved the best, I agreed. And I wondered to myself what quality was to be found in Wanstead. Maybe Mrs Mehitabel was quality enough.

That I know first-hand, Tony. If I can share a secret with you.

You can, Ma'am.

My own sister bore a child, without the benefit of wedlock.

And I wondered would the great comedian ever see the blessed snowdrop cheeks and the red lips so like those of his dead Elizabeth. It was Mrs Mehitabel Canning would have all the rearing and the only visitor to date had been me. So I agreed with all of it and planted a birth tree for her, the tiny elm that would grow as she grew.

I inscribed her name in the bark around the root.

Mary.

Lady Emily was preoccupied by other concerns.

America, she murmured, as I hoed. Something happened to him there.

Yes, I thought. We paddled the bayous. I met my father. He opened a letter from Georgiana.

Nothing good comes from America. Apart from your good self. And your father, Edward told me, hailed from Mayo?

Skinner Mayo.

A trapper, I believe?

So they told me.

An odd journey for you. From America to home. And this is home now, Tony?

There was only so much I could tell her. But I agreed that it was.

Do you believe in revolutions, Tony?

I told her that it was running from a revolution that had led me to that field in Eutaw Springs where I first met her son and that revolutions gave me no freedom papers – it was her son and his mad King did that. So revolutions, I supposed, were good for some and not so good for others.

Will you tell him that, Tony? Guide his judgment in these matters?

I told her that if he asks my opinion, I would readily give it.

But he rarely asks for my opinion. He regards me as a wonder of the natural world, occupying some space beyond opinion. And then he asks me to shine his boots.

You have a rival, Ogilvie said to me some days later, in the field of mud that would become a rose garden.

A rival?

For your Lord's affections.

I have many, good sir, I told him. Since his Maid of Bath died.

But one in particular, who may have taken more than his heart.

What else did this one take?

His imagination. His soul. His ambition.

It was a lot to take, I had to admit. And as I dug another planting hole, I asked him who this rival might be.

Thomas Paine, he said. Who would scatter foreign seeds through this garden of ours.

And I understood something, at last. This garden was more than an endeavour of calloused hands and muddied boots. It was an endeavour of the mind. Or, if I was to believe this earnest Scotsman, of the soul.

Edward spent his childhood here. This garden is his soul. And your task, Tony Small, is to see that it doesn't turn into a garden of weeds.

A garden of weeds. I was captivated by the thought. Even more, by the thought of my rival, Thomas Paine. This scatterer of seed. This thief of souls.

Thomas Paine

Still, my gardening duties were irksome enough already, under the tutelage of Mr Ogilvie. I was relieved of them some days later, by a letter from my Lieutenant asking me to join him in London after collecting various items from Patrick Byrne's bookshop, 108 Grafton Street. So I finished what I could of the actual garden, went back to Leinster House and while Molly packed his various trunks, made my way down those streets of glittering windows, to the bookshop, with its view of Trinity College. Mr Byrne handed me four cigar boxes and wrapped them in a satchel and when I enquired of him why a vendor of pamphlets was trading in cigars, was told in no uncertain terms to mind my own business. The less I knew of what I was carrying, the better.

There was a storm approaching and the Liffey waves were crashing over the piles along the Ballast wall, but I made it to the Pigeon House, where, with all of the wind blowing, the packet would have to wait. So I settled myself between barrels in the forecourt arch, in for the long wait. And while the storm did its best with the booming sea, I thought I might solve the mystery, of why Mr Byrne, that vendor of bound volumes, was trading in cigars.

I opened the satchel and removed a fine tobacco specimen and felt the presence of something else beneath the greased paper. I lifted the paper gingerly and found a well-hidden pile of pamphlets. I extracted one and saw the printed name:

Thomas Paine

I cadged a light from a passing sailor. I then sank between the barrels and began to read Thomas Paine's *Rights of Man*.

RIGHTS OF MAN:

PART THE FIRST

BEING AN
ANSWER TO MR. BURKE'S ATTACK
ON THE
FRENCH REVOLUTION

TO GEORGE WASHINGTON: PRESIDENT OF THE UNITED STATES OF AMERICA.

Sir,

 I present you a small treatise in defence of those principles of freedom which your exemplary virtue hath so eminently contributed to establish. That the Rights of Man may become as universal as your benevolence can wish, and that you may enjoy the happiness of seeing the New World regenerate the Old, is the prayer of
 Sir,
 Your much obliged, and Obedient humble Servant,
 Thomas Paine.

It was hard reading. Much harder than Crusoe on his island adventures. And I wondered had George Washington extended the rights that Mr Paine extolled to the plantations in which I spent my boyhood and my youth. Did Old Montgomery and his sons and overseers still open the backs of their slaves to the air as they plucked the suckers from the tobacco plants? And I puffed on my cigar, made from good handrolled leaves of the kind I once plucked myself. I wondered was Sally still working in St Lucia or had she escaped once more to live out what remained of her life with Rupez Roche and his maroons. When one cigar was finished, I lit another from the stub. And by the time the storm had eased, I had made good inroads on both pamphlet and cigars.

But the *Rights of Man* now had no hiding place. And Mr Paine's words seemed dangerous indeed. So I wrapped them in my greatcoat, walking down the wharf in Holyhead. And I kept the satchel tightly closed on the coach to London. And when I met my Lieutenant in Harley Street, I apologized for my over-consumption.

He laughed, and said he hoped I enjoyed them. The cigars, that is. The pamphlets were for distribution amongst his friends. The cigars I could keep for the journey ahead of us both.

Which was, he informed me, to my great astonishment, to Dover then to Le Havre and on to Paris, France.

He wore his military cloak to the York Hotel in Dover and cautioned me on having any conversation about the *Rights of Man* while I dragged his cases to the rooms. There were government agents about, posing as excise officials and customs officers who checked our cases before I carried them on board yet another packet. It was the first inkling I had of the new life we were about to lead. So I kept my mouth shut with yet another cigar amongst the comings and goings on the wharf. And it was only as the cliffs of Dover withdrew from our view that I questioned him about Thomas Paine. Did the rights he extolled to George Washington extend to my brothers in the Carolinas? My Lieutenant assured me that if Paine had his way they would. But Paine, he said, can no more speak for Washington than he can for the Assembly in Paris.

There was a crush of souls around the wharfs of Calais that reminded me of Charleston Harbour. All in uniform, though none of these coats were red. All black, it appeared to me, an army in black, the crush from behind towards the boats arriving so great that the front figures fell, tumbling in the water like ninepins.

What army is this, I asked my Lieutenant and he replied that it was an army of God, priests and the occasional nobleman, running from the blade of the revolution. I would see this blade later, in the Place du Carrousel and wonder would my own neck be ever deemed worthy of a shave. Why do so many fear the rights of man? I asked and he told me that was the question we were here to answer. Perhaps, only those whose privileges were threatened by them. Kings, queens, lords of the church and of the manor.

But you, my Lord, are a lord, I reminded him.

I have a title, he said, that is valueless.

You are the son of a duke.

And I have lived to regret that fact, dear Tony.

So we left the ship and made our way through that privileged rabble and I wondered what else he might regret, as we travelled by coach through a landscape that could have been the Carolinas. I was on the road to Charleston again, passing lines of battered infantry, cannon dragged through the mud by oxen, through villages where every church was a smouldering ruin and starving children flocked like pigeons round a millwheel at every carriage-stop.

Does this remind you of anything? I asked him, as we passed a village fountain with bodies floating in the bloodied water.

Eutaw Springs, he said, the Carolinas.

You fought against a revolution there.

I was a soldier, then.

And now?

A citizen.

Citizen

He was not a citizen yet, though in a city full of them. And it was a fine city, if you could turn your eyes from the severed heads on the Tuileries railings and the sight of Madame Guillotine on the Place du Carrousel.

We met Mr Paine, who was a citizen, in the garden of White's Hotel. He made a most pleasing rival. I was surprised by his English accent, his small stature and his tolerance for brandy. He was surprised by what he called my fussing about my Lieutenant whom he addressed as Citizen Fitzgerald, or simply, as Ned.

So I was relieved of all duty, a citizen myself. I found these duties hard to relinquish, at first. The waking at first light, to have his boots cleaned, his coffee ready with its small tincture of honey. So his boots went uncleaned until I taught him how to polish them himself. Coffee, we enjoyed together in the garden, as often as not with Thomas Paine.

The habit of following two steps behind them was harder to break. Until Paine took my elbow, walking through the gardens of the Palais-Royal. Which was now called, he told me, the Palais-Égalité. Owned, if ownership of this garden of citizenship could mean anything, by the Duc d'Orléans, now the Duc d'Égalité.

I asked him did his rights of man extend to those who pulled the suckers off tobacco fields in the Carolinas and he told me that if they did not, they meant nothing. There was a slave revolt in Hispaniola, which, by God's grace, could extend to the whole of the Caribbean, into Louisiana and the Carolinas, and make the Continentals live up to their promises. And I wondered was Sally in St Lucia wielding a musket as we spoke.

His current pamphlet, he told me, was a response to a pamphlet which itself was a scurrilous diatribe against the good William Wilberforce and his abolitionist movement. And was not the fact that I, with my freedom papers, and he, once a poor Thetford farmer, could walk arm in arm through these gardens of equality, evidence that the world was changing?

You were a farmer, sir? I asked him.

I was, sir. Like my father. And he smiled. And like him, after that a staymaker.

Staymaker?

He ran a corset shop. I was his apprentice. Have you not heard the invective? Tom Paine, the bodice maker?

I told him, no, that my first acquaintance with his name was on a pamphlet, hidden underneath a box cigars.

He slipped another pamphlet underneath my door that night. And I read what I could, this time without the benefit of tobacco.

TO AMERICANS:

That some desperate wretches should be willing to steal and enslave men by violence and murder for gain is rather lamentable than strange. But that many Christianised people should approve, and be concerned in this savage practice …

And the pamphlets kept coming. They even addressed one another, the next one being an 'Answer to a very new PAMPHLET indeed!' And however much I struggled with them, I grew fond of my rival – Tom the bodice maker. Fonder than anyone, other than Sally, Molly and my Lord Ned.

There were bodices enough on view in the Palais-Égalité, the next morning. A parade of womanhood which my Lieutenant, his heart still being broken, took time to view. And while he lost himself in the palace gardens, Tom Paine guided me towards a crowd of citizens, growing by the minute. A speaker, balancing himself on barrels, an oration, in a language I did not understand.

He recommends Madame Guillotine, Tom translated, for the trial of King Louis XVI – rather than hanging.

I was intrigued, that a king could be tried, let alone hanged. I thought of Molly's Oscar, dangling from the drop. King Louis of France, dancing the Kilmainham Minnit. Where would he be laid, to take his ground sweat?

And now Tom Paine proposed his own solution.

That King Louis be sent to the United States where he could live his remaining days as a decent citizen. Where every citizen is king.

I made so bold as to tell him that if every citizen was king there, I should never have left. My suspicion was, though, that if I had remained in the land of the free, I would still be pulling the suckers of tobacco in Old Montgomery's field. And, I continued, the only guarantor of my freedom was a lord and a king.

Where did you learn your politics? He asked me. From your countryman, Mr Burke?

I told him then, I knew of no Mr Burke.

Edmund Burke. Would agree with you. Wants a manly, moral and regulated liberty. Under a king, however mad.

And, I was so bold as to add, I didn't have a country.

And he told me if my Lieutenant had his way, that soon I would.

And in that country, he would no longer be Lord Edward. He would be Citizen Fitzgerald.

Part of which came to pass. The citizen part.

But first, he had to give away his privileges. And I watched him do just that, some nights later. At a dinner, in White's Hotel. He had already resigned his military commission. He now tore off his epaulets. He would no longer be a lieutenant of the 54th Regiment. He then renounced his lordship. It was as if an egret had dipped itself in oil to imitate a crow. Henceforth he would be Citizen Fitzgerald. And as the whole table erupted into raucous wine-soaked cheers, Tom Paine leaned into my ear and begged me to share in the celebration. Drink, to the obliteration of all distinction.

So I drank. To the newborn citizen, who, I was sure, could still employ a manservant. But I thought of my promise to his mother. I thought, how strange this game of distinction is. I knew my burden of care had grown.

He needed looking after.

Pamela

And then the ghost of Elizabeth made an appearance. It was odd, in that city where the future was being constructed daily, to see a ghost from the past, but that's what Pamela de Genlis seemed, to me at least.

I watched her from the shadows of the pillars of the Palais-Égalité, walking with my Citizen in the torchlit gardens beyond. Although her gown gave her far too much distinction, amongst those citoyennes. Her face moved from one pool of light to the other, my Citizen held her arm and I had to wonder was this business of love really a procession of ghosts? Each imitating the other, back to a dimly recognizable original. Or was it just the way it appeared to me, with my peculiar eyes? Whatever it was, the resemblance to Elizabeth was uncanny, in everything except the hair. Cropped, in that new way, a few delicate strands tumbling round her neck.

I saw her next in the theatre, where else? Beside him in the opera box of the Comédie Française. Her fan, doing its business in time to the overture. I had been invited there by a Captain Monroe, who was forever chasing gossip amongst les anglais in White's hotel. The play was a procession of triumphant banners waved by actors dressed as Jacobins and laid at the feet of a near-naked Liberté.

Six months ago, Captain Monroe confided, they would have been dressed as Girondins.

It would never have played in Sheridan's Drury Lane, I told him.

And the name set something off in him.

Sheridan, he said, who pursued the same Pamela to France? He nodded towards the box across the way. Pamela de Genlis with whom your Lord seems quite enamoured?

My Citizen, I corrected him.

He'll be a lord again soon enough, if Pamela has her way.

He was fishing, I could feel that already. The kind of gossip for whom one bite of information demands another.

I decided to try my hand at it.

And where will that leave Sheridan?

Back in his cups in London. Mother and daughter met him there. With Talleyrand, would you believe?

I was embarrassed to ask who this Talleyrand was.

Sheridan thought she was his dead wife, reborn. He chased her round the coast of Normandy.

So the comedy became a ghost story. I resolved to tell Cecil, if I ever met him again.

And her origins, he told me, are as mysterious as your own.

What did you know of my origins?

Only what your Lord Citizen told me. Mother from Sierra Leone? Father lost in the savannah bayous?

So I had some secrets left. I was glad of my Citizen's discretion. And I thought it best to ask for information, rather than offer any.

And her origins? Pamela de Genlis?

The name comes from the mother. Madame de Genlis. Tutor to the children of the Duc d'Orléans. Before he changed his name to the Duc d'Égalité. But as to her origins? As with yourself, Tony Small. No one knows the father.

The finale was deafening, so the captain came closer. I felt his breath in my ear. It stank of cloves.

Maybe her mother was more than tutor to the Duc's children? Then there's the rumour of the fisherman father in Newfoundland. And in these uncertain times, a pick of fathers could well turn out to be a blessing. The Duc d'Orléans could one day wish his own father was a fisherman.

Madame Guillotine would shave the Duc's beard soon after. So maybe he did.

It would do us well, Tony Small, to penetrate this mystery. Because your Lord Citizen is in deep. And not only with Pamela de Genlis.

In deep?

Observe the company he keeps –

He nodded, towards the box across the way, as the curtains were drawn. A crowd was gathering in my Citizen's box. Amongst them, two burly brothers from Cork city.

– United Irishmen –

It was the first time I heard that term. It wouldn't be the last.

– John and Henry Sheares –

One would later dip his handkerchief in the guillotined king's blood. And both would beg for the guillotine when they were hung, drawn and quartered in Newgate.

The captain wanted an introduction, but I managed to lose him in the foyer, amongst the crowd. So I was introduced to Pamela myself some mornings later, in the Café des Anglais, looking out on the Palais gardens. And I had to wonder was it all my poor imagination at work, as she talked with him over glasses of strawberried champagne. There was not a lot of Elizabeth in those eyes. Maybe the ghost was my own invention. Or Sheridan's. And my Citizen was in love with Pamela de Genlis, not the memory of Sheridan's wife.

But the citizen loved the way the lord did. Revolutions didn't change that.

I will marry her, Tony.

You will, my Lord?

I had brought him coffee in the morning. And now boiling water, in preparation for shaving. I knew I shouldn't, but the habit persisted. I missed the ritual. And I think my Citizen missed it too.

Ned, Tony. Ned. Do I have to remind you?

Only with your mother's blessing surely?

The Ned was unspoken. It was more comfortable that way.

I have written to her, asking for the same.

Well then.

But I realized, in the act of writing, that there was one other blessing I needed.

The bells were ringing from the church across the square. They should have been blessing enough.

Yours.

Then I can only give it my Lord.

You don't understand. I don't want it as a matter of command. I want it freely given.

My blessing?

You loved Elizabeth?

I did.

The echo of the dying bell was more telling than the bell itself.

Your mother's blessing surely is of more consequence than mine.

He turned, towards my lathering brush. I began scraping with the blade.

That's the oddness of the thing. Maybe not.

The oddness of it. I had to think about that phrase, as I cleared those cheeks of soap. I felt the twinge of something new that I didn't recognize.

Tom Paine filled me in.

Those were happier times, before he was trundled off to the Prison de Luxembourg. I remember the church bells, from Notre Dame of the Ascension, in the cobbled square outside White's Hotel.

Madame de Genlis, he told me, has a certain reputation. For theories of education, barely readable books, for a past that she continually reinvents. She may need all her powers of invention, soon enough.

As would Tom Paine, it turned out.

And whoever Pamela's father turns out to be, Duc or fisherman, whoever her mother is cannot be questioned. And as I can't claim to be a genealogist, why are you asking?

Because my Citizen's mother asked me, I thought, to guide his judgment in some matters. And those matters might include you. Your *Rights of Man*.

Curiosity, I said.

But that was a lie. I knew this new twinge, this blush, this emotion, enough to be embarrassed by it. Jealousy.

But at least she took him out of Paris. I was getting tired of shuttered meetings and closed doors, gatherings where my skills as manservant were no longer necessary. Maybe the business of revolution didn't need them? The business of love, however, did. It needed a shave, it needed a laundered cravat and a white shirt front, it needed polished boots. It needed letters ferried, from the foyer of White's to the rooms above the Palais gardens, where I waited in the Café des Anglais while Madame de Genlis composed her reply.

I was surprised to be joined by the same captain, George Monroe. Still chasing gossip amongst les anglais. He had heard of the dinner, where lords became citizens. He had heard Tom Paine had had an altercation with a certain Grimstone some nights later. Yes, I told him, Grimstone had struck my dear Tom Paine across the face. He was not used to being struck, being a bodice maker. The two United Irishmen from Cork, John and Henry Sheares had intervened and sent Grimstone packing.

And your own Lord Edward?

Citizen, I corrected him. Gone, back to Isleworth, to present his case for marriage to his mother.

But I lied. He was at the convention, with the same Paine. I would get used to lying. And this captain was too curious. He was the first of a type I would come to know intimately, back home. In the pay of the Sham Squire. Informers.

And I had just realized I called it home. I was missing those Dublin streets.

Did I take part in these great events? I did. I beat Grimstone to a pulp in the cobbled square beneath his hotel window. It was easier than I thought. I imagined I was bloodying old Montgomery. I drove my Lord Citizen and Tom Paine out to the convention, where he delivered his solution to the problem of the King. I saw the spiked heads in the Tuileries gardens. And I saw Pamela de Genlis make a fast exit from her Paris quarters, while waiting with another of my Citizen's letters of endearment.

Her problem was not her 'fisherman father'. It was the noble one, Philippe Égalité. It was not a good time to be noble.

So my Citizen Lord needed my help again. He was never good at packing.

Your blessing, Tony, he said. I need it more than ever.

You have it, my Lord.

Your Ned. Tell your Ned he has it.

Does your mother approve?

He shrugged. And I could only conclude she didn't. I felt the ghost of Elizabeth, saying, bless him now.

So I gave it to him. I gave my Lord, Lieutenant and my Citizen my benediction. And he was so moved, he knelt before me. There were two fools, I realized, met in that forest. And I told him we needed horses more than blessings.

It was a challenge to find horses in Paris that November, let alone a cart. But with the help of the Sheares brothers, we got our hands on both. And his impatience was such that he rode on ahead of me, on the road north out of the city, towards the border with the Austrian Netherlands. I followed, with my cart of baggage. Along the river, through the crush of citizens. Through the city gates, where the crush grew, if anything, even greater.

Carts like mine. Coaches and four, phaetons, families walking, their households on their heads. Soldiers, marching to the great defensive berms being dug, ringing the city. There had been a war, with Austria, and there would be another. So I trundled on, no need of maps, there was only one direction in which these pilgrims were travelling. And towards nightfall I came upon a baggage cart, parked by the roadside. The canvas coverings did their best to hide the insignia of the House of Orléans, but the two phaetons and the coach and four gave the game away, to me at least. A succession of vehicles then, leading to a riverside inn. And there a young, brown-haired servant girl waved my baggage cart to a halt.

Are you his dear Tony? She asked, all teeth and smiles.

I was once, I told her, and hope to be again.

Well, he's inside, with his betrothed.

So, my Citizen was to be married. I wondered would that make his mother happy. And would that make him Lord Edward again.

They were a motley crew. Her mother, Madame de Genlis, servants of the Duc d'Égalité, an assortment of governesses, household retainers, whose absence of livery only served to make them more conspicuous. The Duke himself was absent, busy being equal somewhere else.

And then there was the brown-haired servant girl, who made so bold as to take my hand as she led me to my sleeping quarters. Her name was Julie, and I wondered how much she knew of jealousy.

United

There was a wedding then, somewhere over the border, past the huge mountains of earthworks with the cannons poking between the gaps like blackened fingers. Past the military camps, the soldiers burning braziers by the flapping tents in the early morning mists, the muskets stacked like the barley sheaves I'd seen back in the Irish fields. The horses tied together, ten or so to a post, their breath rising in the cold air like steaming kettles. Everything was like something else for some reason, nothing seemed itself, as if a huge tempest was waiting to blow the familiar away and replace it with something that had never been.

A town then, filled with soldiers, Austrian, I was told by this little Julie, a fountainhead of information. And there was a fountain, in the square in Tournai before you came to the cathedral, also called Notre Dame, like the one in Paris, the great one by the river and the smaller one by White's Hotel. And in the same cathedral, some weeks later, finally, a wedding.

There were many reasons for the wait, young Julie told me. Permissions to be granted, by Pamela's father and Lord Edward's mother. And I wondered aloud which of her fathers would grant permission, the fisherman or the duke. She laughed and whacked what she would later call my dusky hand and asked me where I learned my wit. I thought it wise not to mention Molly and so I told her, the streets of Dublin.

She had heard the rumours but refused to believe them. She bet me a turn on the dancefloor that it would be a duke and not a fisherman that gave her mistress Pamela away.

So we waited. And some days later when we saw the carts trundling through the cobbled streets they didn't bear any fishing nets, they were piled high with plate and gilded mirror and cloth and bore the three odd little flowers, the fleur-de-lis, Julie called it, of the Duc d'Orléans, now Duc d'Égalité, she told me, but maybe, beyond the borders of France, he could be Orléans again. Anyway, there was a wedding some days later, again in the great cathedral, an unseen choir singing from the upper reaches, an organ that shook the pews from its massive pipes, pointing towards the heavens, a grand aristocratic gathering and small Julie and me, Tony Small.

It was odd to sit alone in that great cathedral, with pigeons cooing round the high windows as if they knew the absurdity below. The clouds of incense gathering round the couple on the altar, the left side of the cathedral pews filled with the bedecked and bejewelled members of her apparent family and the right side with one attendant, me.

He had dressed me in a uniform that was a pale reflection of his own. A green cape and a cockaded hat which I perched on my silken blue breeches.

There were others in his family, I assured the same Julie, during the later festivities. There were Dukes of Leinster and Richmond, there were kings and queens, Irish and English, there was a Silken Thomas who was hung and quartered, but apparently not drawn and the reasons for their non-attendance were many and various. Less to do with the rumours of the fisherman father of the bride, more to do with reasons her other father changed his name from Orléans to Égalité. They were no doubt disapproving of the cause the Duc had embraced so ardently. So in place of his family, there was me, the runaway from Old Montgomery's plantation in the Carolinas, and the one thing we had in common was that, like them, I was beholden to the King.

Which King? She asked, the King who's sitting in prison in Paris?

No, I told her. The other King, of England, who was mad enough to sign my papers of freedom.

England, she said. Where we're headed.

On the way to Ireland, I told her.

And you're from Ireland?

I thought I might be, once. But I was disabused of that notion.

So, from where?

A place I call Elsewhere.

I watched them dance, the groom with his cap of freedom and the bride with her blue and white ribbons threaded through her hair. I watched small Julie dance with the Duc d'Égalité's boy servant and was wondering when she would make good on her bet and ask me up, when, to general amazement, the bride came and took my hand.

She had her husband's permission to ask me to dance. I told her I knew very few steps, apart from the quadrille Molly and I had danced in the Leinster House kitchens. She promised to lead me, and as she did, I came to realize she wanted to whisper as much as dance, and all of her whispers were enquiries about someone else.

How can I gain her approval, dear Tony? She asked me, and I could only wonder how I had so suddenly become dear to her. I made so bold as to ask the same, and was told that my Lord, her new husband, had only one form of address for me, hence the dear.

In fact, in the first days of our acquaintance, I feared I had only one rival – and that was you.

If I could have blushed I would. So instead I expressed my confusion by stepping on her toes.

And, as time went on, she said, stepping adroitly aside, I realized I had another. Far more formidable one. His mother.

At the mention of his mother, I felt the need to blush again, but managed, this time, not to step on those delicate feet.

Had I betrayed her? I had befriended Tom Paine. I had watched him cultivate company she herself would have baulked at. She had asked me to guide her son's judgment in such matters. I had seen him tear off his epaulettes, throw off his privileges, renounce the title that alone gave him distinction.

There are ghosts around you, I thought. Poor thing. You will have to dance between them.

You could never be a rival to his mother, I replied.

No? Why not?

Because, I wanted to reply, she was the original. The first outline I had seen in that gloamy forest. All the rest were imitations, each fainter than the other.

Because, I actually replied, she gave birth to a lord. You married a Citizen.

Are you speaking in riddles, Tony Small?

I was. A riddle without an answer. As yet.

I was to get my answer soon enough. After a ball or two and a riot of packing, we headed to the coast. Four of us. The Citizen and Pamela, me and little Julie, often clinging to the luggage on the carriage roof as the newlyweds explored their wedded status down below us. Julie did her best to teach me French, and I wondered to myself did I need another language. My balladspeak was serving me quite well. But I do remember the word for the blue green vista that met us at Ostend.

La Mer

Never had the sea looked less inviting. A cold wind was blowing from Crusoe's native shore. I wondered where York was across that mariner's vista. We boarded a merchant ship and allowed that English wind batter us towards Dover. We disembarked at night and after one night's rest and one more day's travel, I found myself again in London. The carriage horses' hooves echoed round the white frontages of Harley Street. Cecil opened the door to my knock and his wide eyes understood enough not to ask any questions.

Lady Pamela was wearing white for the occasion, with red and blue sashes threaded through her cloak, and a hat decorated with freedom lilies. If clothes could speak, I whispered to Cecil, as we wrangled the cases inside and he assured me they did, they spoke louder than words.

But if her clothes could speak, the only answer they received was silence. I would get used to that silence, the hush that fell on a gathering, a drawing room, a ball. The whispers that preceded it, as the onlookers parted. It greeted her now, as she entered the great drawing room, and I settled the tea things on the small oriental table. The Scottish master sat to one side, my Citizen's mother on the other. I had wrested the serving duties from Cecil to be a mute observer. I wanted to see did Lady Emily see anything of herself in the daughter-in-law's profile. The search had been long, after all, and up to this point, painful. And while the hair of Citoyenne Pamela might not have had the perfection of Elizabeth's, the etched shadow of the nose and mouth would have fitted the locket well.

But I was ill-prepared for the silence. Whatever words were spoken went back to that ocean of stillness. The sea of what remained unsaid.

I took to calling it La Mer. It hid so many things in its embarrassed hush. His mother's glance to me, as she sipped from the cup I had poured, and enquired from Pamela after the health of Madame de Genlis.

They knew each other? It seemed impossible, but they did.

Mama is well, Pamela replied. Writing, as always –
    But Lady Emily's glance expressed regret, sadness, some kind of infinite disappointment.
    I had asked you, it seemed to say, to guide his judgment in such matters.

And then the silence returned.
    Ogilvie broke it, since books were his world.
    Adèle et Théodore is, for many, a rival to Rousseau.
    And the mention of that Rousseau brought another silence.
    I backed out of that drawing room, glad to occupy myself with a cold teapot.

I almost tumbled over Julie, who had her ear to the keyhole.

I gave the pot to Cecil to refill.

You have both been listening?

They nodded, guiltily.

And what did you hear?

Not a lot, said Cecil.

La Mer, I said to Julie.

What does that mean? Asked Cecil.

A great silence.

Irishman

So, back to Dublin and I realized the thing about the place. It was like a tiny mirror to the wider world. There were wars, revolutions, revolts for kings and against them, wigs were discarded for towheads, crowns for three-cornered hats, satin knee britches for pantaloons. The waves that tore across the ocean of the world just rippled in this little pool. Still and all, the smaller the puddle, the bigger the splash. I was getting confused between things small and big, but there was no confusing the effect of my Citizen's re-entry to the place.

It began with a murmur as we stepped off the packet to the Pigeon House. It grew into a chant of cockle-picking Irishtown children as we made our way along the Pile ends and the Ballast Wall. To the city then and College Green, where someone had rebuilt the House of Parliament and the whole street had its rhymes already composed for our arrival. To the rusting gates of Leinster House, where they made one solid mass against the railings. And back inside that great retreat of empty rooms, where all we could hear was the echo of the world outside.

The place seemed empty. No one to greet us.

Where is everybody? I asked him.

My brother the Duke, he told me, has retired to Carton. So we must make do as best we can.

Servants appeared and disappeared like remembered ghosts. There were cobwebbed staircases, the smell of mildew. I searched through the corridors for Molly, but of her, not a sign. I found my Leinster duds in my old attic room, dusted them off, did my best with the room. The Duke had shuttered the place I was told. There was mutton in the scullery, sour milk in the kitchen, all of the honey had gone. I wakened the cook from what seemed like a month's slumber, and sent him out for supplies. Julie served them what he cooked then, with buttermilk to wash the mutton stew down.

Is it always like this? She asked me, as I showed her once again the way to her room. She had lost herself twice, in the tangle of staircases.

Like what?

Like a great empty cathedral?

It will be better, I told her, in Frescati.

She had her choice of rooms in the servants' quarters, most of the servants having vanished.

The Duke drew in the purse strings, the cook told me, after the French business.

And Molly?

Molly, he told me, was the first to be sent packing.

So I slept, in my attic room, and in my dreams heard the wind moaning in the rigging, as if the whole of Leinster House was a ship of the line, adrift at sea. There was a wooden carving on the prow, with Molly's face.

I awoke and knew already I would find neither tea, coffee, milk nor honey, but I searched the scullery all the same. I found a lemon rind and a bar of soap and managed to flavour my Citizen's water with the first, and shave him with the second, as small Julie dressed her mistress in the way I'd seen in France. A flowing white dress and a jacket trimmed with tiny stripes of blue.

All for the parliamentary session.

No fleur-de-lis? I asked Julie, as she took a blue bonnet from the cases.

Rien, she said.

Which I assumed meant no.

Was it to be Lady now or Madame? Or Citoyenne, to stick with Julie's French?

Lady Pamela it had to be I thought, as I guided her out through the great rusted gates onto the half-built street with the fields of Stephen's Green and the bare fingers of trees scratching the sky.

Will they always hate me, Tony? she asked.

Nobody hates you, my Lady, I replied, though I had to picture to myself the strange sight we must have made, me in my Leinster duds following her in her cockaded glory down towards Parliament House.

She took her place in the gallery then and listened to what she can't have realized was the last gasp of his parliamentary breath. He had embraced Liberté and while the crowds outside the house might have welcomed it, the crowd inside the house most definitely did not.

I could hear the roars, from inside, behind the railings.

What had he said? small Julie asked me, later.

Something about the King and Liberty. The whole of Ireland would soon have its freedom papers.

He had me cut his hair, that night. Cropped it, again in the French way. The cabinet of wigs would gather dust, like the discarded ghosts of his privilege.

Is this safe? I asked him, as the reddish curls drifted towards the floor.

Safety is not the issue, Tony. Principle is.

It drew attention alright as he walked down towards College Green, I walked behind him, leading the horses. Where the Lord once rode, I realized, the Citizen walked.

Was he the first croppy? The first in parliament, I would wager. The first to stride around College Green, the first to attend the theatre in Crow Street.

And at night I searched the town for Molly. The pushing shops in Temple Bar, where the whores sat on the steps in their petticoats in the evening light. The taverns round the Liberties. The hanging tree in Stephen's Green where her Oscar dangled. No sign. No word. Maybe she had moved to The Naul, to tend his grave.

Until, some nights after, I drove them both to the Theatre Royal.

A carriage for this event, which I guided down Crow Street, and watched them disappear into the crowds around the entrance. Amongst which I got a glimpse of a tumble of brown hair and a pair of blue eyes.

Molly, at last. Her bodice full of pins.

Where is the ceremonial gear, Tony? She asked as I tied the horses round the back.

Gathering dust somewhere in Leinster House.

So you were spared that ribbing, she said.

And what happened to you?

I grew a bit too big for service, she said.

You have a child, Molly?

No. I had a witch take care of it. If I'd bore a child I'd be on a pushing block now in Barrack Street.

And you have a job?

I'm a seamstress, she said, half smiling. In there.

She nodded her head towards the stage entrance.

You always loved the theatre, Tony.

I did. And still do.

Come in then, backstage, behind the flats. Have a look.

What's the play? I asked her.

The Beggar's Opera. Polly Peachum and Macheath. They lock him in London's Newgate. You remember our Newgate, Tony?

I did. The smell of porter and pies and the tassels of her skirts.

But unlike mine and Oscar's story, there's a happy ending. I do love a happy ending.

As did I. And she led me in.

Into the shadow world behind. Once more I got that smell of sawdust and greasepaint. I remembered Cecil, who would have envied me, then.

Shadows on the canvas backing. A dance, which Molly told me, was one of whores and thieves. A song. And suddenly, a riot, in the stalls.

It happens every night, Molly whispered. Macheath tells them he is ready to be hanged. Someone else shouts 'guillotined'. There's a shouting match between supporters of the drop and Madame Guillotine.

I had to imagine the happy ending. My Citizen emerged with his Lady, amongst a throng from the gods who approved of his green scarf and his cropped hair, while the stalls continued their riot.

I drove them back to the cold wastes of Leinster House, where, some days later, we received news from Paris.

Madame Guillotine had shaved the French King's head. Half of Paris had reddened their kerchiefs with his blood. And I was surprised to find small Julie weeping.

I put my arms around her, underneath the skylight.

Is your mistress crying, too?

She shook her head. She dipped her hands in a ceramic bowl, and they came out red.

I felt a pain in my chest. I thought she had found her own small guillotine.

Are you bleeding, Julie? I asked.

No, she said. Je tiens en rouge.

She took a white handkerchief then and dipped it in the bowl. One after the other, laid them in the sunlight coming through the glass window to dry.

They steamed slowly, dyed to a crisp red.

For the Lord Lieutenant's ball, she said.

She had me find a scissors then and help her cut them into strips.

Ribbons, she said. For my Lady's hair. As if dipped in the dead King's blood.

This isn't your idea, Julie?

No, she said. Hers. Do you think the Lord Lieutenant will appreciate?

I could imagine Lady Camden's frozen face. The icy blue of the Lord Lieutenant's eyes.

They needed a carriage for the journey. So I drove them, in the open-topped phaeton, past the Trinity gates, past Parliament House. Past the cavern of Crow Street, where I could see the crowds outside the theatre. Into the Castle Yard, where every carriage was draped in black, every lord and lady dressed in mourning.

I thought of dipping down to Crow Street to waste some time with Molly. But something told me their quadrille would not last long.

I was right. It was as if they had danced the 'Kilmainham Minnit' on the Castle floor. Neither Lord nor Lady Camden appreciated the gesture. The carriage was required.

She wept on the way back, tearing the ribbons from her hair. And although I couldn't understand her teary French, I could picture the scene.

After that came the closing of the houses. To us, not to others. I observed the hurt on his face. As a lord he was welcome, as a citizen, not. No balls at Dublin Castle, the Lord Lieutenant's lodge. No country house weekends.

So it was a cold wind that made us say goodbye to Leinster House and say hello to the blustery breezes of Frescati. I laboured in the garden under my Citizen's direction, until summer ended. Ogilvie came to visit and announce he had let Frescati to a banker from Greystones named La Touche. We made our way out to Carton, and after various changes of dwelling we ended up in a demesne house in Kildare, close to his brother the Duke's estate but far from the grandeur of his dwelling. And I began finally to understand the reality of Captain Moonlight and the blackened faces and the women's shifts worn by muscular young men, the burning hayricks and the cattle sliced below the gut. A rambling farmhouse set amongst muddy Kildare fields, where I first heard that word for twilight. The twilight I remembered from the Eutaw forest. Gloaming.

We lived in the gloaming now. Lady Pamela, Julie and their dear and faithful Tony, as their Citizen visited Belfast and Portadown and Newry where the 'Rights of Man' proclaimed themselves in gatherings public and for the most part private. And old Sheil who managed the lands for my Citizen gave us lessons in Irish which we promised to have mastered on his return.

And so I delved into the tongue that I once thought would be mine. Damn 'Primero de Mayo', bayou Spanish and French, I tried to dream in the language and the landscape that my imagined father would have left behind him.

Low muddy fields, like those around Old Montgomery's. Words that felt like pebbles in the mouth, thick phlegmy consonants that rolled together.

Rain – báisteach
Black – dubh
Blue – gorm
Barley – eorna

We practised it together as my Citizen came and went, the leaving always at night and the coming in the daytime. He brought new friends with him, dissenters from the flaxen mills in Larne and Belfast, lawyers and pamphleteers, the cigar salesman I once met in Parliament Street. Men of the cloth, Presbyterian ministers, a Catholic priest or two. I had heard names I would come to recognize, and some to like, some to hate. Bond, O'Connor, Higgins, Magan, Neilson. She was hungry for company, I could tell, the three of us alone together for the most part, the kind of company a lady should keep. She was with child soon enough, old Lawlor noticed it before I did, we were working the potato drills together and she came to the farmhouse door, up late, around mid-morning. He nudged me, tá sí ag iompair, and when I questioned his argot, he translated. Can't you see the signs, he said, up late in the morning with the crúiscíní lán.

But my Citizen returned and he noticed it too. Their joy was infectious. A trip back to Dublin then, Sheil driving the carriage, I was confined to the roof with Julie while they both rested in the cabin inside.

I saw the city again from my juddering perch, the river came into view around the Black Dog prison and I remembered the children's rhymes when we first crossed it. As black as the bellows the bould Tony Small. Then the smell of hops and offal over the Essex Bridge and the crush of barges and the forest of masts beyond the bridges and the Customs House on the North Quays. We turned right past the parliament buildings and right again towards Leinster House.

The gates were open, thank God. The Duke sent his regards. His mother sent a letter of congratulation and delight. Lady Pamela's condition – for she was a lady again, bearing an heir – worked wonders. But she found the house too cold. I was left there, to kick my heels and warm it, while they returned to their Kildare gloaming.

It was a week or so later that I kicked my heels down Joshua Dawson's Street, down the newly built thoroughfares of glass and sandy brick, past the grafters on the wooden struts of scaffolding who whistled their abuse, down to Crow Street where I knocked on the backstage door. Where my darling Molly answered, and gave me a prickly embrace, her bodice like a porcupine with pins and needles.

To what do I owe the privilege, Tony?

To Macheath, I told her.

I wanted to know more of *The Beggar's Opera*.

It's long gone, she said. But you can know more of Romeo.

Romeo? I asked her.

Romeo, Romeo, where the Jasus are you? And Juliet. Daly plays Mercutio, though he's getting a bit old.

Daly?

Dasher Daly. Took over after Spranger Barry. Tears his britches open every night in the knockabouts onstage, which I stitch the next day. As I'm doing at the moment. Hold that thread, would you?

So I held it. And she got me a seat on a bench that evening from where I saw the Montagues and Capulets go at it like the croppies and the yeomen would a few years after. And after Juliet had killed herself with Romeo's flask, I got the whiff of strong tobacco from my left and a voice muttered: it would draw a tear from a stone.

I agreed it would. I turned to look at him but could hardly see him for the mist in my eyes. Or hear him, for the applause.

Mercutio took the bulk of it. Dasher Daly bowed, his britches torn once more. He owned the theatre, after all and owned the stage that night.

Well-liked.

I agreed he was.

A duellist, I am told.

I had no idea.

Three with pistol, three with sword. Prevailed in five. Lucky we never met —

He tried to rise, with the aid of a stick.

And if you could help me, kind sir —

So I did. I gripped his free hand and my own hand froze.

Yes. You've noticed. A bullet took that thumb away. Another did good work on this knee. But you should see —

And he smiled, gritting his teeth, as I helped him upwards.

— the other fellows. But ever since my own duelling days, crowds can be a problem —

So we waited, while the benches emptied.

Offend my friends. Offend my cause. You offend me.

So I vowed never to offend him. And as I helped him through the foyer and out onto the cobbles of Temple Bar I could only wonder did that tapping stick of his conceal a blade. And if it did, would he be steadier with it.

And we have friends in common.

We do?

Sheridan, amongst them. Although I sometimes wonder, can Sheridan be a friend to anyone but himself?

Tap tap. Broad shoulders, a sagging face. Then tap again. I would become used to that sound.

The child died, he whispered. Almost to himself.

I wondered if I'd heard him right.

Mary?

Yes. You cared for her. How do I know that? Your own Lord told me. Who is waiting for me now, in the Gentleman's Theatre in Fishamble Street.

Why had he not told me? But there were other secrets he hadn't shared. As I realized when that tapping stick rapped on the door of another theatre. The Gentleman's Theatre, Fishamble Street.

The door was opened by a face I knew from Paris. Henry Sheares. I had last seen him admiring the spiked heads in the Tuileries gardens. Behind him was his brother John, displaying a red handkerchief. Which, the duellist whispered to me, had been dipped in the blood of the French King. After his head had been shaved by Madame Guillotine. And amongst the group gathered on the empty stage was my Citizen Lord.

The cane tapped its way in. Could I enter behind him? I wasn't invited. The door closed again. I was left on the cobbled street, wondering how many other secrets had been withheld.

I made my way back, amongst the shadows, hoping that I had heard him wrong. But I learned, from the kitchen gossip of Leinster House, that it was the truth.

Little Mary had died, indeed.

And Lord Edward had returned, for his wife's lying-in.

I rode out the next evening to Frescati, past the cockle-pickers and the rhyming children. There were new gardeners tending the lawns. But they allowed me to visit the little elm tree, now three years old. I cleared the long grass to reveal the name I inscribed in the bark. It was elongated, misshapen, barely legible. But it still said Mary.

I would love to say I watered her elm with tears. But I didn't. It was a misshapen piece of bark now, with four carved letters. Nobody to see it. Nobody to notice it but me. I felt fury, more than loss. More than agony. What's wrong with this race, this place, that allows the accident of birth define who a child is and how a child is mourned. Maybe I had no tears left in me. So I carved some more.

RIP 1794.

I slept in the Frescati gardens, afraid that if I rode back to Leinster House I would drag my Citizen from his bed over those cockle fields, force him to weep over his daughter's elm, drag him all the way to Wandsworth even, to that Mrs Malaprop who had had all of his child's rearing.

I was woken by the gardeners the next morning. I was asked had I no home to go to? It was a good question to which I had no answer. So I rode back along the dawn shore, came through the Merrion fields, settled the horse in the stables, came into that house through the scullery. Empty of servants. A low, haunted moan sounded through the dumb waiter. I followed the sound, through the arched kitchens, up the stone steps, into the great staircase by the entrance. It was louder there and touched with some kind of pain. No light but the moon through the leaded windows and that moan again, as if a ghost had possessed that mansion, the ghost of a child forgotten by everyone but me. A servant girl scurried by then, a candle in one hand, a bowl of water in the other.

Have the dead awoken? I asked her.

No, she told me. Lady Pamela's time has come.

Conspiracy

You met McNally?

He was writing a letter at his library desk. I had his child crooked in my arms, wrapped in what little Julie told me was Breton lace.

One thumb missing, and an injured knee?

A duel, with Jonah Barrington. The first of many, I was told. McNally will defend our cause, at whatever cost to his person.

He sealed the letter while little Eddy's tiny fingers grasped at my thumb. I had two for him to play with.

He enjoyed your company. And I need him to read this. Which can't be sent by the Dublin post.

Why not, my Lord?

Tony, Tony. Do I have to explain why?

He didn't. Conspiracy was like love, I was learning. It involved much ferrying of letters back and forth. This one to Dame Street where I put it into McNally's thumbless hand.

I accompanied him some nights later across the river to Kilmainham Prison and while Leonard McNally occupied the Sergeant at Arms with conversation, I shimmied up the wall as Molly had done with her Oscar. I placed another letter between the teeth of a manacled giant who met me at the bars.

I almost took you for Olaudah, he said.

Olaudah?

Olaudah Equiano –

And he might have said more, had the conversation not been cut short by a whistle from below. McNally, with his good thumb in his mouth.

Samuel Neilson was his name, McNally told me, as we tapped our way back by the river. Editor of the Northern Star, whose opinions had led to his incarceration. For McNally was barrister to him, and to others in what he called 'the brotherhood'. McNally's duelling days were over. As were his days of doing battle with the pen. He was a poet once. And a playwright, hence his friendship with the comedian, Sheridan.

Although, he said wistfully, as his stick scraped along the quay wall, he may never forgive me *The Apotheosis of Punch*.

Punch? I asked.

A satire, he said. On Sheridan's style.

And he quoted, looking down at the brown water.

> *Now, indeed may Genius mourn and weep*
> *Since Tragedy and Comedy both sleep*
> *Since dullness has besotted the two wenches*
> *No wonder actors play to empty benches.*

You sir, he looked at me. Would you have forgiven me that?

I was at a loss to know what would be forgiven.

This sewer was a river once. And Sheridan once had wit.

Conspiracy was introducing my Citizen to a city quite new to him. Skinner's Row, Dirty Lane, the tangle of the Liberties. Astley's Circus, where a half-naked giant, in trunks emblazoned with the Union Jack took on all comers. The challenge was accepted by a face that I recognized from behind the bars of Kilmainham Prison. So McNally's pleas had worked. Samuel Neilson, now blood-spattered, was giving back as good as he got. And after an elbow and an uppercut, the giant hit the floor and Samuel Neilson raised the fist of victory and the assemblage went wild, bellowing in French 'ça ira, ça ira, ça ira' which, my Citizen informed me, was the refrain of the Parisian sans-culottes and meant 'everything will be fine'. And I had to doubt this assurance, as the strains of 'God Save The King' sounded out from the rear, the refrains in French tried to drown them out and the bouts of fisticuffs spread far beyond the stage.

I wrestled my Citizen through the mayhem to a backstage room, where McNally was bathing Neilson's bloodied face in a bowl of steaming water.

Olaudah, Neilson said. Did I acquit myself manfully?

Olaudah who?

Forgive me, he said. Olaudah Equiano. Was my guest in Belfast. A lover of freedom, like everyone here. From Africa, the kingdom of Benin. You know the kingdom of Benin?

I told him I did not, being from the King's lost kingdom of Carolina.

Tony is his name, my Citizen said. Tony Small.

Surely he deserves a better name than Small?

If I do, sir, I wasn't given it.

And who christened you, Tony Small?

My mother, I said.

From the Kingdom of Benin?

No, I said. From the Kingdom of Sierra Leone.

He spat some blood into the bowl.

Forgive me again. One tooth seems loose. My friend Olaudah had a name forced on him. Gustavus Vassa. Till he found his freedom and rechristened himself. I suggest a renaming, Tony Small. When you take the oath. Have you taken the oath?

The oath?

I had heard of it, of course. The oath of the United Irishmen. But I hadn't taken it. I hadn't been asked. And the room was filling up with those who must have.

When you do, we can rechristen you. Baptize you, into your new kingdom. But until then, Tony Small –

The implication was clear. I had to leave.

Conspiracy was indeed like love. It involved letters, meetings in secret and oaths of eternal fidelity.

I walked home alone. The mention of my mother had caught at my heart. What was her name, I wondered, amongst her Temne people, in Sierra Leone?

I knew her by one name only. April. And I wondered once more, how can you come to miss a charnel house?

I called this city home, but I knew it wasn't. It was my Citizen's home, not mine.

He could make it mine, I thought. He could share this journey with me. It is taking him to streets you never knew existed. If Luke Caffrey and Larry didn't survive them, I am not sure he will either.

Meanwhile, the Dublin sun did what the burning logs from the Kildare forests could never manage. It warmed Leinster House.

My Citizen slept late. His meetings needed the protection of the dark. Lady Pamela was often confined to her shuttered room. But the city squares were drenched in sunlight and I thought that little Eddy should enjoy them. And since he couldn't walk yet and was growing too heavy for little Julie to carry him, I dreamed up a miniature carriage that might do the same.

I wrangled a set of small wheels, from four garden wheel-barrows. I bound them together with a frame and axle, greased like a carriage shaft. I had the blacksmith fashion a bowed handle, to arch above them. I had Julie bring me little Eddy's bassinet and tried to fit it to them. The wheels were too wide, the handle too heavy. It pulled the bassinet to the floor, and then to the ceiling. I had the blacksmith begin again, adjust the axle on the wheels, shorten the bowed handle. And the bassinet then fit, as snugly as Cinderella's foot into her slipper.

Come Julie, I said, take little Eddy for a walk.

How? she asked.

In his baby carriage.

So, she carried him down and set him inside. She made him snug with blankets, pillows and a hanging row of coloured beads.

He gurgled, happily, fingered the beads above his blue eyes.

And we took him for an amble down Joshua Dawson's Street and on to Stephen's Green. The wheels squeaked. The vehicle shook. But the infant loved the adventure. I had to imagine how it looked to him. The blue sky framed by the passing trees, the random flurries of pigeons and doves.

A crowd had gathered, viewing the fives of tennis on the open field. And we soon had an audience.

Has it a name, this vehicle? A gentleman enquired.

It is its first outing, I told him.

An ambulator, he suggested.

But it does more than amble, his partner said. It walks all over. It perambulates.

A perambulator, then.

So, perambulator it became.

It became our habit. To walk little Eddy in his perambulator around the squares of Dublin. Fitzwilliam, Merrion, around the hanging tree, the artificial pond of Stephen's Green, then across the Essex Bridge, down Sackville Street and Gardiner's Mall to the squares of Rutland and Mountjoy.

We drew crowds, wherever we walked. And soon every fashionable lady wanted a perambulator. And maybe even a Moorish servant to push it.

But by then the conspiracy moved on. To Sussex, where little Eddy and his perambulator were left in Goodwood House. And on to Hamburg, with its log jam of ships.

Hamburg

Another grand house, with gardens stretching down towards a river, which, he told me, was called the Elbe.

It could have been the Liffey, with its cast of arrivals and departures. With the wind, which whipped over a sea they called the Baltic, setting that forest of masts in motion.

Why Hamburg? I asked him.

Because, he told me, Madame de Genlis has made her home here. Because her niece, Henriette de Sercey, was marrying the Hamburg merchant, Johann-Conrad Mattieson, whose guest we were.

So, there were secrets. And the plot had thickened.

I felt a pang that I recognized. Like jealousy, but thicker again. The pang of exclusion. Others knew something I didn't.

But it was something to do with those ships, I knew. Their clatter kept me awake at night. They were still clattering in the morning, like woodpeckers in the Savannah bayous. I brought his coffee to the terrace, with a spoonful of honey to sweeten it and found him gone.

It was to become his rhythm in Hamburg. Here for a few days, and then gone, for another week.

I served it to Henriette de Sercey instead.

You're from Carolina? She asked me.

Yes, I answered. By way of St Lucia.

Was it her voice or her complexion? I recognized something.

St Lucia, she answered. The volcanoes. Soufrière.

You are acquainted, Madame?

I was born in Santo Domingo. My father owned a sugar enterprise.

And your mother?

What made me so bold? Something darkened her face. And it wasn't a blush.

Ah. So you can tell. Or you wouldn't have asked that question. So let it be our secret, Tony Small.

I know no secret, Madame.

I fear you do. By sugar enterprise, I meant plantation. My mother worked in one. He made so bold as to marry her.

His —

Yes, say the word. His property. His slave. She was beautiful, but quadroon. Which makes me quarteronne. Or sang-mêlé. Or simply Creole. Take your pick. Are you good with secrets, Tony Small?

I do my best with them, Madame.

So, do your best with this one. And I would have more coffee, if you please.

I made my way through the many halls to the kitchen and replenished her cup. I had to wonder. Her face was as pale as any of the bewigged servants that passed me. As any of the portraits that hung on the walls. When I made my way back out, she gestured to the seat beside her.

Sit with me Tony.

And so I sat.

What is it with secrets? She asked.

A trick of memory, I said. Keeps them sleeping.

They can sleep, but they'll someday wake. My father lost his enterprise. His sugar. His fields. His plantation learned the lessons of the French, you see. Revolted. Long after we had left. But I can still smell the frangipani and hear the buzzing round my cot at night. Another net of wings. It frightened me then, but I miss it now. Do you miss your Carolina?

There was little for me to miss there, I told her. Apart from the smell of tobacco.

So you won't mind if I smoke?

She took a thin cigarillo from her handbag and a tinder box.

Do you believe it will take? Their revolution?

In Santo Domingo?

I thought of Sally and Rupez Roche. I had to hope it would.

No, she answered. Closer to home. In Ireland.

What do you know, I asked her, of their revolution in Ireland?

The reason they are here, surely. My cousin Pamela can't love her supposed mother that much. Although she will need all the support she can get, in her condition.

I pretended I knew. And I remembered my lessons in Irish, from old Mr Sheil.

Tá sí ag iompair arís, I thought. And I must have said it out loud, because she then asked –

It that Carolina patois?

No, I told her. It's Gaelic. For my Lady's condition.

Gaelic, she said. Maybe we should all speak in Gaelic. Or in Creole. It would save us the trouble of being understood.

And although we spoke neither, our conversations continued, as the wedding preparations, like Lady Pamela, grew.

And she knew well, too well, the trouble of being understood. What was said was like a tap that dripped, into the great well of what was unsaid. And what was unsaid was to do with that forest of masts in the river beyond. My Citizen's companions were in need of ships, but not these ones, as it turned out. These ones merely set the scene.

Like the de Loutherbourg backdrops I would see later in Drury Lane, in a play of revolution and betrayal, they were wrapped around by the Baltic mists and they wrapped around him, in his three-cornered hat, his greatcoat and his military boots.

My Citizen asked me to walk with him amongst them, as they tinkled in the evening light. Rigging against masts. He liked the sound.

They call Hamburg the Venice of the North. Though you have never been to Venice, dear Tony.

I agreed, I hadn't. There were so many places I hadn't been. So many things I didn't know.

To know nothing is the sweetest life, he told me, as old Erasmus said.

I didn't know this Erasmus. But I liked the sentiment.

The wedding came and went. And his meetings were always at night, amongst that wilderness of masts.

The talk was of ships, my new Creole friend told me. What numbers and munitions could fit upon them, when they could embark and disembark. Her husband would finance them.

Admiral de Hoche and Bonaparte would provide them. I should keep this knowledge between us. And I would do well to look, in my Lord's absence, after his Lady's protection.

He vanished then, somewhere south. So I walked with Lady Pamela, along the moonlit quays of Hamburg as I had once walked with Elizabeth along the wharves of Southampton.

Shadows often followed us, like ghosts. Footsteps echoed, with the tinkle of the rigging.

I carried a sword stick now, as Henriette had advised, in case steel was needed. And a lady's pistol, in case lead.

I keep myself in ignorance of all of his affairs, Pamela said. I hope you do too?

I assured her that I worked hard at it.

So, if questioned – and she paused – the footsteps following us paused too – I can swear on oath that I know nothing.

To know nothing is the sweetest life, I agreed with her. Those footsteps behind, that kettledrum of masts above them were all saying too much.

I brought her an omelette in the morning. She thanked me for it but ate little.

Small Julie scoffed whatever remained.

Where will she have the infant? She wondered, Hamburg or Kildare?

That depends, I told her, on whether the French are on the main or not.

As it happened, they were not. At least, not yet.

I wheeled her mistress Pamela along the quays to the music of that rigging. In a wheelchair, now that she found walking such a chore. There were footsteps following, along the wet cobbles, in and out of the mist.

Ignore them, Tony, she said.

But I recognized the step. I turned and saw him against the panoply of masts.

May I wheel my wife a little way? Dear Tony?

A baggage cart trundled up behind him.

Give them what help you can?

And as he walked her into the harbour mists, I gave them what help I could. There were bayonets, jutting from the canvas wrapping. I helped them unload, onto a waiting skiff. I realized ignorance would be hard to maintain.

So, the French were coming, Julie told me. She had access to the secret denied me. She had her own informant. The empty chimney, after a late-night dinner down below. So much for secrets. Echoing talk, in a language I didn't understand. She could be more specific, she told me, if I allowed her underneath the covers with me. I shook my head. There was only so much I wanted to know. I didn't yet want to learn her French. And I still missed Sally. I was already missing Molly.

I listened at the same chimney two nights later. What is the word. Eavesdropped. The language was again French. But the cries were in a tongue anyone could understand. Lady Pamela was giving birth.

A girl, my Citizen told me the next morning, walking in the garden of that house above the Elbe. I could hear the tiny cries from the room inside. All I could think of was Elizabeth and Mary.

Should we count our blessings, Tony? He asked.

We should, I thought. We should head to that Elsewhere, if it ever existed.

Or back to that forest in Eutaw.

But we would return to London, when her Ladyship was able.

I brought her cousin Henriette coffee, on the terrace. And as I lit her thin cigar, she whispered, secre mwen an secrete avec ou. Creole, she said.

And I understood. The sense, if not the words.

Her secret would be safe with me.

The Silence

I have to leave you for a while, he said.

Why, why do you have to leave me?

Because, he said, some business takes me elsewhere.

Can I not come elsewhere too?

I wish you could. And maybe you can someday. But not today.

It would have broken anybody's heart. Or perhaps only mine. Even more so, because the words were not addressed to me.

To little Eddy, on the lawns of Goodwood House.

The Duchess stood by the great open doors, waiting. She had moved there, with Ogilvie, for the season.

Can I say my goodbyes, my Lord? Or are you leaving me too?

No, take him to her Tony. But the carriage is waiting. Make it brief.

So I took little Eddy's hand, then lifted him and walked him in my arms towards the house.

Where is elsewhere, Tony?

I've spent a lifetime wondering the same, little Eddy. And all I can tell you is, it's not here.

They were good at leaving children, I was coming to realize. Little Mary in Wandsworth. Little Eddy in Goodwood. And as I walked the boy over, I hoped I would not have to plant another elm.

It was odd, to see someone vanish in plain sight. Maybe it was a trick of the light. But my Lieutenant, my Citizen, my Lord, seemed to vanish, by the carriage door, beyond the lawns.

I have lost him, Tony, the Duchess said.

Do you ever really lose a child, Ma'am? I asked.

The boy's cheek was soft against my own. Soft with tears.

I think you know, dear Tony, she answered. One can.

Perhaps I do, Ma'am.

I asked you to guide him in some matters. An impossible task.

Maybe, Ma'am.

So I have lost one Edward. And gained another.

She was wise, that lady. She knew what the transaction was. Maybe more than her son did. And little Eddy left my arms and ran to her embrace. I had made my goodbyes, so there was no point in dallying. I passed out into the forecourt. I took the reins and whipped the horse towards the London road. I wondered what the silence was like, in the carriage behind me.

It persisted, on the packet back to Dublin, the journey to Kildare. Back to Leinster House. To Frescati, which the banker had left empty again. He spoke to the plants. The flowers that he planted. If he spoke to anyone, he didn't speak to me.

And maybe it was the need for talk that drew me into the web of the Sham Squire. Old Shambolo.

The Beggar's Opera

The theatre, as usual, was to blame. And, I was missing Molly. Or maybe it was that silence. From Frescati to Leinster House, where his brother would barely speak to him. The Duke had little time for citizens. So rather than endure that cloak of what Julie called froideur I headed down to Crow Street, and the backstage door.

There was a threesome now, readying the costumes. Molly, Mary Kate and Lizzie Poole, who was stitching her own. She was to play Polly Peachum, in *The Beggar's Opera*. So I could finally get to know the end.

No riots tonight, then? I asked Molly.

Not tonight, Molly answered. Play to the finish. Dasher Daly and the Squire will see to that.

It was the first I had heard of this squire.

He is playing Macheath?

Who? Old Shambolo? Who wants to hear him sing?

Dasher Daly, then? I asked. The duellist?

No, she said. Some lad from across the water. Bowden. These are his breeches.

And she held up a garment.

Beggars and thieves. But even beggars and thieves can wear satin.

So I got to see Macheath again, with his five pregnant love-lies. I got to hear him sing 'How Happy I Could be with Either'. And I got to know the end, which, as Molly had promised, insisted on being happy as well. A positive fountain of happiness. I wondered could happiness ever be that infectious. Or could it be lathered onto a ramshackle play, like the soap in a morning shave. And I got to repair to the pushing house in Crane Lane, where the Sham Squire held court.

Lizzie was doing double duty as a player and a prissey and all Molly wanted to do was play billiards and drink.

So we did both, in the gloomy basement, where the guttering candlelight provided me with a disguise, everyone being dark or red-faced down there anyway. Or too drunk to care.

She pointed out the Squire, who was bending over a hazard table. A magistrate's wig curled into dovetails round the ears, a face like a pomegranate that sweated beneath it, one large pugilist's hand throwing the dice, while the other played with Lizzie's bodice.

He was a justice of the peace, Molly told me. And a newspaper proprietor. And a jailbird. He knew the cells of Newgate well enough to keep them filled. He charged for entry there, and exit, and everything consumed inside.

To be avoided, Molly cautioned me, which proved impossible, since he caught her eye. He pushed through the crush to Molly's side and requested an introduction.

Lord Edward's savage, I have been told.

Enchanté, I said, in my best savage tone, and bowed. I don't know why I said it. Perhaps it was a better choice of word now than indeed.

Fluent in French, as well.

I have two French words, I told him. Enchanté and froideur. And forgive me, a third. Rien.

And what is a runaway slave doing in the environs of Leinster House?

I could ask a similar question.

Maybe it was the whiskey talking.

Which would be?

What is a justice of the peace doing in a pushing house?

Easily answered. I own it. And it's a pushing house by night, a staymakers by day. We make bodices in the light so they can be undone in the dark.

He brought his face close. I had to recoil from the odour of sweat.

Like your good Lord's friend, Tom Paine. I was a bodice maker once.

Indeed, I answered.

I could feel conspiracy approaching.

And he was a friend to your Lord?

And to me.

You keep interesting company, he said.

Kept, I added. We left Tom Paine in Paris.

We should converse, he said, in a less rowdy setting.

Perhaps the staymakers? In the daytime?

No, he said. The *Freeman's Journal*. In Clarendon Street. I could make it worth your while.

I had my own way in now. To conspiracy, if not to secrets. And I realized how lonely I had been. Exclusion was a cold condition.

I told my Citizen the story in the gardens of Frescati. He was planting snowdrops, in the clay around Mary's elm. And I had to wonder had he read the carved inscription.

No. It was covered by a tangle of grass.

But at least the mention of the Squire drew him out of his silence. Conspiracy, I was to find, warmed us both.

Higgins, he said. Squire Francis Higgins.

The Sham, they call him.

And what does this Sham want?

What everyone wants, it seems. Information.

He dropped a bulb in the grass. He pulled the earthy gloves from his fingers. He smiled, for the first time in a long time.

Let us humour him then. Perhaps the Sham is worth shamming, dear Tony?

And I was dear again. I was a confidant, again. I found the Sham repellent, but my Citizen gardener, with his instinct for noxious weeds, bade me keep in his good favour.

And as Molly would have put it, I gave it a go. Another round of billiards, after the playhouses closed. The Sham had half the cast amongst his harem now. Mrs Peachum, Polly herself, Lucy Lockit, Suky Tawdry, Molly Brazen, Betty Doxey all double jobbing as doxies, working well into the night. I was glad to see Molly kept herself clean. A whispered conversation beneath the sweaty stairwell, and another invite for a cup of afternoon coffee to the editorial premises of the *Freeman's Journal*.

But, he advised, don't come as yourself.

Whom should I come as? Man Friday?

No, he muttered. Do as the actors do. You've heard of blackface? Come in whiteface.

An intriguing concept. Tony Small, with his dusky countenance was deemed too conspicuous. So as the Sham suggested, Molly and myself went to work. On the empty stage
of the Theatre Royal, we created a sham Tony. Face and
neck and hands whitened with a mixture of beeswax and
theatrical whitening.

Molly concocted the recipe. We tried whitewash at first,
builders' lime and water, but it burnt my eyes and caused
sneezing fits. So I dipped my hands in a sack of fuller's earth
and Molly whooped her approval. A tincture of wax to
make the fuller's congeal, the resultant paste smeared over
my visible skin and behold –

Tony Small became Antaine 'Skinner' Beag from west of
the Shannon, late of the Carolinas.

It was as if the Skinner had been from Mayo after all. I had
renamed myself at last. I was white and unremarkable. I
sauntered down the Dublin streets, somewhat unsettled by
my sudden invisibility. I began to wonder. Did I miss all of
that rhyming invective? Black as an umbrella, that saunter-
ing fella. But it served its purpose. The anonymous Antaine
'Skinner' Beag could go where he wanted. With no rhyming
couplets in his wake, no street ballads to celebrate his itinerary.

Which was, to be specific, the editorial premises of the
Freeman's Journal in Clarendon Street. The outside all run
down, crumbling brick and cracked windows and the inside
stinking of lead alphabets and newsprint. Did Judas run a
newspaper, I wondered, and were those clattering printing
presses a gateway to the underworld?

The Sham at first didn't recognize me. Dismissed me as just
another guttersnipe. And when I reminded the good squire
of our conversations, and of the savage nature underneath

this fuller's earth, he went overboard in his embraces, his sweaty pomegranate of a face threatening to wipe me clean.

Easy, I cautioned.

Genius, he said. We can do some business together. And what do I call you?

Antaine 'Skinner' Beag.

Gaelic, he chortled. As spoken in Shamrógshire. And here's to excellent pseudonymous endeavours.

He poured me a whiskey. And when I expressed a preference for coffee, I was told to take a running jump. I was an Irishman now. A savage no more.

Eringobragh.

So I swallowed my whiskey as the squire gulped his own, his rheumy cheeks crushing themselves with the bite of it, more like a lemon now than a pomegranate, paroxysms of coughing taking him over. He lit a cigar to stifle the cough and turned to the leaded window, as if to throw away his apparently anodyne suggestion.

That some of those in the Lord's household should be worried about the company he keeps.

Antaine agreed.

Indeed they were. Eringobraghers and the titled of Leinster made an unhappy mix.

Let's call them what they are, the Sham almost spat. United Irelanders. Croppies. Traitors to the realm.

Perhaps they merely love their country?

As we all do. The question is, how?

The squire finished one glass and poured himself another.

His brother the Duke shares your concern?

I wondered how much to tell him. Then remembered the silence.

So Antaine told the Squire about froideur. How the Duke and the Citizen rarely speak, of late.

But the Duke has spoken. To his friends in Dublin Castle. The Lord Lieutenant is most anxious to confine your Lord's ambitions to the House of Parliament, where they rightly belong.

Another 'indeed' from me. Or Antaine. It suited the white countenance.

Lord Camden, the Squire continued, the Lord Lieutenant, would appreciate any information that would help sunder your master from his more hot-headed companions.

The Eringobraghers?

Again, let's call them what they are. United Irelanders. Croppies. The Belfast Brigade.

Traitors to the realm, I added. Helpfully, I could only hope.

Indeed.

And the word was the Squire's, now.

Let us weed them out.

Then I knew an offer of money was forthcoming.

They would pay. Generously.

So it came.

Lord Camden?

The very same.

But the savage in Antaine smelt a rat. Or a commission. How much would Shambolo take from the Lord Lieutenant's purse?

So I tested the waters.

Would the payment be from the Lord Lieutenant to myself? I asked.

Good God no. He could never be associated with such a procedure. I would act as intermediary.

So, the answer was, a lot. But still, they came to an agreement. Between Antaine 'Skinner' Beag and Squire Francis Higgins, for certain transactions of a patriotic nature. I was given a down payment of seven guineas, the said sum to be revisited at weekly intervals. I repaired then to Crow Street where darling Molly washed off my whiteface and refused to take a penny for her service.

So I gave her a guinea instead.

Are you an agent of the Crown now, Tony? She asked.

A double agent. Antaine 'Skinner' Beag. In the service of my Citizen gardener.

I headed out to Frescati to share the news and found not one, but three gardeners there. My Citizen Lord, the Belfast giant, Samuel Neilson and his barrister, McNally. But the garden they were cultivating did not yet exist. United Irishmen, all. Their garden, Samuel Neilson informed me, in that voice that seemed to emerge from a barrel of oak, was infested with weeds from across the water, with an organizational design that favoured the few English roses and left the native grasses criminally untilled.

I told them I had been offered a species of garden duty myself. By the Sham Squire, Francis Higgins.

McNally was fascinated. Less by the proposal, than by the use to which it could be put.

I repeated the Squire's phrase.

Let us weed them out.

He began to devise a plot. A black comedy, he called it. That could have been written by Shambolo.

Or written by McNally himself and played by the great Shambolo.

And my Ned begged to differ. Written by, if anyone, his own dear Tony. Or, as his pseudonym now goes, Antaine 'Skinner' Beag.

The silence had broken. I felt the warm flush of companionship, again. I joined them in the spadework, around the

Scot's rose garden. And as the sun went down, we had the beginnings of a plan. And I realized how devilishly complicated this business of betrayal could become.

I was to feed Higgins fantasies, of training meets and movement plans. Tall tales of revolution and rebellion, oaths sworn by burning hayricks, transports of pike and muskets, dates decided and abandoned.

And to make sure I received payment for the same.

And so began my career as Antaine Beag. The money earned bought tobacco, porter, down payments on meeting halls and printed broadsheets. Seditious, all of them, facilitated by the keg-shaped printer, Phelim 'Gargle' McCann, who alone amongst the staff of the Sham Squire's *Freeman's Journal*, seemed to know what game was afoot, and more, became a willing accomplice.

Antaine out shammed the Sham by day and learned the mysteries of print by night. He proposed meetings in the demesne of Lord Malahide, by the graves of Diarmuid and Gráinne, by the Lia Fáil on the Hill of Tara.

He sent the yeomanry in the worst of weathers across mountainous waves to Dalkey island and Ireland's Eye. Mayo figured large in the croppy plans. He sent them tramping across bogs unknown to himself or anyone, keeping watch for imaginary ships on the Atlantic horizon. The paltry results of their efforts made them doubt the very existence of subversion and plot, so he proceeded to lay the bait more carefully. He got Molly to deposit handfuls of the printed broadsheets and tattered copies of the *Rights of Man* in the pushing shop in Crane Lane at night. So the staymaker's shop was raided in the daytime, and copies of the bodice maker's pamphlet were found enhancing the bosoms of the milliner's mannequins.

That the shop's owner, the Sham, found himself borne off to Newgate for a night of enquiry only strengthened the claims of Antaine 'Skinner' Beag. Sedition was everywhere.

Was the Sham himself aware of being shammed? Never. Antaine came to realize that self-love is like no other love. Nothing could puncture its illusions. That sweating face could love no other. If anything, the shadow of what he called 'eringobraghism' falling on him merely helped his cause. It helped to quell the rumours that swirled around him, that he was spymaster to the viceregal apartments. That he had now served his time, done his duty, held his hand to the flame, unlike what he called those counter-jumpers, those late arrivistes, those pretenders to the legacy of the Great O'Neill.

But that was all before the ballad of the poor old lady.

Who had written it? The printer Phelim 'Gargle' McCann had no idea. Who first called him Gargle? Ballads were like nicknames. They were written by the wind.

The Shan Van Vocht

My true rival, if the Scot had only known.

I held the print block in my hand. I could see the outlines of her greying hair, above the serried letters of her ballad below.

I walked from Leinster House to Clarendon Street at night, with the block tucked in the vest of my Leinster livery. No need for whiteface now, as the shadows consumed me.

Three knocks on the leaded window of the *Freeman's Journal* and Antaine 'Skinner' Beag was admitted by Phelim 'Gargle' McCann.

She was an old lady, Gargle informed me, as he brushed the block with printer's ink, older than that patchwork of idealized fields that surrounded her. And those fields spread like the quilt of her skirts, all the way to the coast of Mayo, to the wilds of Cork, to Antrim's Giant's Causeway. We were all of us, Irishmen and women, her children.

I wasn't sure that I liked this ancient, by whom, I was assured, all of the United Irishmen swore their oath.

But she hadn't always been old, the printer said, just as I haven't always been shaped like a barrel of porter.

He pulled the metal lever of the press and she fluttered in piles to the floor. She was once as young and fragrant as the Lord's Pamela, her back straight and tall, her hair with its own golden sheen, and could be young again. And she was waiting for the arrival of the French to revive her.

I liked her ballad even less. Which McCann insisted on humming as the stack of broadsides grew.

> Oh the French are on the bay
> They'll be here without delay
> And the orange will decay
> says the Shan Van Vocht

I walked to The Yellow Lion in Thomas Street. I left one stack of broadsheets with the publican, Moore. Who told me to scatter the rest like seeds of hope around the Liberties. I walked back, close to dawn. I remembered the docks in Hamburg. A French fleet, in the service of the same old lady.

She seemed to stare back at me, her engraved gouges of flowing hair and her ancient face.

> On the Curragh of Kildare
> The boys they will be there
> With their pikes in good repair
> Says the Shan Van Vocht

The French arrived around her tattered hem in late December, had their boats dashed against her heels and wandered around her sodden skirts for a day or two. They were back home by January.

So, whatever else she did, the old lady managed to ruin my Citizen's Christmas.

We huddled in Kildare where there were no pikes in good repair, as she had promised. There were no balls in Castletown or Carton House, either. Or if there were, we weren't invited. Lady Pamela fretted at the absence of society. But the society that her husband kept now didn't dance the cotillion. It danced jigs and reels to old Sheil's fiddle. It assembled in barns and marched around moonlit hayricks. It had its secret oaths and passwords and its business eventually drew us back to Dublin.

Frescati was out of bounds. His brother the Duke had abandoned Leinster House. That left its maze of ghostly, half-finished corridors to us. An endless stretch of rooms, keening with the late winter winds, so that even I couldn't find my Citizen some days, and if the yeomen questioned me about his whereabouts, I could honestly claim to know nothing of them.

Lady Pamela perfected her English with learning her ballads, but they had none of the spit and wit of the 'Kilmainham Minnit'. The Old Lady promised a lot but delivered little. And her rhymes were no match for Luke Caffrey's. Or Larry's. Even Antaine 'Skinner' Beag found them wanting.

> *What will the yeomen do*
> *but throw off the red and blue*
> *And swear that they'll be true*
> *Says the Shan Van Vocht*

She was better at promises than Antaine, and like him, had perfected the art of disappointment. And she never got paid.

But my Citizen came and went at her service, Samuel Neilson, his aide-de-camp. As commander in chief of the United Irishmen, my Citizen needed a uniform. A jacket, a cape, britches of gold and a cap of liberty like a French boat itself, with a dangling tassel.

> *What colours shall be seen*
> *Where their father's homes have been*
> *but their own immortal green*
> *says the Shan Van Vocht*

So I brought the sketch and measurements to quite another lady for stitching. Darling Molly, back of the Crow Street theatre, who gave a giggle when she saw it.

> *And will Ireland be free?*
> *Yes Ireland shall be free*
> *From the centre to the sea*

Says who? She asked.

Says the Shan Van Vocht, I told her.

I'll squeeze it in, she said, between *The Recruiting Officer* and *The Deuce Is in Him*. But I suppose a fitting is out of the question?

It was. He would emerge from the windswept corridors, like a ghost, slip out of the stables into the adjoining fields, and tread his way down to the river, on foot.

So is it any wonder I couldn't warm to her? The old lady, never Molly. This succubus that could have come from the mists around the volcano above Morne Fortune, this rain-wrapped old skeleton with her tales of fadó fadó which means, if I'm to remember my lessons from old Sheil, long ago long ago. She had many graveyards, but none of them in sweet Bully's Acre. And all of her acolytes ended up the same in the end. Pushing barley or dancing the Kilmain-ham Minnit.

But my Citizen was now her servant, and I was his. And, because of that, hers. There were meetings to be scurried to in cottages in the Liberties, passwords whispered: where's McCann? Is Ivers from Carlow come?

Ivers from Carlow was never there, but who did get wind of the password was the bold Major Swann. Who turned up at a meeting of the brotherhood's in Oliver Bond's. Who sent the sheriff round to Leinster House with a party of yeomen. I bundled my Lord – he was my Lord again, the 'citizen' was gone in the panic – down the corridors, across the stable-yard and led him towards the river.

Reynolds, he said, wondering who betrayed him.

Maybe. Or Magan.

Any one of them, he said. Not you, Tony, never you.

Not me. Antaine Beag had made enough shillings.

Higgins, I thought. Was maybe no sham after all.

Neilson met us by the Ha'penny Bridge, told me my Citizen Lord would be safe in any one of a dozen houses and led him off to the Liberties.

And the silence began again. He was a runaway, as I had once been. His forests and swamps weren't the bayous of Carolina, they were the Liberties, the Coombe, the barges on the muddy banks around Usher's Island, and whoever was lucky enough to track him down was promised a reward of more than a pair of muddy boots. Molly showed me the printed sheet nailed to the door of Dasher Daly's coffee house. One thousand pounds for information leading to the capture of Lord Edward Fitzgerald, formerly Lieutenant of the 54th Regiment of Foot.

Betrayal. It made its own forest. Its own tangle of brambles, its own swamp. We moved from Leinster House to Usher's Island, by the river. Every time the window shook, we thought it might be him. I'd pull back the drapes, to see only the poplar tree outside, the watchmen beyond it by the river.

And while my Citizen couldn't be found, the Sham Squire couldn't be avoided. He cornered me in Stephen's Green, kissed my unpasted cheek and dragged me through a crawl of taverns and ended up in his own pushing place in Crane Lane. Lord Edward, the Sham surmised, was engineering his own capture and his subsequent escape to preserve Ireland from the clutches of the Lord Lieutenant and the viceregal lodge with the help of the Prince Regent who alone know the secret wishes of the mad King. Which was for the restoration of an Irish kinship under the Geraldines and their absent son, King Edward of Erin. The only question being, where could he be found?

I could only admire these elaborations of conspiracy and betrayal, but had to admit, with much regret, that even I didn't know.

Perhaps you have heard, then, of the servants' plot?

I hadn't but was all ears.

Surely you of all people, would have gotten wind of it?

It must have passed me by.

That on a certain night a password would be whispered and the combined servants of every great Dublin house would murder their masters in their beds?

An excellent plan, I thought.

It is a great weakness, I agreed with him, to have your breakfast served by those who hate your guts. To be given your morning shave by the one who could cut your throat.

Strange that Tony Small has been kept in the dark? Given that his master is the duke of these designs?

Strange indeed, I agreed.

But I would happily murder others, I thought. Including yourself.

If there was a password, I told him, I would surely get wind of it. If it could be shared.

Doonvara, he muttered. I have been told. By various informants of mine. I have no way of knowing what it means.

Murder, I told him. In Gaelic. As spoken in Shamrógshire.

Ah. The wickedness of it! The devilish affrontery. To use the very word at issue. In the full knowledge their betters would never understand.

They could always take lessons, I told him. As could you yourself.

Do you think it would help?

Immeasurably. To live in an ocean of incomprehension is not only terrifying. Dangerous, too.

He drank and gave it some thought.

The reward, he muttered. Will draw him out. Lance the boil. Surely.

But the only one it drew out was the Scot, who came visiting from London.

His hair almost gone now. One dark curl, like a duck's tail, attempting to disguise the fact.

One thousand pounds, Tony.

So I have heard, sir.

His voice was sadder, older, full of loss. I wondered had I always misjudged him.

Would that not tempt you?

No, sir, it would not.

But it would surely tempt some of his associates.

I have no doubt it would, sir.

There is honour amongst them, I am sure. But dishonour, too.

I had no doubt there was. When he disclosed another offer. What he called a discreet one, from the First Secretary, Castlereagh. Lord Edward could leave the country, for America, in secret, with the King's agreement. Otherwise, kick his heels in Newgate or Kilmainham. Before the hanging and the quartering. And unlike his forbear, Silken Thomas, he wouldn't be spared the drawing.

If only he could be found.

Perhaps he will listen to his Tony?

Could I trust him? I wasn't sure. His lessons in natural man and horticulture always left me uneasy. But then, could I trust anyone, now?

It was the letter that did it. He drew it from his worsted Norwich jacket and spread it on the scullery table.

Like my certificate of service to the British Crown, but with wax seals and imprints, a small garden of signatures and the promise of safe delivery back to the America we had come from.

If I didn't trust the Scot, I thought, I had to trust that.

So I took old Ogilvie down towards Blind Quay and began an elaborate wander through a city foreign to him – one he never would have had cause to encounter. Past the Elephant and up Fishamble Street and took in old Shambolo's pushing shop along the way. Then back behind the Castle, Skinner's Row, Dirty Lane and along Cork Hill, all to make sure there was no one else behind. And when I was convinced it was just the two of us, I led him up to the canal and guided him across the broken barges to Portobello. All we learned there was that our quarry had moved on.

Back to the Liffey then, through the tangle of the Liberties and Thomas Street. And we found him there in an upstairs room, in what they called a huddle.

There was a lamp burning. It made a silhouette of my lost Citizen at the door. Above the narrow staircase.

He came down and kissed me. Made me promise we were alone.

I can swear to it.

He looked paler than he had ever been. Thin, like that wounded lieutenant. If I could find a salmon-leap, I thought, or a burnt chicken-coop, maybe I could feed him.

Then you should listen to your tutor.

And he took Ogilvie upstairs while I sat, amongst the piles of broadsheets, scattered on the floor. Somebody, besides Shambolo, had a printing press.

I could hear the voices in a subdued storm above me and had little to do below. So I picked up a sheet, to see how much my reading had progressed.

To all United friends. Half a million heroes await the second coming of the French to commence the millennium of Freedom.

The first coming hadn't worked too well, I thought. Then I saw another crumpled sheet below. I picked it up, uncrumpled it and saw her face again. I had been there at its printing.

> *Yes Ireland shall be free*
> *From the centre to the sea*
> *And hurrah for Liberty*
> *Says the Shan Van Vocht*

The storm of voices, from above. The sound of a chair overturned.

Do you believe it, Tony?

My Citizen Lord was at the sagging half door, above the staircase. A guttering candle, in a saucer, lighting his ghost of a face.

He meant the broadsheet. The old lady's promise.

I would believe anything, my Lord.

Though truly, I felt her rhyme could have done with more swagger.

Call me Ned.

Back to our refrain, since the stables in Charleston. Like the rhymes of street children.

Of course, my Lord, my Lieutenant, I can call you Ned.

And then there were footsteps above, as the door swung back again.

Try to remind him of his better self.

This from the Scot, who pushed his way past his stepson.

He descended the stairs and stood amongst the same mess of pamphlets, brushing back what remained of his hair.

We all of us placed such trust in you.

You did, sir.

His noble savage.

I was that once, I agreed.

But, no longer, I thought to myself.

He pulled the letter once more from his pocket and handed it over.

Make him see reason.

But reason, I now knew, had nothing to do with it.

The front door banged, as he made his way back out into the Liberties night.

How will he find his way home? I wondered.

And I must have said it out loud. Because my Ned smiled, at last.

How will any of us find our way home?

Abhaile, I said. Or was it Antaine Beag? I had learnt that word in the gloaming. The muddy fields of Kildare.

Home. Maybe that was what was needed. The appeal. The refrain.

There is a boat waiting, I told him, that could take us to Liverpool.

And from there?

I handed over the letter of freedom. Another promise, from the mad King.

The great passage, I told him. Home. That my mother once made, in chains. But we could walk the decks together. We could see the albatross once more. You could play the mandolin. Sing 'Lilliburlero' in your hammock. On our journey to America. We could paddle down the Mississippi, hunt and trap like Skinner Mayo in the bayou. We could listen to the rain dripping in the Eutaw forest.

You're dreaming, dear Tony.

I am. But you taught me to dream.

America was your prison.

Until I met you.

And I tried to remind him. Of those three good days in the forest with the jays and the woodpeckers chattering and the Cherokee children pulling salmon from the river. How the morning sun through the umbrella of trees did that strange thing and turned prison into paradise.

And England was my prison. Until I met you.

But it was perfect once. There was a church spire peeking through the trees and the purr of a turtle dove and a pheasant taking to the air from a silvery tuft and each blade of grass was touched with its own piece of frost. Even if I saw it from the carriage roof, among the cases.

I thought I could keep the tears at bay. But they were falling now, smudging the broadsheet print.

The tears were mine, and then his.

I thought of those boots I could have robbed, dancing the Kilmainham Minnit.

So I am to blame, my Lord?

For what?

For your undoing? For this?

I crumpled the broadsheet between my savage fingers.

He tore his own letter to pieces between his.

The King will not forgive, my Lord, however mad he is.

He's been cured of his madness Tony. For some time now. And his promises mean nothing.

So my letter of freedom meant nothing as well?

No one gave you your freedom, Tony dear. You took what was always yours. And it took me some time to learn it. But what a lesson you taught me.

So I was to blame. And she had won, that Shan Van Vocht.

It will start with the burning mail coaches. We will turn the city into their charnel house. Their regiments will be useless to them. Half of them are sworn to us.

And the other half?

Barricaded streets and hot lead from the rooftops. And when we next meet, this land will have its freedom papers. And until then look after my little ones. And say goodbye to your Ned.

Could I bring myself to say it? The goodbye, whatever about the Ned?

But I managed them both.

Goodbye. My Ned.

I left then, walked through the Liberties night where it smelt of tanning cowhide. Down by the Liffey, where it smelt of hops and barley.

Where I first learned my balladspeak.
And I wondered would this be the saddest verse.
Or the happiest? He was a soldier, after all.

Crow Street

Did I see him again? In a manner of speaking.

We were staying in that house on Usher's Island when I was given word that he wanted his commander's uniform. And, as the pamphlet told me, half a million heroes would commence the second millennium of freedom.

I made my way to the stage door of the theatre in Crow Street. Molly had had ample time to finish it, and I found her down amongst the flies busy with the costumes for the night ahead. Which would be Robin Hood, she told me. Robin Hood with singing.

She had my Ned's uniform stitched to perfection and neatly folded in a hiding place in that underground bit beneath the stage. Where the orchestra sits, two little panels removed and out it came. It was some garment, green jacket and a green cape with red and gold braids, much better than the Robin Hood tights and the huntsman's cap with the feather that would later entertain Dublin's finest.

I didn't bring him his uniform. Couldn't, since I didn't know where he was. The word was that Samuel Neilson would meet me in The Yellow Lion in Thomas Street but I knew better than to carry it there. So carried myself there, without it. And as I left the stage door and passed around the front, I saw the playbill, posted by the entrance.

Robin Hood, or *Sherwood*,
a comic opera by Leonard McNally.
As performed before the Prince of Wales
in the Theatre Royal, Drury Lane.

I thought, how odd. On this of all nights. Was this another version of the servants' plot? I didn't know whether it was genius or folly. McNally's rhymes entertain the masters in their theatre boxes while their servants join the half a million heroes on the streets. I wondered had Cecil seen it already, in his beloved Drury Lane. And if the mayhem that was promised pulled down this theatre with it, maybe Cecil, if I ever saw him again, could fill me in on the story. Did Robin Hood win his battle with the forces of the Crown? I made my way down to the Liberties where the streets were strangely empty. I thought again, how odd. Were these half a million heroes in hiding?

So into The Yellow Lion and its clouds of tobacco smoke. Every head turned and I did my best to ignore them. I found an empty table near the back.

Neilson had to bend his head coming in, he was even bigger than me and I had a good head on most of them Gaels. He gave me one of those brief Belfast nods and he bought us both some porter and eyed me as he smoked his pipe.

Tony Small, he said. Time to change that name of yours.

I haven't yet taken the oath.

Then tell me. Why aren't you with us?

Because, I told him, I might stand out a little.

Olaudah Equiano would have said, what does it matter?

What does what matter? I asked him.

If the hands wielding the pike are white or brown?

I never met this Olaudah, I said. And the Lord has a wife and two children that need looking after.

Fair enough then, he said and puffed for a bit.

But I had lied. Like all of those informers, I had lied. I wasn't with them because I feared the whole enterprise might be folly.

I had met a fool in that forest, in the bloodied uniform of a Lieutenant of the 19th Foot. I had given the job of this hero's uniform to Molly and her seamstress prisseys. I had carried the galleon-shaped hat from the hatter's in Newbridge and all I could think of sitting with Neilson in that hostelry was one question. How would the hat fit? He had moved so many times, from Oliver Bond's on Thomas Street to the place by the canal in Portobello with all of the other hideouts in between that I had never the time to try it on him for size.

I was with his Lady and the baby Pamela in that Usher's Island house and every knock outside drew her running down the stairs with all of that operatic expectation on her face. I rocked the child to sleep and couldn't help wondering if every clip of hoof outside was him, every creak of the leafless poplar tree outside the window, every time the windowpane rattled, was it him, was it him, like a ghost in one of old Shakespeare's stories. How can you fit a hat on a phantom? And the night before we had heard rumours of him moving hideout once again with his group of merry men and the story was, he was almost caught heading to Usher's Island in the environs of the Coombe. He was coming to see us, his darling wife and children and his faithful Tony, and almost lost his life in the attempt. That same Lieutenant Sirr, who we had last met by the Moorish Wall in Gibraltar, who had played Duke to his fool on the regimental stage was now Town Major to the city of Dublin. He was waiting in the shadows of the Barrack Street Bridge. There was a call out and a scuffle and one of the United men died or was taken away to sing like another blackbird while my Ned made his escape into the Liberties, where the streets wound round themselves like threads of an old woman's hair and none of them had any name. He lodged well with a feather merchant that night, I was later told, and slept on a bed of goose down.

And now all I could think of was his galleon-shaped hat and the feathered cap of Robin Hood, in The Yellow Lion. Where I sipped my porter and nodded back at Neilson and he said, after a thoughtful number of puffs, the business is about to start, and your Lord has requested his regalia.

Tell me where he is, I answered, and I'll gladly bring him his duds.

Don't call them duds, he riposted, a uniform.

His uniform, I corrected myself. Which I'll gladly carry to him.

Do you think I was born yesterday? He asked and I riposted, why should I trust you any more than you trust me?

Because, he said, I know where he is, and you don't.

And he had me there. But he was as faithful as myself, I knew that, behind the porter and the bluster. He would have died for him readily, then.

So, he said, tell me where it is and I can guarantee he wears it.

I walked him out then, past Christ Church and down Dame Street. I pulled the cloak around me as we passed the castle, where the portcullis was down and the triangle was visible through it, red with yesterday's blood.

I was invited inside there, Neilson said, too often. Never want that invite again.

So you have a plan? I asked him.

We have a plan, he said, that will start with the mail coaches and will end with the whole country up in arms and the citadel of freedom set up inside those castle gates. We have a leader, hidden well. And you said you had a uniform.

Yes, I said. Just follow me. And I crossed the broad street where the first mail coach was raising up the dust, down the side street to the theatre and the tradesmen's entrance.

I had my own key. I opened the bent wooden door and led us both inside.

I heard my boots echoing around the empty stalls. I had always loved theatres since my first sight of Old Prospero in Drury Lane. Even the days when they were empty, since I was free to wander through the stalls and climb onto the boards and raise the dust on them myself, as if I was one of the players. So I led him down through the wooden seats and ascended the stage and saw Molly and Mary Kate stitching away amongst the flies.

The big night tonight, one of them said – Molly or Mary Kate.

And I said yes, I hope they all break a leg which was the theatre argot I was proud like them to use.

But there's another big night coming, Molly said with that knowing smile.

A big day, I said, and bigger, greater days to follow.

You've brought another giant, Mary Kate added.

Yes, I said, this is my Lord's friend and mine, who will remain nameless.

She shook her head and smiled up at Neilson.

But I'd recognize this one anywhere.

Just keep your mouth shut then, I said, we've come for the costume for a performance the like of which this place has never seen.

Haha.

And if anyone asks, you saw nothing.

I'm blind with stitching anyways she says, and I stepped down to the orchestra pit and opened the small door of my hidey hole and saw the small curved cellar of bricks with the mound of hemp sackcloth. I took the costume out then, the braided suit and the green cape and cap of liberty shaped like the boat that took us from old Charleston. And Neilson had to put it on, the cape swinging round his shoulder and the cap too small for the size of his head.

French, he said as he strutted round the empty boards in his porterhouse boots.

Yes, where are the French? Asked Mary Kate. We heard they were coming.

They were. Till they blew away home, Molly muttered, her lovely mouth full of needles.

Who needs the French, replied Neilson, whereupon I told him he was tempting fate with his strutting, it was high time to get out of there and I began wrapping my Ned's uniform in the old hemp and took the cape and wrapped it too and last of all took that ridiculous hat which seemed to have been designed to catch a cannonball or at the very least a bullet and gave it a hemp sack all to itself.

Goodbye now, I said to Neilson, and give my Lord my blessing.

If you follow me, he said, I'll have to cut your throat.

Then I won't follow, I said. But there were tears in my eyes. I had a feeling, you see. That the last memory of my Ned would be of his liberty hat on another one's head on that empty stage. And it was as if the whole journey had been a dream, an unreal play written by another, maybe that Shakespeare himself and I had met nothing but his fool in that forest so long ago.

Neilson walked back down the stalls, his arms full of wrapped around canvas as if it was any other bundle. Then I heard the stage door slam, and he was gone.

I walked outside, leaving a decent interval, so I wouldn't get my throat cut. And I was reading the playbill again when I heard a tapping behind me. I could see McNally's reflection in the glass.

Have you come, I asked him, to check is your name spelt right?

No, he said. To leave some tickets with the front of house.

You're going to miss your own performance?

Seen it too many times, he said. And besides, as you might be aware, I shall be busy elsewhere.

He reached into his pocket then and took an envelope out between his two good fingers.

Here. For you.

What is it?

A ticket for tonight. The best of seats.

I took it. Opened it. An embossed card, for a performance at seven.

I've been told that you're quite the thingamabob.

What thingamabob?

The stage Johnny.

So that's what I was, I remember thinking, as he tapped his way to the backstage door.

And I walked back then, towards the river and sat outside the house on Usher's Island and watched the weeds snaking under the brown water.

The Performance

It would begin with the burning mail coaches, my Citizen told me. And end with the citadel of freedom set up inside the Castle gates. And I had a ticket for the playhouse for once. No more rapping at the stage door or hiding in the flies. So I took my time dressing that night while Julie attended to the lady and her child.

I had best be well appointed, for the curtain call or the advent of freedom, whichever happened first. But there was the problem of choice. Mine was limited, to those well-worn Leinster duds, a greatcoat and some collarless shirts. There were of course the oriental pantaloons and orange jacket designed by Lady Emily herself, but I was hoping to be in the audience, not on the stage.

And then I saw the case of his own clothes, which I had dragged all the way from Leinster House. I thought, he wouldn't mind me wearing his. On this night of all nights. I opened the clasps and the smell of those moth balls I had spread around the garments filled the room. I lifted a shirt of Holland linen to my nostrils, and the smell of camphor was overwhelmed by one of starch, and another, which was faintly, but unmistakably his. A sleeved waistcoat, then, lined with fustian and silk. A velvet dress coat, of a deep Prussian blue.

They were a tight fit, but I took a deep breath and managed the buttons. I could walk, I imagined, without the seams splitting, and as I turned to the mirror to judge the spectacle, I wondered was he himself trying on his commander's uniform in the feather merchant's, the green cape with the red and gold braids and the liberty hat, which I hoped wasn't as tight a fit as this waistcoat of fustian and silk.

I had dressed him and now he was dressing me.

And when the sun was setting, I treaded my way back past the Castle and reached it in time to see the portcullis pulled up and the Lord Lieutenant's coach pull out. I could see old Camden, the Lord Lieutenant himself, inside with his two ladies, Camden and Castlereagh, dressed for the evening.

I followed the coach, saw it turn left at Crow Street and saw it stop outside the Theatre Royal entrance.

So they were bound for the same play.

It was a great palaver for so short a journey, I thought, as I watched Camden's boots hit the pavement and after them the elegant heels of Lady Camden and Lady Castlereagh, followed by the Sergeant at Arms.

But these were dangerous days. In earlier times I would have guided my own Lord's coach to join them. And all I could think of now was should I kill them all with my bare hands in their theatre box. While the orchestra struck up the overture, as the curtains pulled back, with all eyes on the stage. I had a murderous vision, of bloodied epaulettes and eyeballs and bejewelled, broken necks. I could have brought all of Shambolo's fears to light. Doonvara indeed.

But I stilled those treasonous thoughts and was about to walk round to the stage door when I remembered my ticket. Of course. There would be no backstage knocking tonight. So I made my way with the best of them through the main entrance, endured the stares of the Dublin swells as seat after seat rose in the parterre. I belonged in the gods or the groundlings, those basilisk eyes told me. But I chose not to care. I folded his dress coat over my Leinster britches and waited for the overture to begin.

It was a poor play indeed. Sheridan would have done better. But the real show, as I heard later, took place elsewhere.

Neilson had been followed.

Followed by whom would be the question. But as McNally was my witness, it wasn't by me. He made it to the Liberties, to the feather merchant Murphy's where he delivered his costume and my Lord Citizen no doubt tried it on and was happy that it fitted. And around the time of the first interval as I was watching the curtain come down, the feather merchant's door was opened by a Major Swann.

Was he in uniform, or in disguise, did he use the password, is Ivers from Carlow come? No one told me, but Swann made his entrance, and made it up the stairs, where he confronted my Lord Citizen and however I picture what happened next, all I can see is the green cape swirling as my own Ned turns to face him. Major Swann fires his pistol, no doubt at that liberty hat, missing its target and hitting the pillows of goose down and my Ned draws his blade to protect himself and stabs Swann so many times that his guts are hanging as another called Ryan makes his entrance, to be gutted in turn.

And he falls backwards through the door, crying murder, and tumbles down the stairs while my Ned stabs him all the time.

Then Major Sirr, who had set the trap, joins the action from outside and sets upon the melancholy Jacques he had last met in the fake forest of Arden on the regimental stage in Gibraltar.

He shoots him twice, on the stairway. And is it my imagination or did someone tell me that the fury of the moment was doused in a cascade of goose feathers, from above? Anyway, all I can see are those feathers, falling like snow as they finally subdue him and wrestle the stiletto from his bleeding hand.

He's done good work with the blade though, left two almost dead, one that would die later. And he's tied then onto a kitchen chair and carried through the streets back to the Castle while the bunch of other yeomen followed, wearing his green cape, his braided uniform and his cap of liberty like trophies of the fallen.

All this while the curtain was raised again, and Robin Hood took the stage and the chorus sang and two officers made their way into the Lord Lieutenant's box. There was a whispered consultation and all the eyes in the stalls, the gods, the parterre were on Camden's face. There was a drama somewhere else, other than on the stage below them, and I could only admire their performance as they kept it hidden. Faces impassive as a mask, the only hint of disturbance being the gentle movement of Lady Castlereagh's fan.

CHORUS

Newgate

The chorus is the bit that repeats. In every ballad. In case you've forgotten the beginning.

So here it goes.

I had come back for what my betters would have called sentimental reasons, on the Holyhead packet to the Pigeon House.

I had hopes when I last saw him. Of course I had. Hopes of seeing him again. But they were ghostly hopes, like my vanishing breath in that empty church.

Where I've scraped his name and my title on the slate that covered his coffin.

LEF.

I get a shiver of loss, closing the door of that church. As if the ghost of himself doesn't want to be abandoned. But it was you, I have to remind the ghostly Lord, abandoned me.

I walk back now, through that dead city. The yeomen had done good work on it. So many ghosts, it's a job to keep them quiet. More dead, it seems, than living.

I've got some hours to spend before the packet leaves for Holyhead, and so I think I'll amble round the walls of Newgate Prison.

They took my Ned there, from the Castle. Carried him in the kitchen chair, like a captured trophy.

I try to picture the spectacle. Did they pass the Theatre Royal door?

An illustration like in a printed garland.

The flapping cape stained with blood from the bullet wound. The hat shaped like the ship from St Lucia, at last on his head. And I wondered again, did it fit?

But then I remember what McNally told me. The yeomen passed it from one head to another, like a fool's cap and bells.

They carried my Ned down to the Liffey. Across the Essex Bridge and up to Green Street.

The Black Dog Gaol is no more. Newgate makes a fine substitute.

The mechanical drop awaited him there. It would have been long finished by then.

Neilson attempted a rescue but was nabbed by the yeomen. It took ten to hold him down. Or so I was told.

And while I'm wondering what cell they put Neilson in, I begin to count the windows. Twelve on each side and four more in the middle.

Two towers to hem them in and a triangle over the door.

I hoped he hadn't joined the ranks of my Ned's betrayers. The temptation, they told me, had been great.

For soon after his capture, the bloodletting began. Those half a million heroes that answered the call to the millennium of freedom were hunted down. Those croppies got no letters from the mad King. They died on their green fields with homemade pikes in their hands and ears of barley in their pockets. Cannon shot and cavalry sabres turned their hillsides red. The triangle and the pitch cap saw to the families they had left behind. And then I knew hadn't met a fool in that forest in old Carolina. I had met a hero. Their hero.

Could it all have been different? Yes. My Ned could have emerged from the feather merchant's, dressed in full uniform, the mail coaches could have carried the word and the citadel of freedom been set up within the Castle gates. And I could have strangled Camden, the Lord Lieutenant, in his theatre box with my bare hands to the music of Robin Hood.

But someone betrayed him, and I kept my hands to myself.

As the blood began to flow, even Lady Pamela left. And as always, I carried the bags.

Why did she leave? Hundreds have asked that question, but I tried not to. So much blood was flowing by then, it would have made Madame Guillotine proud. My Ned's sister, Lady Louisa, tried to arrange a meeting, which Lady Pamela forbade, being of the opinion that if the sight of him in that cell didn't kill her, the sight of her in the cell would surely kill him.

She obeyed the orders of the Privy Council and took herself to London. At least there, she told me, she could see little Eddy. She said little on the journey over, writing letters and I walked the deck with baby Pamela and Julie. Julie wondered what would happen to our perambulator. I told it her was never ours and I was happy to carry this little one while her mother wrote letters, as I'd once carried little Mary, like an unread letter, her tiny self.

Lady Pamela loved him, in her way, but her way was to leave. They all loved him in their different ways, and even that Privy Council claimed to be serving his best interests, if he had only known them himself.

There was a comedy yet to be played. A grotesque comedy of concern and caring, of lords and ladies, dukes, duchesses and demented Irish rebels.

Too savage for Sheridan to write.

The building that now looms over me, the backdrop.

And some of the players are still inside.

I bellow out his name, now, loud as I can. NEILSON!

There's no response from any of the windows.

The turnkey by the door jerks round his head. He mutters something to the two men-at-arms.

But they soon lose interest.

My Ned breathed his last two weeks after his capture. He's my Ned now, since no one else would claim him. Unlike poor Larry, he was spared the drop. I can only hope that he died with his legs to the city.

I make my way towards Ringsend, then along the road we had often ridden, on our journey to Frescati. The packet that delivered the rebel Napper Tandy from Chester is due to return. I'm to be sneaked back on with the horses.

The Pigeon House looms over the pearly bay.

The cockle-pickers are retreating, as the tide comes in.
And I wonder did old Shambolo have the last laugh after all. Was the Sham Squire ever shammed indeed, or did he do all the shamming. There were more informers in the end than sovereigns to pay them. But perhaps he needed no sovereigns for his last act. And maybe the play was Shambolo's all along. And we all led Major Sirr to that merchant of goose feathers.

LAST VERSE

The Holyhead Packet

I hang on to the mane of a horse and do my best not to slip, in the mix of seawater and dung. And when I hear the cannon boom from the Bull Lighthouse, I consider it safe to try my luck on the deck.

There's a crush around the stern, looking back at the place we are leaving. The fairy-tale city and the thin line of the Dublin hills, rising and falling with the waves.

Maguire, the seaman who snuck me aboard, avoids my eye.

Alone again, now.

All the croppies are dead and the ballads about them are just beginning. The barley they filled their pockets with will be sprouting on Vinegar Hill.

I make a seat for myself in a whorl of ship's rope, lick the pencil and begin to scribble. My betters stroll the deck as the evening fades and the pitching Elsewhere settles into a tranquil line, lit by that same bottle-green light wherein I first saw it.

I like that 'wherein', don't you? It's a word like 'indeed', one of the many I learnt on my travels, you're never sure what it means, but it makes a good, even weighty sound, giving a smidgeon of learning to that basic balladspeak I mastered. And it doesn't have to mean anything, which is a strange kind of relief.

Meaning can be hard to bear.

Can the dead sing? No, but they can be sung about.

> But what harasses Larry the most
> And makes his poor soul melancholy
> When he thinks on the time that his ghost
> Shall come in a sheet to his Molly.
> O sure it will kill her alive.

Did his ghost come to Lady Pamela? If so, it didn't harm her. She soon relieved herself of both grief and devotion with the help of Sheridan, the great comedian. She then joined her mother in Hamburg, who may or may not have been the Duc d'Orléan's pushing block prissey.

I couldn't join them. I couldn't forget. And anyway, I wasn't asked. I said goodbye to Julie and my Ned's children somewhere on the road to Richmond.

But there was just one child I had given my heart to. And she was lying in her own sweet Bully's Acre.

If only I could track it down. In the England still ahead of me. Without money, from Ogilvie or Lawlor.

There's the flare of a match, and sparks from the bowl of a pipe.

I want you back below, Maguire says.

Why? I ask. I've only the moon to look at me?

Maybe, he says. It's your place. Below with the horses. The few shillings you paid are not worth my hide.

I could toss him into the moonlit waters, the way I had tossed Tallentire. But something makes me sorry for him.

I talked with Tandy on the way over. He could hardly move for the chains. He didn't want to be stretched. A lot of bravado fades, Maguire continues, when you're faced with the drop.

He turns then, the moon cutting his face in two.

But your master died well.

He died. No one dies well.

The dream is over, Tandy told me. It died with your Lord Edward.

You mean my Ned.

So go below, Tony Small. With the beasts of burden. Where you won't be noticed.

And I slide back down below with the horses as the South Stack outside Holyhead comes out of the mist.

I remember that silence, amongst the shifting hooves.

I remember that word, froideur.

Why did it feel like death to me?

Worse than death, when the living don't talk.

At least the dead would if they could.

But the living? You know they can. And they don't.

And I hear a ghost whisper an apology, as a foghorn blew.

I can't sleep, Tony. I wish I could.

I thought death was nothing but a sleep, my Lord.

It's a troubled one. Knowing who betrayed me.

And who was that?

It's better you don't know.

Just give me some assurance then. Nothing that I did led them to you.

Nothing. Rien. Nada.

If I'd only known there were so many words for nothing.

I have met my little Mary, the ghost says.

So you can talk to her. At least. At last.

There was so much I didn't know. But I know it now.

What do you know?

This gorgeous pantomime. How much of it I missed.

And I like that phrase. This gorgeous pantomime. I make a note to use it. And not to miss any of it.

She has apple blossoms in her hair.

And then his ghost goes silent. But a horse whinnies, and I wake up.

Horses do make good cover, I realize when we get off the packet at Holyhead. There are soldiers on the quayside checking all of my betters that disembark, and England belongs to them. I busy myself amongst the beasts as Maguire had advised, and I'm given a seat on a cattle-cart by a drover with sympathies. Republican sympathies, that is. There were United Englishmen, he tells me, as well as United Irishmen. Though the united Caribbean men may have done better than both. They threw off real chains.

He fills me in on Santo Domingo, Toussaint Louverture and the great slave revolution as he drives towards the slaughterhouse in Bristol. I ask about St Lucia, Rupez Roche and Sally, but the drover doesn't know much of either.

And you, he asks, as his whip lazily rises bluebottles from the horse's back, how did you end up here? Or there, he says, and nodded his head in the direction of the Irish Sea.

By reason of a promise, I tell him, from your very own King.

A promise of what?

Freedom.

And did you find it?

I found a home of sorts. I found a gorgeous pantomime. I found something like love.

And love, after all, the drover says, is the greatest of these.

I like that phrase, the greatest of these. I ask him where he learned it.

The Bible, he says. Corinthians 13:13.

The Greatest of These

The drover gives me the 'Epistles of Paul' to read, on my journey to London. I have little use for most of it, but towards the end I find something like the wisdom of Tom Paine. And love, I'm sure my friend Ned would have agreed, must be the greatest of them all.

And all around me the low hills of England pass by.

Things always changed, when we journeyed through his England. He became more Lord than Lieutenant.

As if there was a dusting of frost between us, a small shimmering layer of ice that separated one from the other.

What had I gained by the journey? Not what I was owed. Unless I was owed memory. And you can't eat memory.

I make my way from Charing Cross to Marylebone through the heart of bedlam. I get my share of stares and once again wonder how Crusoe's Friday had managed in this place.

But I have my suit, my stick and my ghost to keep me company.

Wandering, that dawn, but I don't know where. And only when I arrive do I realize my destination.

The house in Harley Street.

All the carriages gone, the stables empty, the only evidence of life being the one in a servant boy's outfit, lounging on the front steps.

No longer a boy, though, a man now, his frame straining his livery to ripping point.

Lo, Cecil, I ask him, would they not take the care to get you a new suit?

He looks up and blinks in the sunlight. Sunlight everywhere, that morning.

Tony, he says, is it you?

Hard to miss, I would wager.

By God a face, he says, from beyond the grave. Are you living still?

Come here till I prove it to you.

He leaps up and wraps his arms around me.

Where are they?

Gone, he says. When the Lord went. They shuttered the house.

Where?

Who knows? He shrugs. Richmond, Surrey, Goodwood. The Duke's? They're sitting it out. The shame … of the whole business …

And you?

I'm houseboy to a shuttered house. No more than you.

And who pays you, Cecil?

Nobody. I live in hope.

Ogilvie?

He sits on the steps, by the railings. He pulls on his tattered sleeves.

And little Eddy?

Gone wherever the Duchess is gone, he shivers, and says softly. Lady Pamela crossed the water. With the two girls.

What will you do, Cecil? Sit and starve?

They need stagehands, Tony. In Drury Lane. Do you remember Drury Lane?

How could I forget?

Work is work, we both agree. So we walk across the many parks to where the theatre stands, like a pillared wedding cake, in the morning sun.

A playbill is fixed to the glass door of the entrance.

Pizarro, a Tragedy in Five Acts by Richard Brinsley Sheridan.

So the great comedian has changed his tune.

A tragedy.

You do love the stage, Cecil, I remember.

I do, he says. From wherever I can watch it.

And this 'wherever' is the backstage, the great doors open to all of the dust of bedlam and the dray carts coming and going, huge bits of scenery to be trundled and lifted, palm trees in man-sized pots. They need muscle. Cecil knows the ganger and before lunchtime we are wrestling whole landscapes into the dark interior.

And once more I can enjoy the empty stage, the dust wheeling above it from some conduit of light above, the boxes rising around like tiers of marzipan. And this is the best stage of all, the great London sun throwing its cathedral of light through the opened doors, the ropes hanging in their black lines from the flies above, pieces of other 'elsewheres' lying discarded in triangular and rectangular piles. Here a Scottish castle, there a Venetian lagoon and I'm sure, if I had taken care to look, I'd have uncovered a piece of Prospero's own isle, with the ghost of Ariel attached.

We work till the sun goes down and are given our orders for the morrow and I feel good, heartened by the prospect of employment but uncertain as to where to lay my head.

And as if reading my thoughts, Cecil pipes up.

Where to now Tony? Have you a home to go to?

Lo, Cecil, my only home lately has been the ground beneath my feet.

You could bed down with me, good Tony.

Where, Cecil?

The only place they left for me. The stables.

My old home?

Your old home, indeed.

So, the stables. Cecil sleeps in the byre above. I clear my old bed in the straw, below.

Empty of horses now. Empty of everything but us.

Orezembo

Little Julie turns up. No longer little, since she found herself with child. Mine, she tells me. She had felt an odd ache when she returned to Hamburg and assumed it was the ache of missing me. But, no, it was quite a happier complaint.

Neither Madame de Genlis nor Lady Pamela welcomed her condition. So from Hamburg to Harley Street in search of me, who does, welcome it and more. I find a hovel in Air Street, Soho, with my Drury Lane earnings and leave the stables to Cecil.

At first, we sleep on straw and wooden pallets. I make a bed, then, out of detritus from the stage of Drury Lane. The headboard, a mermaid, with branches for her hair, painted seaweed green. The legs, dragon feet, from some melodrama of knights and monsters, long ago. Julie sews a patchwork quilt from the stolen costumes of old kings and queens. So we bed down in a universe of stolen dreams. And love, I find, is indeed the greatest of these.

Is there a reason for everything? Is there a ghost, guiding my hand? We're building a forest on that stage, giant trees like tormented ancients, canopies that join boughs and hands above rivers of silk, painted canvas mountains in the background, echoing themselves into rose-coloured mists. Nothing like the rubber and banana planted Arden in the regimental hall in Gibraltar. And my only question is, whose forest will it turn out to be?

So I'm whitening the plaster rocks with a pot of fuller's earth when a pear-shaped figure steps from the wings.

Let me weep, I hear. I know that face.

And I know that voice. Sheridan's.

I turn, in a cloud of white chalk.

The great comedian himself, with de Loutherbourg, the supervisor of all of these illusions.

Orezembo? He says.

I shake myself free of the fuller's earth. Who on earth is this Orezembo?

You're building his habitat. His trees. His forests. His paradise. And you know it already, Tony Small.

So where is it? Is it the Carolinas I grew up in? That the mad King lost?

It could have been, he says. It could have been the Ireland I grew up in. Maybe it should have been. All paradises, lost.

Then he shakes his head.

But that would have taken courage, Tony dear. I'm a scribbler and sometime politicker. Unlike your good Lord. We work with the head, not the heart.

He smiled. He thought I understood.

You must know, there is only so much reality the Lord Chancellor can bear. And, besides, I need to keep my seat in Parliament. So my parable of blood and conquest doesn't happen in Ireland. Or in Carolina. It happens in Peru.

And maybe he's drunk, as he often was, maybe he has tired of his Harlequin Fridays, maybe I'm suited to the role, maybe my skin was the same hue as the Peruvian native, for whatever reason, out of all these maybes there arises one certainty. I'm called one day on the stage, pages are thrust into my hand and I read the part of Orezembo, some lines of which I can still remember.

'My life is a withered tree – it is not worth preserving.'

And Sheridan's voice booms from the auditorium.

How does the playbill read?

Pizarro, I answer. *A Tragedy in Five Acts*.

So make me feel it. Tragedy. Pathos.

Pathos. It's a new word to me. But I know it has something to do with sadness. So I weep, as I read again.

'My life is a withered tree – it is not worth preserving.'

And the next:

'Strike, Christian! Then boast among thy fellows – I too have murdered a Peruvian.'

I mimic a wound. Bent double. I know pain, and for once show it. After which I hear an unfamiliar sound.

Applause.

From Cecil. From the stagehands. But most of all from Sheridan, deep in the auditorium.

The play revives his fortunes. I become that Peruvian for as long as it lasts.

Did I become his Tony, afterwards? No, he wouldn't have presumed to usurp that title, but he did delight in calling me his Orezembo. And he, I suppose, becomes my comedian.

I would carry him from his sleeping quarters in the great palace of illusions, Drury Lane, to what he called the sister palace of illusions, the House of Parliament. Then haul him back from whatever gaming house he ended up in.

Shambolo, he would say. Tell me again.

I get sick of the tale of the Sham Squire. But he never does. The Squire has the aura of his own creations. Could well have been invented by him. And who knows, maybe was.

For we are nothing if not a story, Tony.

This, on a carriage down to Somerset. To Wells Cathedral, where the daughter he claims as his, Mary, lay buried.

With Elizabeth. Tony. You remember Elizabeth?

I do. And her story, too.

My Maid of Bath.

Does he know? Of course he knows. But he needs the comfort of illusions, now. And of my arm, as he weeps over both of their graves.

Consummation

Orezembo bows his last, as my little Moirisco is born. I work from home, to be closer to his cries. I carve a bassinet, out of an oaken trunk. But Sheridan's Peru has left me an unwanted gift.

A cough.

The lead and sawdust have gotten to my lungs. With all of that fuller's earth, it reduces me. I wonder how advanced what Mrs Mehitabel Canning would have called my consummation is.

I don't want to write. But Julie persuades me. If I could write a ballad, I can surely manage a begging letter. And Cecil told me they had returned. And a debt, after all, is a debt. She calls me Anthony now, it has the murmur of respectability. She writes the details of my debt in a borrowed ledger. The family, she assures me, will honour what is owed.

So she hires a scribe, who knows the way of begging letters …

London, October 1st, 1803

My Lady,

I hope you will pardon the liberty I take in writing but having a great favour to ask and knowing your Ladyship's goodness makes me take this freedom. I am at present in a very bad state of health and not able to do anything to support myself or family. I applied to Mr Ogilvie for what is owing to me by Lawlor and he told me that as soon as the estates in Ireland would afford it he would let me have a hundred pounds, now being so ill and having no money I am drove to the greatest distress, for what little money I have has been spent on doctors, the favour I have to ask your Ladyship is if you could make insteps for me in the family to make up a sum of money for me so that I may be able to keep the business for my Wife and Children which is my greatest trouble, or if it was in your Ladyship's power to advance me some, I make no doubt but that Mr Ogilvie will keep his word for it for really if I was not the way that I am at present I would not trouble your Ladyship on any account or the Family – I am at home at present under the hands of surgeon John Heaviside he gives me every hope of recovery and desires me to take all the nourishing food and asks I take but little exercise. I hope your Ladyship is well and Miss Lucy.

> *Remain your Ladyship's servant,*
>
> *Anthony Small.*
>
> *Number 10 Air Street, Soho, London.*

The Curtain Call

Do I expect a reply? Not really. But my consumption turns out to be unconsummated. All that is needed for my recovery is a respite from the greasepaint, the dust, the fuller's earth.

I open a chandler's shop. My theatrical days might be over. But the stage still needs candles.

Light is the lifeblood of Sheridan's theatre, it consumes it the way the players consume applause, huge chandeliers swaying from the tiered ceiling, candle sconces lining every box, magnesium flares above the pit, whole banks of candle-wick behind the backdrops with mirrors to multiply them, waxing and waning with sunset and sunrise, lanterns that circle and throw ghostly shadows and need flares to throw them, lightning that flashes and scorches while Cecil rolls the thunderclaps, basins of candle wax for the footlights, with floating wicks. And it was from these, Cecil told me later, that the curtains caught flame and the fire began.

I see it from across the river, a cloud of black smoke at first, then of orange, as I cross the river, then of flames so bright they make Lambeth Palace look like an illuminated set. Hoses scattering drops like diamonds from the river hand-pumps, all of them useless.

So the London crowd gathers and stays, to enjoy the spectacle of an inferno the whole length of the theatre façade, the heat so intense it forces us back to the Strand side and it's from there, by the Piazza Coffee House, that I hear the comedian's voice.

You're blocking my view, Orezembo.

I turn and there's Sheridan himself, a bottle of claret on the table beside him.

Sit down, at least, if you can't put it out.

So I sit, as my comedian drinks and mutters.

Might a body not enjoy a glass of wine by his own fireside?

And he pours me one.

Time has not been kind to him. There are crusts of spittle round his lips and his waistcoat is stained with so much detritus, it seems to have a life of its own. But his speech is still resonant enough to fill the air around.

I had another play in mind, he says. The tale of the Sham Squire and the informers of '98.

A comedy?

A pantomime, he says, and drinks some more.

Will it tell us who betrayed him? I asked.

There'll be a guessing game. At the end. As in any pantomime. We can play it now.

Magan? I ask him, and he shakes his head.

All he gave away was passwords. The question is, who betrayed his hiding place?

Neilson?

Samuel Neilson manfully served his time.

He shakes his head again.

No, he says, as he labours to his feet.

There's been a request to the Lord Lieutenant. For a pension. Betrayal, it seems, pays better than the stage.

The portico of Drury Lane collapses. The rumble that follows is like a stage thunder sheet.

So you have to look to the theatre for your Lord's Judas. The play's the thing –

And he limps, comically, over the flame-lit cobbles. All that is missing is the stick.

You don't mean –

But I do. My old pupil. The wretched versifier. McNally.

A blast of smoke from the burning theatre envelopes him. When it clears, he is gone.

ACKNOWLEDGEMENTS

Thanks to Jennifer Brady, who read the manuscript with more care and provided more editorial advice than any author deserves. Thanks to Antony Farrell, Ruth Hallinan and the staff at Lilliput Press who gave me the kind of support I thought had vanished from publishing. Thanks to Adekunle Gomez from the African Cultural Project at the Africa Institute in Ireland for insight on the culture of Temne people and their history. Thanks to David Dickson who provided valuable insight into many historical details, to Bridget Farrell for proofing, to Stephen Rea, Caryl Phillips and Brenda Rawn for their invaluable responses to early drafts of this novel.

Thanks also to the staff of the National Library of Ireland who provided access to the Leinster Papers, among them the letter of Tony Small to Lady Sophia Fitzgerald. Thanks to the biographers of Lord Edward: Thomas Moore, *The Life and Death of Lord Edward* (London, 1831); I.A. Taylor, *The Life of Lord Edward Fitzgerald, 1763–1798* (Wentworth

Press, 2019) but chief amongst them, Stella Tillyard, *Citizen Lord* (Chatto & Windus, 1997).

Thanks also for Andrew Carpenter's *Verse in English from Eighteenth-Century Ireland* (Cork University Press, 1998), a text that gave a vivid portrait of life as lived, written, sung and spoken in Dublin of that period. Thomas Bartlett's *Revolutionary Dublin: The Letters of Francis Higgins to Dublin Castle, 1795–1801* (Four Courts Press, 2004) provided an invaluable source of insight while writing this novel, as did the following texts: *Rough Crossings: Britain, the Slaves and the American Revolution* by Simon Schama (Vintage, 2009); *The Interesting Narrative of Olaudah Equiano or Gustavo Vassa, the African* by Olaudah Equiano (London, 1798); *The Black Jacobins* by C.L.R. James (Penguin, 2001); *A Traitor's Kiss: The Life of Richard Brinsley Sheridan* by Fintan O'Toole (Granta Books, 1998); *The Linleys of Bath* by Clementina Black (Ulan Press, 2012) and 'The Life and Networks of Pamela Fitzgerald, 1773–1831' by Laura Mather – University of Limerick M.A. thesis, 2017.

And too many others to mention here.